I Want Everybody
To Like Me

Holly E. Jones

Cover design by Jennifer Crafton

FOR JESSICA

A fighter, friend, weirdo and muse.

ACKNOWLEDGEMENTS

My husband encouraged me.

My children inspired me.

My friends helped me.

My parents raised and educated me.

My siblings gave me endless ideas.

My Grandpa Curly set an example for storytelling that I hope to uphold.

Thank you all.

"This is the kind of spontaneous publicity—your name in print—that makes people. I'm in print! Things are going to start happening to me now."

-Navin R. Johnson, "The Jerk" (1979)

CHAPTER ONE

"Can I braid your hair?" I asked Sara. She had long, blonde hair with pop bottle curls that bounced from her shoulders to the middle of her back. My mom taught me to braid hair over the summer and I wanted to make sure the rest of the sixth grade knew of my abilities right away. Sara stared out the window of the bus as we rode through our neighborhood on a bright, late-August morning. With both hands, I gathered her curls into a loose ponytail.

"Actually, could we wait until after school?" She asked, shaking her hair loose from my hands. "I kind of did my hair special for today."

I knew what was up. She wanted to impress one, if not all of the boys at school. I couldn't remember exactly which boys were going to be in Mrs. Saltor's class with us. All I cared about was that my best friend and I were going to be together. The only time Sara and I hadn't been in the same class was in second grade—but that had just been for the first few weeks of the school year. Sara's teacher got really sick and they couldn't find a long-term sub, so they divided all the students among the rest of the second grade classes. As luck would have it, Sara ended up in mine, which helped keep our streak alive.

My name is Violet Karchefski, but everybody calls me Vy. All through the summer, my best friend in the whole world, Sara Anderson and I planned out how we were going to make the sixth grade our best year ever. It just *had* to be, because in the seventh grade we'd be busted apart by middle school. Seventh graders had five different classes every day and the chances that you'd be in any of them with your best friend were pretty slim. It was 1990—the dawn of a new decade and it was the last chance for Sara and me to really cement ourselves as *best friends forever.*

A few weeks before school started, Sara seemed to get distracted. She was talking a lot about boys. I couldn't think of one single redeeming thing about boys. Now, don't get me wrong, I had some friends who were boys, but they weren't boys to me in the way that some boys were *boys* to Sara. I think something happened toward the end of the summer that changed her. Maybe it was the overnight camping trip her youth group took to Blue Lake. Maybe it was the week she spent at her grandparents' after that. Whatever it was, as we sat together on the bus the morning of the first day of school, I knew my best friend was in danger of becoming boy-crazy and ruining everything.

"Do you think we'll have assigned seats?" I asked.

Sara stared out the window. The bus cruised along the river road, passing the swimming holes where we'd spent so many hot days over the course of the summer jumping off rocks, catching crawdads, playing in the water and making our best-year-ever plans.

2

"Sara?" I nudged her, bringing her attention back from whatever daydream she was in.

"Yeah?"

"I said, do you think we'll have assigned seats?"

"Oh, I don't know," she shook her head. "Do you think we will?"

"Well, we're sixth graders now," I said, "so they'll probably just let us sit wherever we want, right? I mean, it's not like we're little kids anymore, so we should be able to sit anywhere."

Sara straightened her shirt on her shoulders and looked down at her chest.

"Um, yeah," she said. "That makes sense." She looked back out the window.

At the beginning of the summer, my mom made me start wearing a training bra. I let Sara try it on during a sleepover. She filled it out and then some. The next day when we were out for a bike ride, Sara showed me her strap. She had told her mom that I was wearing a training bra and that it was too small for her, so her mom took her to the mall that day to get her fitted for her own. When she showed me what she got, it wasn't even a training bra—it was the real thing. She told me her mom said,

"You're just a little more *developed*."

Back on the bus, I looked down at my own chest. It was as flat as a pancake behind my double-layered orange and yellow collared shirts. I tied both shirts at my waist instead of buttoning the last three buttons, so it poofed out a bit to hide my flatness. I wasn't too worried, though.

Boobs weren't that much of a concern for me. I was focused on more important things, like having the best sixth grade year ever with my best friend in the whole wide world.

"So, if they *do* let us pick our own seats, let's sit together, okay? Like we planned. Somewhere in the back," I recalled our conversations in the river. Maybe that'd help shake her back to reality. "Remember?"

Sara nodded.

"Sure," she replied, squinting in the early morning sunlight.

The brakes on the bus squealed as we pulled up in front of the school. Kids and parents lined the sidewalks carrying backpacks and bags full of fresh supplies for the year. Pencils would never be sharper. Tissue boxes would never be more readily available. Markers would be full of ink and crayons would have smooth edges and perfect points. This, the first day of school, was the last day that everything would be absolutely perfect. I had no idea how right I was about that.

Sara and I stood up, waiting for our turn to step out into the aisle of the bus and shuffle toward the door. We both stooped over to peer out the window at everyone on the sidewalk. I saw a few friends and a new kid here and there, but nothing too exciting. Sara seemed to be looking for someone specific in the crowd. I could tell because she squinted and leaned forward over the side of the seats as she looked out the window. I felt someone push on my backpack from behind me.

"Hey!" I exclaimed at the person behind me as I bumped Sara's side with my stomach.

Sara looked over her shoulder at me and then at the line of other kids waiting.

"Sorry," she mumbled to us all, slowly walking forward. She continued to look out the window.

"Who are you looking for?" I asked.

"Nobody," she replied. But she kept looking.

As we stepped off of the bus I was surrounded by the unique smells of the first day of school. Diesel exhaust from the busses, the smell of new plastics, and coffee in the commuter mugs of every teacher, staff member and parent. I was so busy taking in the moment that I hadn't noticed Sara walking away.

"Can you smell that?" I asked. My question was met with a dull, blunt punch to the shoulder.

"What, didja fart?" laughed Jake Coughlin, the source of the blow to my arm.

"Shut up, Jake," I snipped, punching him back. "I was talking to Sara."

Jake pointed toward the front doors of the school where I saw Sara walking toward a boy I had never seen before. She tucked her hair behind her ear and smiled while this boy sat on the handrail talking to her.

"Who is that?" I asked with a sneer as I stepped up onto the sidewalk.

"New guy," answered Jake, who followed just behind me.

5

"How do you know him?"

"I don't," Jake said. "That's how I know he's new." Jake shifted his backpack on his shoulders, which were enormous. Jake was tall and muscular. Some kids thought he had been held back a grade or two because of his size but my mom assured me that he was born just three days before I was. She had been there when his mom went into labor. Our moms were really close friends, so we spent a lot of time together when we were growing up. Jake lived just a few houses away from mine and was a lot like a brother to me. He knew most of my secrets and, if it weren't for Sara, he would probably be my very best friend. Since I had Sara though, he was just my best *guy* friend. My dad once called Jake my *boy*friend, which I made sure he knew was absolutely not what we called our friendship. It took a lot of retching sounds and vomiting gestures to explain, but I think my dad eventually understood.

This new guy didn't look like anybody else around. In my town we all sort of blended in together. There was only one mall nearby and everybody got their school clothes from the same stores. Any deviation from those styles really stood out and this guy most definitely stood out. He had black jeans that were tight around the ankles, high-top shoes with three different colored laces in each shoe, and an olive green military-style coat with the name "NELSON" stitched onto the breast pocket.

"Name's Nelson, it looks like," Jake said.

"I can read," I shot back in a sarcastic tone. I didn't so much care about the guy's name. I wanted to know why my best friend was talking to him. How did she know him? Did she meet him this summer? Was he the reason why she wouldn't let me braid her hair? What grade was he in? Whose class was he in? Most importantly, *where was he going to sit?*

The bell rang and we quickly filed into the building. Jake and I walked together past the apple vending machine and to the left, down the north hallway. We passed the library, which I heard got a new computer over the summer. I was looking forward to showing off what I had learned using my dad's new personal computer that he brought home from work. It was ivory-colored and almost bigger than our TV. It was supposed to be for my mom, who was writing her master's thesis, but one day in late July something happened and all of the hard work she had put into it was suddenly gone. There was nothing saved, nothing printed, and no way to find the 88 pages she had already written. Mom cried for a long time that day. I did too, since I had to give back the electric typewriter she handed down to me on the day Dad gave her the computer.

I could see Sara's blonde hair up ahead in the crowd as we moved through the hallway like a school of salmon through the spillway of a dam. Our school was old and hadn't been updated since my parents went there in the 1960s. The walls were painted a creamy off-white from the floor to about halfway up, where it switched to mint green. The floor tiles were also green, just slightly darker than the paint on the walls but with orange, gray, and white speckles. The soles of my new shoes made sticky sounds on the tile as I walked. I passed two doors on the left and two more on the right before arriving outside my new classroom. I saw Sara and the new guy walk in together. I froze in the hall. Jake took a few steps ahead of me and then looked back.

"What's the matter, Vy? You *are* in Mrs. Saltor's class, aren't you?" he asked.

I nodded.

"So, what's the hold up?" he asked, waiting for me.

I could tell he was antsy for me to follow him in. I pointed to the doorway.

"Where did they sit?" I asked flatly, staring at the floor and pursing my lips.

"Who?"

"Sara and Nelson. Where did they sit?"

"Um…" Jake leaned over and looked through the door. "Last two seats in the back row."

"Next to each other?"

"Yeah. In the corner. He's closest to the window."

"So, it's not assigned seating," I confirmed.

"Doesn't look like it," Jake shook his head.

"Oh." I sank. I let my head hang and my shoulders drop. The final bell rang and I scuffed my feet along the green tile floor as I walked into the room. Jake hopped past me and claimed the last seat that was available near the back of the class. Looking up, I saw one desk left.

Dead center, front row. This year was going to be absolutely horrible, I just knew it.

CHAPTER TWO

"How was the first day of sixth grade?" Dad asked at dinner that night. I shrugged and shoveled potatoes au gratin into my mouth. Mom tapped on her plate with her fork.

"Your father asked you a question," she said, giving me a look that I knew was meant to remind me that dinner was a time for polite conversation, and no matter how bad my day had been, participation was required. I set my fork down and put my hands in my lap.

"The first day was fine. Mrs. Saltor was fine. Lunch was fine, recess was fine, it's all just fine," I snapped, annoyed. I just wanted to finish eating as quickly as possible so I could meet Sara for our walk. She was going to have a lot of explaining to do about what happened that day. I barely saw her. After the seating fiasco, I spent the whole day either by myself or floating between other groups of friends while Sara was joined at the hip with the new kid.

"Just fine?" my dad asked. "Oh, good. I can tell Mr. Saltor that tomorrow morning—my daughter thinks his wife's class is just 'fine.'"

Mr. Saltor was my dad's boss. We took a family vacation with the Saltors every summer to a dude ranch in central Oregon. Their daughter was my age. Her name was Alice and she was an only child. She had horses, four-wheelers and a pool at her house. I sometimes dreamed about how pleasant her life was with all that stuff. Sara and I begged our parents to do whatever they could to get us into Mrs. Saltor's class for sixth grade. I knew Mrs. Saltor would be extra-nice to me—I mean, how could she not be? I'd been to her house outside of school and was friends with her daughter. It had all been part of my plan to make sixth grade the best year ever. It was a plan I could feel starting to slip away.

"It's great, Dad," I reassured my father and finished the last few bites of pork chops on my plate. "I'm sitting in the front row."

"Front row, huh? That's great!" Dad seemed surprised and pleased to hear that. I knew he would be, which was why I said it—I needed to get myself excused from this dinner table quickly.

Most evenings, Sara and I went for walks across town. Staying mainly on the back roads, we would meet halfway between our houses after dinner and head west. We continued until the streetlights came on, which was our signal to turn around and head for home. Phone time was limited for both of us and she only had one TV at her house, so walking was how we hung out.

As fall approached the days would only start getting shorter, which meant there would soon be no time in the evenings for walks with Sara. The high school football games were coming up and my family always went together. I couldn't be entirely independent there, what with my mom, dad, older sister Victoria and little brother Calvin in the stands spying on me. I liked to walk around the track with my friends during the games but since I knew my parents would be watching I'd have to be careful about who I walked with and what I said. One time, when I was walking around the track with a few friends I used the "S" word as I passed the 40-yard line. By the time I made it back to the bleachers, Mom already knew what I'd said and stripped me of my track-walking privileges.

"May I be excused?" I asked, piling my fork and napkin onto my plate. I was halfway out of my seat when Mom finally nodded.

"Yes, you may," she said. I raced to the kitchen and quickly cleaned off my dishes. Kicking the dishwasher closed, I leaned back into the dining room.

"Is it okay if I go for a walk with Sara?"

"Be *home* when the streetlights come on," Mom instructed.

"What!?" I whined. "Are you kidding? That's not the deal!"

She wasn't having any of my protests.

"Or just stay here," she offered.

"But Sara is already meeting me!"

"Then be home by the time the lights come on."

This was going to cut my walking time in half at least. I'd have to carefully read the sunset if I was going to make it home in time. Just another thing adding to the stress of the night. There was enough on my mind with all of the questions I had for Sara. I agreed to Mom's terms with a dramatic sigh and eye roll.

"Not even twelve years old yet and she's already acting like a teenager." My mom muttered to my father across the table as I walked away. Whatever.

Sara wasn't anywhere in sight as I rounded the corner out of the cul-de-sac and started down the hill. The halfway point between our houses was the sidewalk in front of a yellow split-level house that was owned by the high school's chemistry teacher. As I approached his driveway I could see that the front window was open. I heard the sound of dishes being washed and loaded into a dishwasher along with the closing music of the local newscast. Six-thirty. Sara was nowhere to be seen.

I got all the way to Sara's house. I marched up onto the porch. Before I rang the doorbell I checked to see if the door was unlocked. All summer I just opened the door and let myself in, but that was when she was home alone with her brother and sisters. I didn't think her parents would mind much if I just walked in, but since I knew my folks would have totally freaked out if someone just let themselves into our house, I used the doorbell this time.

Sara's family was big. She had two older sisters and an older brother. I heard her parents talking about adopting a baby at some point too. The Andersons all had shiny blonde hair, except for Sara's brother, Sam. Mrs. Anderson worked in the school district office and Mr. Anderson taught fourth grade. He was also an inventor. Every now and then, when I was over at Sara's house, her dad would pop his head into the room and ask for our help with his latest contraption. He built these rocking horses that "walked" and Sara and I liked to race them up and down the hallway. One time, her dad made this electric-powered bouncing doorway that a person could be strapped into and tossed up and down—he called that one an "exercise machine for paraplegics." Their family took a lot of vitamins and read a lot of books. Sometimes I imagined what it would be like to be adopted by Sara's family.

My hand had just barely reached the doorbell when Sara's dad flung the front door open. It surprised me so much I nearly fell off the porch.

"There she is," he greeted me with a smile and then announced, "Sara? You have a visitor!"

"Who is it?" I heard Sara shout from the other room.

Her dad gestured for me to step inside, which I did, as I called out to Sara,

"It's me! Are we walking?"

"Oh," she said, with a hint of disappointment in her voice. "Yeah, I'll be right there."

Her dad closed the door behind me and went back into the dining room.

"Do you want to join us for dessert?" he asked. "Fresh berries?"

I smiled and shook my head. Partly because I didn't have time to waste, but also because I'd never thought fruit should be considered "dessert."

"No, thanks," I said, patting my belly, "I'm stuffed." I could see Sara's brother Sam's feet sticking out over the armrest of the couch. Her two sisters, Judy and Julie, were still at the dinner table. I slowly paced in front of the door, looking at the family photos that lined the stairway in front of me. The Anderson girls were all very pretty. Sam wasn't ugly by any stretch, either.

"Mom? Have you seen my green sneakers?" Sara yelled from upstairs.

I looked around for Mrs. Anderson. I heard her before I saw her.

"Look in the basket at the end of the hallway," she replied. Mrs. Anderson was laying inverted on an ironing board that had been propped up against the hearth in the living room. She was a petite woman with big eyes and thick glasses. She looked up at me and waved. "Hi dear," she smiled, "just getting some time in on my slant-board."

I smiled and waved back, trying not to let my impatience show. Finally Sara came skipping down the stairs.

"Ready?" she asked.

I nodded and we both said "good-bye" to her family.

"I have to be back home by the time the lights turn on tonight," I told her as we crossed the porch, "So we should get moving."

"That's okay," she said, sounding a little relieved. "I'm expecting a phone call later on, so it's probably good."

We set out from her house and headed west toward the high school on our usual route. Our first few steps were in silence while I tried to think of the best way to start the conversation. Luckily she started talking first.

"I'm sorry we didn't get to sit together today," she said.

"Yeah," I said, "that's okay." I lied. It wasn't okay. It blew our plans before we even put them into action, but I didn't know what else to say to her at that moment. Plus, she was my best friend and it was just kind of expected that we forgive each other quickly. "So, who's Nelson?" I jumped right in.

"You mean Jason?"

"Yeah, Jason," I remembered that Mrs. Saltor introduced him by that name to our class, but I had a hard time paying attention to anything. Sitting in the front row made it easier for me to daydream because the teacher was usually looking over my head or pacing up and down the aisles of desks. "Where's he from?" I asked.

"Lake Minnifeld," she answered, pointing north.

"Oh, up by your grandparents."

"Uh-huh."

"You meet him this summer?"

"Uh-huh." She said with a happy tone in her voice.

16

I couldn't believe this was the first I'd ever heard about him. How long had she been planning on keeping her summer romance a secret from her best friend? I felt so betrayed. My mind raced to find a way to handle my feelings. I couldn't think of anything except for how angry I was.

We approached the outfield fence around the high school baseball field and I was still trying to figure it out. Looking to the south we could see the football field and track. The varsity football players and cheerleaders were cleaning up after practice. In tandem rhythm, we bounced our backs against the chain link fence.

"It sounds a lot like that movie we watched at Alice's sleepover," I said. "You know, where the girl meets the boy at the beach over summer vacation and he shows up at her school and makes things really weird with her friends. Remember? *Grease?*"

Sara stopped bouncing and stood up straight.

"You mean *she* shows up at *his* school," she corrected me.

"Oh, right," I accepted her correction.

Sara stared at me and pursed her lips together. I kept bouncing against the fence and squinted at the sunset, pretending not to notice her expression.

"Are you mad at me?" she asked boldly.

I shook my head and played dumb.

"Mad? No!" I laughed. "I'm not mad." I lied again. I was furious. Why didn't she tell me about this guy? Why was she choosing him over me? Had my placement among her priorities changed? What did I do to her to deserve this? I wasn't going to ask her any of these things directly, of course. I still wanted her to like me. There was a hint of spite to it, though—if she couldn't tell me about this boy, then I wasn't about to let her see how much it affected me.

We watched the last cheerleader sling a gym bag over her shoulder and follow the rest of the squad across the track toward the locker rooms. Sara sighed.

"We'd better get back," she said, pointing at the street lights.

"Yep," I said with a twinge of bitterness in my voice. I kicked a weed growing in the lawn, sending little white tufty seeds flying through the air at our ankles. We walked a few steps together in silence.

"Look, Violet," Sara said, stopping me in my tracks.

She used my whole name. She never used my whole name. Nobody but my grandmother used my whole name. Everybody always called me "Vy." I even signed my schoolwork "Vy." I gave Sara a shocked stare. She looked annoyed.

"Just because we're friends doesn't mean that I can't meet other friends," She said as she walked ahead. The parking lot lights turned on above us. The street lights were still dark.

I would have stayed put just to show her how mad I was, but Sara had been my closest friend for so long I couldn't risk losing her. I already felt like she was slipping away, right into Nelson's arms.

"No, you're right. It doesn't," I said, jogging to catch up, "and I didn't say that it did. Look, Sara, I'm sorry, I just—I just got a little jealous, that's all."

"You don't have to be jealous. We're best friends! And best friends can share each other with boys," she said. "It's just part of life."

I didn't like it, but I didn't want to drive her away. I wanted Sara to like me. I wanted everybody to like me—that's always been my thing.

"Why didn't you tell me about Nelson earlier?" I asked.

"I didn't think you'd want to hear about me spending time with a boy," she said, "what with all the barfing sounds you usually make when we talk about them like that."

"Ugh," I said, pretending to hurl on the pavement. "So it's like *that* with you two?"

"Yeah," Sara laughed, pushing my shoulder with both of her hands. "It's like *that*."

"Gross." I shrugged. "Next time, no secrets?"

"Okay," Sara agreed. "Hug?" She extended her arms.

I gladly took the hug. It was a little distant but it was still a best friend hug. Sort of.

CHAPTER THREE

Mrs. Saltor's daughter, Alice, made an amazing discovery on the playground over the summer. There was a set of bars we called the *flip bars*. The P.E. classes used them to do chin-ups but at recess we used them to do gymnastic tricks with varying degrees of difficulty and risk. Each trick had a name, like the *seahorse*, which was when you'd bend a knee over the bar with the other leg making a figure 4 behind it and you'd spin around using a kicking motion while holding the bar in your hands next to your knee. There was the *cherry drop*, where you'd sit with both legs over the bar and your hands holding the bar beside you, then sort of fall backwards and around, releasing your legs and hands at the perfect moment to do an Olympic-style dismount, landing on the ground with both feet. Finally there was the *death drop*, which was like the cherry drop except you started out squatting with your feet balancing on the bar. You'd drop to your legs to do the same falling-back motion as the cherry drop, but with the death drop you never grabbed the bar—it was a no-handed trick and probably the most difficult one anybody could do on the bars.

While Mrs. Saltor was stapling construction paper letters and pictures to bulletin boards in her classroom, Alice played on the playground by herself. Her mom worried a lot, so even when it was warmer than 80 degrees outside, she still made Alice take a sweater. Alice used her sweater to fashion a sling with which she could tie herself to one of the flip bars, thereby elevating her trick capabilities. The brilliance of the sweater-sling was that it provided a sense of security as she whipped around the horizontal bars at great speeds with no hands. Alice taught us all how to tie our sweaters during lunch recess on the first day of school. All of us except for Sara, of course, who wasn't there.

Sitting atop the highest of the three horizontal bars during morning recess on the second day of school, I watched clusters of kids playing together. Some weren't really playing as much as they were just wandering around in groups, and then there were those who leaned against poles and playground equipment talking to each other. All last year, at just about every recess, Sara played on the bars with Alice and me. So far, her sixth grade track record wasn't so great. Alice stopped the seahorse spin she was doing and hung upside down by her knees, catching her breath.

"Where's Sara?" she asked.

I scanned the playground and found her over by the tetherballs, sitting on the grass while Jason Nelson swatted aggressively at the ball that was attached to the rope hanging from the pole. He hit it from the right, then he hit it from the left—then right, and then left again. The rope wound around the back side of the pole. He had no opponent. Sara watched with big eyes. She had that same look on her face that I saw the day before when we got off the bus. It was glassy and daydreamy. Barf.

"She's over there," I said, pointing toward the tetherball poles.

The recess duty blew the five-minute warning whistle and I started to untie the sweater that held me to the bar.

"Why doesn't she like the bars anymore?" Alice asked, flipping herself over backwards and onto the ground with a thump. Alice always landed on her feet.

I wasn't so coordinated. In my first cherry drop attempt my grip on the bars wasn't tight enough and I let go too soon, causing me to flop to the ground chest first. Sara had been sick that day and Alice had gotten in trouble so she was on the wall. There was a painted line on the blacktop perpendicular to the exterior of the school about two feet from the wall. During recess, if you were on the side of the line that was farthest from the school, you were ok. You couldn't cross the line and be on the other side until the bell rang. If you got in trouble you'd first get a warning whistle. The little "fweet-fweet" from the recess duty meant *hey, knock that off.* If you didn't immediately comply, you got a long whistle blast and she'd point to the wall. You'd have to go to the wrong side of the painted line and lean against the building until recess was over. That's where Alice was on the day I had the wind knocked out of me attempting a cherry drop, leaving me alone and unable to breathe, stumbling toward the swings as the final bell rang.

"Probably because she's too busy with *him*," I said, throwing my sweater to the ground and climbing up into a squatting position on the bar. I extended both of my arms out in front of me and closed my eyes. I slid my feet forward, let my butt hit the bar, and then fell backwards with my arms fully extended over my head. I could feel the beautiful arc my body made as I swooped around and straightened my legs to release the bar. When my feet hit the ground, my eyes were still closed. My arms were outstretched from my sides. I heard applause in my mind. The final bell rang. I scooped up my sweater and ran behind Alice to our classroom.

For the rest of the afternoon I couldn't concentrate. What was so great about this boy? What was so great about boys anyway? They played rough and got into trouble. They smelled weird and were all sweaty in P.E. They liked things like road rash, lizards, and bugs and they made fun of me for liking the spelling bee and taking piano lessons. I had almost forgotten—it was piano lesson day and I would be taking a different bus home.

"Good!" I thought to myself. Then Sara could have her dramatic "good-bye, Nelson" moment to herself. The day before, she had lingered by the door of the bus, letting him put his hand on the side of her face while he said something lovey-dovey to her. I stuck my head out the window to try and hear what they were saying, but there were too many kids running around making noise for me to make out any words. Plus, Jake was kicking the soles of my shoes, which was a total distraction. After watching that googly-eyed good-bye the day before, I planned to turn them in for "hands-on" if I saw them doing it again.

There was a rule at school that you weren't allowed to touch other people. It didn't matter whether you had a good or bad reason for doing it. If you got caught touching someone else, then a teacher or teacher's aide would shout, "Hands-on!" and point at you. After that, they would either put your name on the chalkboard or on a little clipboard. If you had three hands-on offenses in one day (or one really bad one like fighting or, God forbid, *kissing*), you had to report to the office for the next recess where they'd give you a paint scraper, which you were supposed to use to scrape gum off of the asphalt and the bottom of the bleachers in the gym. Maybe if Sara got in trouble for hands-on she'd think twice about spending so much time with Nelson and would get back to hanging out with me. That was a fine plan but I wouldn't be on the bus that day to make it happen, so it didn't matter.

On piano lesson days I rode bus 10 way up and over the side of the mountain to Mrs. Higbee's house. She was a little old lady who played piano and organ for the local Lutheran church services and taught piano lessons out of her home. The bus ride to her house was much longer than my usual ride home. It took almost half an hour to get over the mountain. Bus 10 was much nicer than my usual bus, too. It was newer and it had a real stereo with a cassette deck. If you had a tape that the bus driver decided was acceptable, and if you were the first to get one to her, she'd play it until you got off the bus. The girl who got off at the stop right before Mrs. Higbee's house had a Janet Jackson tape, which, if the driver pushed play before the bus pulled away from the school, my favorite song, *Black Cat*, would finish right before the bus driver popped the tape out and switched back to the radio.

25

"Take one and pass it back," Mrs. Saltor said as she stood in front of my desk holding out a stack of papers.

I took the papers and held it to my nose for a quick sniff of the purple ink from the ditto machine before putting one copy on my desk and handing the rest to the person behind me. Just as I went to write my name on the top right corner of my paper, my pencil lead snapped off. I stood up and walked to the back of the class to use the sharpener on the counter. One of the privileges of being a sixth grader was that you didn't have to raise your hand to get up from your desk if you had to sharpen your pencil or go to the bathroom—you could just do it. You didn't even need to take a hall pass to go to the bathroom. With age came trust and I appreciated that.

From the back of the room, where the hand-crank pencil sharpener was bolted to the countertop, I could see everyone in the class. Sitting in the front, I didn't often get to see what was going on around the room. Sharpening my pencil, I saw Jake whispering an elaborately spun tale of his last summer-league baseball win to a couple of guys sitting nearby. I saw Nicole Thompson standing her math book up on the right side of her desk as a makeshift shield from the spitballs Tom Ryerson was blowing through a straw he'd pocketed from the cafeteria. I saw Justin Haley, who sat right in front of Tom, tearing off little pieces of loose leaf paper and popping them in his mouth as he dismantled a disposable pen, preparing to join the spitball assault. Mya Forrest, Cristina Berg, Jennifer Markham and Mindy Wilson were all applying lip gloss using tiny compact mirrors and fluffing their bangs with their fingers.

I pulled my pencil out of the sharpener and blew on the tip. Not sharp enough yet. Mrs. Saltor was crossing over to her desk so I hurried to finish the job. Once I was satisfied with the point on my pencil I started back toward my desk, purposely walking between Sara and Nelson, intentionally tripping over their feet, which were nestled next to each other in the middle of the aisle.

"Hey!" I exclaimed, dramatically, making sure I flailed enough to draw attention to myself and them.

Sara and Nelson quickly retracted their feet back under their respective desks. Sara blushed and started writing her name on her paper. Nelson tried to smile sweetly at me but I saw right through it. He was a best friend thief and whether he liked it or not, I wasn't going to let a smile change my opinion. Sure, I could go about my business and just let the two of them be happy, but what would that accomplish? Nothing. If I had to be miserable and bestfriendless, then they had to at least be miserable, too.

I sat back down at my desk and began to read the assignment instructions. While I read, Mrs. Saltor announced that we would have visitors joining our class in the coming weeks for a new program called *D.A.R.E*, which stood for "Drug Abuse Resistance Education." It was some partnership the school had with the local police department to teach us kids about drugs. I saw something about the program on a flyer at the library during the summer. There were these all-grade dances held at the grange hall called "*D.A.R.E* dances." The flyer said "Keep our kids OFF the streets and AWAY from drugs!" in big letters. Even though they were all-grade dances, Mom and Dad said my older sister Victoria and I were still too young and we couldn't go.

The visitors to our class included a police officer, a couple of high school students, and a reporter for the local paper. Our town was so small there were really only two police officers and we all knew them by name. Officer John Thompson visited the elementary schools during the year and Officer Mike Edmonds went to the middle and high schools. Officer John was Nicole's uncle and he was always really friendly. Officer Mike had yelled at me and Sara once when we climbed over the fence of the private golf course to pick blackberries one summer.

"Hey, girls!" he shouted from his patrol car, which was pulled over on the other side of the fence from where we were picking berries. He startled Sara so badly that she threw the big green plastic bowl of berries she was holding up into the air. Blackberries rained down, splattering on both of us. Officer Mike yelled, "You're not supposed to be over there!"

"My dad's a member!" I shouted back, arrogantly.

"What?" he called out and turned off the engine of his police car. I swallowed hard, but kept going.

"My dad's a member at the club! He pays dues! That means I can pick berries if I want to! And this is my guest! You can have a guest if you're a member!" I yelled. My heart was racing a million miles a minute. This was some serious backtalk.

Officer Mike shook his head.

"That doesn't matter, young lady," he said.

"Whattayamean it doesn't matter?" I snipped back, knowing that if my mom and dad ever heard me sass an authority figure like that I'd be grounded until I was in high school. "My dad pays hard-earned money for those dues and we come berry picking over here with my parents all the time! It's one of the benefits, like playing golf, or eating at the country club, or using the ball washers!"

Sara hadn't moved since she threw the bowl. She stood frozen with her hands at her sides, her eyes wide and her shoulders trembling. Officer Mike opened the door of his patrol car and stepped out onto the road. He walked toward us with one of his hands on a walkie-talkie and the other on the fastener that held his night stick in place on his belt. He stood with his face just inches from the chain-link fence and lowered his voice.

"It *doesn't matter* that your daddy pays dues, Miss Violet, because you two aren't picking the berries that belong to the golf course. These berries belong to the Ferris family. *They* own this property," he explained, pointing to the beat up old white house just up the hill. "This fence is supposed to be moved back a whole eight feet here in a couple of days. You are *stealing* the Ferris' berries, girls. And you," he said, pulling out the nightstick and pointing it at my nose, "you are getting awfully lippy."

I could feel the fear tears welling up behind my eyes. A knot balled up in my throat and I got the tingle in the back of my neck that I'd always get when I was in trouble or caught doing something I shouldn't have been. I lowered my head.

29

"We're sorry, Sir," I mumbled.

"Go on home," Office Mike said, putting the nightstick back on his belt.

Sara bent down and picked up the bowl. I took her hand and we started running across the fairway of the 16th hole. I could hear a man on the tee box shout,

"FORE!" but we didn't stop running. The man's ball bounced in a few steps front of us. We kept running. We didn't stop until we got to my house.

When we got there, Officer Mike's car was parked out front. I insisted that we go back to Sara's house instead. She shook her head and pushed me on the back.

"No," she said, "we have to face the music, Vy." Sara was a very honest person. I was ready to turn tail and hide for as long as it took for the heat to blow over. She gave me a stern look. I trudged into the house, expecting the worst. My parents would not like this.

"Hi girls!" my dad greeted us cheerfully. My mom only smiled. Officer Mike nodded his greeting.

"Hi Dad," I said, putting the berries we'd picked on the counter.

The adults continued their conversation, paying little mind to me and Sara. Officer Mike was just talking to Dad about the property dispute between the Ferrises and the golf course. He didn't say a single word about me and Sara stealing the Ferris' berries or about me being mouthy. Sara and I passed the front door just as Officer Mike was leaving and he gave us a quick wink. From that moment forward I knew he could be cool.

The assignment Mrs. Saltor had given us was that we were to write a full-page essay describing how much or what we knew about drugs. I really didn't know much. I knew that you could buy medicine, gardening supplies, fabric, Band-Aids, and have your pictures developed at the drugstore downtown, so I wrote about medicines. I much preferred red and purple medicines to the pink stuff I had to take when I got an ear infection. They said it tasted like bubblegum. They lied.

I was just finishing my essay when I got a whiff of the day's hot lunch being prepared in the cafeteria. I could smell the canned vegetables and warm processed cheese along with the aroma of something fried wafting through the halls. The buildings at our school hadn't been updated since my parents were students there and things were pretty outdated.

For example, we had to eat lunch at our desks because the cafeteria wasn't big enough to fit all of us. It was also the gym and the auditorium, with a stage on the side of the room opposite the kitchen. There was a big, outdoor covered area with eight basketball hoops that everybody called the "playshed." Sometimes we'd have indoor recess in there on really rainy days, but it usually flooded, which meant we'd have to stay inside and play something inactive like heads-up-seven-up.

We turned in our essays and lined up for lunch. I pulled my lunch ticket out of my pencil box and pressed it into the palm of my hand, lagging behind to make sure I was the very last in line. Tom and Justin stood directly in front of me. Nelson and Sara stood in front of them. The door opened and we all followed Mrs. Saltor down the hall, talking about our essay assignments.

"Dude, my sister knows a guy who buys pot at the Minute-Mart by the railroad tracks," boasted Tom.

"I heard people buy coke there," Justin added.

"I ride my bike to buy Coke there," I chimed in.

The boys stopped and looked at me with puzzled faces.

"You," Justin asked in disbelief, "buy coke at the Minute-Mart?"

I nodded.

"Yep. I like grape soda better, but I think the last time I was there, I got a Coke. Diet Coke," I said. "Regular Coke makes my teeth feel squeaky."

In the summer, after my sister and I were done with junior golf practice, my parents let us be pretty independent. I could ride my bike all over town so long as I stuck to the back roads. I would raid the old ten-gallon water bottle full of loose change in Dad's closet to go for soda or candy or miniature, collectible fuzzy bears, kittens, and bunnies.

"Oh my God," Justin laughed. Tom doubled over beside him. "Coke! You are such an idiot!" They hooted and howled, laughing at what I'd said. I didn't understand why.

Nelson looked over his shoulder at me. I saw pity on his face. Tom and Justin could laugh at me for whatever reason all they wanted, but there was no way I was going to let stupid Nelson pity me. I couldn't care less if he liked me or not.

"What are you lookin' at?" I snapped, lurching at him.

He left his place in line and let Tom and Justin walk past him. He came up alongside me. He looked like my grandma when she told me my aunt died a few years back.

"Violet," he started, "they're laughing because 'coke' is the name of a really bad drug. You're talking about soda pop. They're talking about something much more dangerous. You didn't know that, did you?" His helpful tone disgusted me. He was condescending in his kindness.

"No, I didn't. Because I'm not a drug dealer," I snipped, speeding up in the hopes it would make it clear that I didn't want to talk to Nelson anymore. I felt a twinge of embarrassment about what Tom and Justin must've thought about me but it paled in comparison to the bitterness I felt toward Nelson.

Our class line met up with the long hot-lunch line and we all stopped. Nelson kept walking, passing me, Justin and Tom on his way back to where he had been earlier, next to Sara.

"Hey!" Tom cried out at Nelson, "No cuts!"

Sara whipped around and gave Tom a dirty look.

"He said 'savesies'," she announced, pulling Nelson into the space in front of her. "Besides, he's cutting in front of me, not you."

"When he cuts in front of you, he cuts in front of all of us," Justin declared. He looked at Tom and then me as if we were supposed to back him up. "No reverse cuts, either. Aren't you gonna get mad, cokehead?" Justin asked me.

I didn't want Nelson back in line next to me. I just wanted to be left alone. I ignored Justin and leaned against the wall.

I could see into one of the third grade classrooms where the little kids were having a story read to them. They all sat on a big green rug. How peaceful and innocent they were, with their heads in their hands and their elbows rested on their knees. They sat Indian-style in a big crescent shape around their teacher, who was reading *A Pocket for Corduroy* in a very animated, sweet voice. I longed to be one of them. I missed the days of simple pleasures like Corduroy Bear and rug time. I missed the times before boys and drugs made life so complicated.

Lunch was tomato soup, French fries, orange wedges and "cheese zombies," which were dough topped with processed cheese topped with more dough and baked until the tops and bottoms were brown and the middle was oozing with molten cheesy goodness. At the condiment table I made my signature blend of mayonnaise and ketchup for fry dipping. Being last in line, I missed out on the opportunity to get chocolate milk or 2% and I had to settle for fat-free, plain white milk. So far, I was right about the year. It was awful.

By the time I returned to the classroom to eat, the cold lunch kids were already nearing the end of their meals. Traditionally, while the hot lunch kids lined up and slowly trudged to the cafeteria, the cold lunch kids performed their daily trade ritual. Someone would pull something out of a lunch that they wanted to trade and hold it in the air. Others would do the same, making offers like "two Oreos for a cupcake" or "bag of carrot sticks for an apple" and so on. They rarely made trades with hot lunch kids, mostly because hot lunches almost never came with desserts, and desserts were hot commodities. I traded a frozen juice pop from a hot lunch for a cold lunch Twinkie once, but it wasn't a very common trade.

I made my way to my seat at the front of the classroom and sat sideways in my chair so I could stare out the window while I ate. Darci Price sat in the desk next to me. She lived in my neighborhood, not far from Sara's house. Her mom taught French at the high school and her Dad owned the only service station in town. She was the tallest girl in class and probably the most developed, too. The first time I ever saw a bra that wasn't my mom's was at Darci's house. She looked and acted older than all of us but we were the same age. Darci had an agent and acted in commercials. She could sing really well and even appeared as a paid extra in the movie *Kindergarten Cop*. I sometimes dreamed about what it would be like to have an agent and get to be in movies and commercials like Darci did. Everybody liked Darci, but she never seemed to care about all of the attention she got. I would have bathed in it.

I listened to the conversations happening around me. I could hear Sara giggling while Nelson mumbled. I could barely make out what he was saying.

"And when we were standing on that log that was sticking out into the river, the one next to the campground?" he asked, and then I

35

couldn't hear the rest but it must have been something really wild based on how Sara reacted.

"Right!" Sara blurted out. She began to laugh with her mouth full of food.

"Gross," I said under my breath. Not only is this boy infringing on my relationship with my best friend, he's forced her manners down the drain.

"What's gross?" Darci asked.

"Oh, nothing," I sighed.

Darci looked back at Sara.

"Are you and Sara still friends?"

Wow. Not even two days into the new school year and we went from being known as inseparable best friends to strangers. The fact that Darci had to ask about us just broke my heart. I made a mental note to remember that moment just in case I needed to bring it up to Sara.

"I don't really know anymore," I admitted.

"Boys can do that to people," Darci said, wiping her hands with a napkin and piling it up on her lunch tray. "Have you ever had a boyfriend?"

I laughed at the question, nearly snorting my milk out my nose.

"No," I scoffed, pointing my finger at the back of my throat and making a barfing gesture. When my puke-acting was through, I looked back at Sara and Nelson. They appeared genuinely happy talking back and forth, like they had their own secret language and world where I wasn't welcome.

"Well, Vy," said Darci, "maybe you should." Darci stood up and took her tray to the coffee can on a rolling cart that served as the slop bucket to take leftovers to the trash.

I watched Darci and the way she moved. She seemed so much older and wiser than the rest of us. She had already had a boyfriend. I heard that she'd had a few and even dumped the ones she didn't like anymore. I was going to have to give this some careful consideration. After all, I loved the idea of being more like Darci. Everybody liked Darci. The hard part was going to be thinking about boys as something other than disgusting enemies of best friendships.

"If you can't beat 'em, join 'em, I guess," I whispered under my breath.

CHAPTER FOUR

If Sara didn't want to be around me anymore, then I'd show her she was missing out because *everybody else did*. I didn't want to be popular. I wanted to be admired. There was a big difference between the two.

Popular girls like Jennifer, Mya, Cristina, and Mindy were the ones that ruled the school. What they wore set the trend for the rest of the class. The music they listened to defined what was cool, and everyone learned the words to the songs that filled the cassette tapes in their Walkmans. They had exclusive slumber parties where boys snuck over to peek in the windows and watch them play Ouija, paint their nails, flip through the pages of *BOP* magazine, and watch *Dirty Dancing* (a movie that was far too explicit for my parents to let me watch at the time). I didn't want that. I wanted to be *on* the pages of *BOP* magazine. I wanted to be the one who Jennifer, Mya, Cristina, Mindy, and everybody else secretly wanted to be. This was my new goal. Nobody ever said it out loud, but we all looked at Darci with that kind of admiration.

It became obvious very quickly that my family would be no help in my efforts to be more confident, independent, famous, and universally liked. My sister, Victoria, was in the eighth grade and it was her experience transitioning from sixth grade into middle school that inspired my need to make sixth grade the best year ever. She and her best friend, Jean Devaney, found other friends between class periods and started following different paths and competing with each other. I watched middle school slowly tearing their friendship apart. In the seventh grade Victoria joined the band and Jean joined the track team. They had different science teachers and went head-to-head in the spring science fair. Jean built a self-regulating irrigation system for her family's vegetable garden. Victoria visited the local TV station and met a weatherman, then used what she learned from him to prepare her own weather forecasting system. Victoria and Jean both received blue ribbons and tied for grand champion. I remember the rage hidden behind both of their smug smiles as they stood on the cafeteria stage together to receive their awards.

When we were younger, Victoria and Jean had been a united force against me. They would mix dirt with water and grass clippings in empty margarine containers and turn them upside down on the big metal utility box where they baked in the sun until they hardened into cakes. Jean held me down while Victoria would try to make me eat their grassy mud pies. They whispered secrets and left me behind every chance they got.

Now that they were eighth graders, Victoria and Jean were all weird. Sometimes they were nice to each other's faces but then spread rumors or said nasty things when the other wasn't around. They would fight on the phone and not talk for days, and then they would write these long make-up notes. It was hard to see the two of them like this, which was what made my fear of middle school's effects on me and Sara so very real. If separate class periods could bust up Victoria and Jean, then Sara and I might be doomed if we didn't do something about it beforehand.

Victoria and I were just barely two years apart in age but we couldn't be more different. She was tall and slender with long, dark, shiny hair that looked like it belonged on a Hawaiian princess. She had these mysterious eyes that gave her an expression of skepticism all of the time. My hair was short, mousy brown and couldn't decide if it wanted to be curly or straight, so I looked like I had constant bed-head, even when I put a lot of effort into my hair. My eyes were big and green, which I thought made me look kind of like a bug. I was short for my age but had a pretty athletic build. I don't know what exactly it was about the way we looked, but when we were together people often assumed Victoria was my little sister instead of the other way around. She said she liked that because when we got old, then I'd be the witchy one.

My brother, Calvin, was in preschool. He was five and still pretty confused about the world. Blonde and cute, Calvin looked a lot like Timmy, the little boy I saw on reruns of the old TV show *Lassie*. His favorite things included his blanket named "fuzzy," his thumb, and asking Victoria and me questions. He cried all the time. Seriously, *all the time*.

Calvin's room had been mine before he was born. When he first came home from the hospital he slept in a basinet in the living room between the easy chair and the couch. I didn't understand why I had to give up my own room and move in with Victoria if the new baby was just going to sleep in the living room. Having Calvin in there put a real damper on my TV-watching schedule. He was usually napping when I got home, so the chances that I'd get to enjoy any *Sesame Street*, *Mr. Roger's Neighborhood*, *Gilligan's Island*, *Little House on the Prairie*, or *Benson* reruns were extremely slim. Mom and Dad made up for it by giving Victoria and me the old black and white TV to put in our room. After a while, Calvin grew out of the basinet and started sleeping in a crib in his room, which helped better explain why I needed to give up my room in the first place.

At dinner, the TV newsman talked about Libya and Lebanon while we passed casserole, Brussels sprouts, and pears filled with jam around the table. Calvin was crying and climbing into his booster seat. Serving utensils clinked against our plates.

"Mom, can I ride my bike to the Minute-Mart tonight?" I asked. "I need to buy a magazine."

"No," she said sternly, wiping jam off of Calvin's hands while he squirmed around. My mom was the most beautiful woman in the world. When she was in high school she was a cheerleader and prom queen. She had long blonde hair and captivating green eyes. It was hard to believe she was only two years away from her fortieth birthday because she still looked like she was only nineteen.

"Shhhhh!" Dad hushed at us as he waved his fork in the air. The newsman was talking about *Voyager 2* passing Neptune. My Dad loved space. He had built his own telescope from scratch, grinding the lenses and everything right there in our garage. I used to carefully pull the clipboard that held the instruction manual and Dad's drawings from the nail on the wall where it hung above his workbench so I could sit on a stack of free weights and pretend I understood the complexity of the design. When he finished it, Dad sat in the driveway all night waiting for Halley's Comet to go by. Since then, on clear nights he would pull out his telescope to show us planets, galaxies, constellations and other exciting things in the night sky. I loved every minute of it. But space was a little too nerdy for my current pursuit, so I rolled my eyes dramatically at Dad's shushing and ate my Brussels sprouts.

After dinner I took my tape player and the Paula Abdul tape I "borrowed" from Victoria out into the garage. I needed some time to think. I had spent the entire summer planning out how to make sixth grade the best year ever for me and my best friend. Now, because my best friend had been distracted and otherwise sidelined by a boy, I only had a few days to figure out how to put myself on a path to greatness and recapture a sense of direction for the year. It was bigger than that, even— I needed to plot out a path for my life. In my mind, the best way to do that was by strapping on my white boot roller skates with purple wheels and rolling around the driveway.

While Paula wailed and crooned over synthesized dance beats I gracefully turned, spun, kicked, and practiced "shooting the duck" up and down the driveway. "Shooting the duck" was when you'd lower yourself into a squatting position and then put one leg straight out in front of you, holding your skate off the ground while you sat on your other heel and rolled. It was really hard to do. I was pretty good at it.

I let my mind wander, fantasizing about how my plans might work. I imagined myself walking into class and proudly sitting at the front, while whispers filled the air behind me.

"Did you hear?"

"She's on that show, right?"

"Yeah, and in that movie, too."

"Should I ask for her autograph?"

"Have you seen her skate?"

Everybody liked me. The attention was awesome but I acted like I didn't even care. Sara would walk in with Nelson right behind her. I'd glance over my shoulder and she'd smile at me with a hint of regret on her face. But before she could walk over and apologize, begging to be a more active part of my life, a mystery boy would woosh in past her and over to me. He'd give me a flower and an intricately folded note that said something like:

My darling Vy,

There's nobody on the planet like you—nobody quite as smart, nobody as interesting, nobody that's anything like you and that's the very best thing you can be.

Love you always forever and even more,

Your guy.

A quick kiss on the cheek and my mystery boy would saunter out of the room. Everyone's jaws would drop and their hearts would fill with jealousy. The girls would want to be me. The boys would want to be that mystery guy who got to love me.

This was less of a plan than it was just a fantasy. I was so overwhelmed by the attention I was getting in my daydream that I neglected to notice Jake and his cousin, Dan, who had parked their bikes at the curb in front of my house. They sat on the utility box next to the bushes that lined our property—the same box where Victoria and Jean baked the mud pies I was forced to eat. I saw the boys, lost my balance and fell into the grass beside the driveway. Dan and Jake applauded.

"Nice work," Jake said, clapping and nodding. He sounded serious but we'd spent a lot of time perfecting our sarcastic tone with each other so I assumed he was just being a jerk.

"Whatever," I shot back, examining the fresh grass stains on my knees. Luckily, my skates didn't do too much damage to the lawn when I landed. My mom was very serious about the condition of our lawn. So serious, in fact, that we weren't allowed to play on it for more than a few minutes at a time. We were encouraged to play in the driveway or the street, especially if we were playing with neighbor kids. One summer when Mom was re-seeding the lawn, we held a three-legged race in the driveway. Victoria tripped and broke her arm. Somehow it ended up being my fault, although I never figured out why.

"You have some pretty nice moves," said Jake's cousin, Dan. Dan Martin was a year older than Victoria and went to school in the next town over. I was pretty sure he liked me, even though I was three years younger than he was.

Until that moment, I had never noticed him as anything other than Jake's cousin who was in our neighborhood every other Wednesday while his parents played cards with Jake's folks. Suddenly, I saw him as a dead ringer for a young Patrick Dempsey. I hadn't really given Patrick Dempsey much thought either, but I did remember really enjoying the movie *Can't Buy Me Love* when Sara and I watched it at a sleepover during the summer. Patrick Dempsey played the main character—a nerd who used his telescope money to replace a girl's suede skirt and jacket so she wouldn't get in trouble with her mom in exchange for her being his girlfriend. I didn't think about it at the time but I must have really liked him because when I realized that Dan looked like Patrick Dempsey, my attitude about them both became clear. I *liked* them.

I stood up and brushed myself off.

"Thanks," I said. I was feeling somewhere in between nervous and happy. I had an overwhelming urge to impress Dan. I had never felt this about a boy before.

"So," Jake said, sliding off the utility box, "how come you aren't walking with Sara tonight? That's kind of an every night thing for you guys." He hopped on his bike and rode up into the driveway.

Being that Jake was my best guy friend, I really wanted to confide in him, but my mind was going in a million different directions and I couldn't just spill my guts with Dan sitting there. I started to skate behind Jake, matching the circle he rode around the driveway. I paid careful attention to my skating, making sure I was doing the most graceful and complicated moves I knew how to do. I did crossover turns, occasionally went backwards, and even did the hourglass-tracing move where my feet were parallel but went wide, then narrow, then wide over and over again. I hoped Dan would be impressed.

"I dunno," I said with an aloof tone, "she's pretty busy with the new guy, so, y'know."

I looked up at Dan and noticed he wasn't paying any attention to me. He was looking back up the street where his older brother, Chris, was talking with Melissa Lockheed, another neighbor girl. Chris and Melissa were in high school. They were in the same grade but went to rival schools. I heard from Jake that Chris and Melissa made out on the golf course and got caught by Officer Mike with their shirts off next to the 15th tee box.

I went into a toe-heel spin in the center of the circle Jake was riding and did at least six turns before coming out of it into a perfect one-legged backwards glide. I looked over at Dan again. He was still watching his brother and Melissa, so he missed the whole thing. I lost my balance rounding the corner by the garage door and slammed into the side of the house. Only then did Dan look over.

"Dang, what a wipeout!" he exclaimed.

I had skinned my palms on the pavement when I fell. I looked at the little specks of red that were starting to appear and brushed my hands together.

"It's okay," I said, getting back up onto my wheels. I heard the front door open.

"Violet?" Mom called through the courtyard.

I was on the opposite side of the house and couldn't see her, but her voice carried quite clearly. She sounded both curious and bothered with a hint of concern in her voice.

"Yes?" I responded.

"Did you hit the house?"

"Yes?"

"Did it leave a mark on the paint?"

"No?"

"Are you okay?"

"Yes."

"Okay, five more minutes," she said, closing the door.

I picked up the tape player. Jake had been standing on his pedals with his hand brake on, trying to do a reverse wheelie on his front tire. When I hit the "stop" button and Paula quit singing, Jake dropped his back tire and started riding around the driveway again.

"Wanna walk with me tomorrow night, then?" he asked.

"Is Dan gonna be here?" I asked, hopefully.

"No, why?"

"Oh, nothing," I said, skating over to the lawn to sit down and take off my skates. "I'll meet you at your house after dinner, okay?"

"Cool. You riding the bus tomorrow?"

"Yeah."

"Okay, see you then." Jake rode in my direction and swerved to miss me at the last minute before jumping the curb into the street. "C'mon, doofus!" he called back after Dan, who was still staring at his brother and Melissa. He swung his leg over his bike and kicked the pedals.

"Later," Dan said, cocking his head backwards at me as he left.

I was going to have to figure out this whole boy thing sooner than I'd thought. Attention from everybody else seemed like an attainable goal with enough talent and self-promotion. Connecting with boys was going to be something totally different—I mean, the whole definition of "like" was changing. I wasn't ready to deal with all that.

As I brushed my teeth that night, I thought about boys. That feeling that overcame me while I was out skating—where did it come from? What was it about Dan? Was it about Patrick Dempsey? What made me feel so awkward and nervous, and why did I suddenly feel like I had to impress either one of them? I had never cared before. I remember a couple of summers ago when we were playing in the sprinklers in Jake's front yard and Dan was teasing me about my swimsuit.

"You're cute, honey, and someday you'll fill that out," he said, splashing water at my face.

Chris was sitting in the grass not too far away, tossing a football in the air to himself.

"Good one, Dan," Chris said, "only you're flirting with a third-grader."

"Fourth grade next month," I smartly corrected him.

"Not better at all," Chris shook his head.

While I worked on my molars, I thought about what Chris had said that day. *Flirting.* I would have called it *insulting*, but I was still learning about the world. I rinsed and went out to the dictionary on the shelf in the living room to look it up.

Flirting: To behave in a way that shows attraction to someone.

I made my way to bed and waited for Mom to pop in and say good night. Most nights, after she'd tuck me in, I'd give it a few minutes, and then sneak out into the hallway, where, if I laid on the floor by the corner, I could peek around through the crack in the door and watch whatever Mom and Dad had on TV until they turned it off.

Mom leaned into my room and said,

"Good night girls," to which Victoria and I replied,

"Night, Mom."

A few minutes later, I was laying on the brown shag carpet, watching an Isuzu commercial during a break in an episode of *M*A*S*H*. Just then, it struck me. When boys chased girls around the playground and threw things at them, hit them, or tried to embarrass them by lifting their skirt on "Friday flip-up day," they were *flirting*. It didn't mean that those boys were jerks, it meant that they *liked* those girls, assuming that's what the dictionary meant by *attraction*.

The next day at school, the *D.A.R.E.* program special guests were in our class. They were two high school boys and a reporter for the local paper. I had my name in the paper once before, when I had taken third place in the second grade spelling bee. I could have taken second or even first place if they hadn't given me the word "molasses." I was too embarrassed to say the letters "A-S-S" out loud in front of my parents and teachers so I threw the bee and settled for third place. Sara took first, correctly spelling the word "accessible."

I hadn't had my picture in the paper before, though. Hanging around his neck, this reporter had the biggest camera I'd ever seen. The lens was bigger than the size of Mrs. Saltor's coffee cup. The two high school boys arranged four chairs in a square for a role-playing exercise. I was only partly paying attention. In my mind, I was running through all of the different ways that I could use the day to my advantage.

The way I saw it, this reporter's camera could be the key to kicking off my efforts toward becoming admired. If I got my picture in the paper, well, you never knew who'd see that. Maybe someone famous. Maybe an agent. Maybe Darci would see it and wish that *she* could be more like *me*. The possibility was out there and I wasn't going to let this opportunity pass me by. If everybody could see me, then maybe everybody could like me.

The high school boys finished setting up the chairs at the front of the room and they called out for volunteers. My hand went up like a shot. Glancing back over my shoulder, I saw nearly every other hand in the class was raised, too. I heard the mechanical clicking of the reporter's camera going off and I instantly took stock of how I looked at that moment. I was reaching my right arm toward the ceiling with all of my might, lifting my butt off of my chair and trying to appear as if I were the highest-reaching student in the class. My left hand was at my elbow, trying to pull my right arm up even higher. I looked ridiculous.

"Um, how about you and you," the blonde high school boy said, pointing at Sara and Nelson. I let my hand fall to my desk. As they made their way to the front of the room, I smoothed my hair with my hands. The reporter's camera flashed and made a quiet but high-pitched whine while he wound the film. I decided I was going to make sure that my picture made it into the story no matter what. While the high school boys play-acted an impaired driving incident with Sara and Nelson in the "back seat," I concentrated on putting myself between the camera and the action at all times. I never took my eyes off of the reporter. I smiled so much my face started to ache. My lips shook and my cheeks nearly swallowed my eyes.

When it was all over, Mrs. Saltor thanked the high school boys and the reporter while everyone went back to their seats. The next edition of the newspaper would be out on the following Tuesday and I was positive that my face would be the first thing people would see when they picked it up from their front porch. The thought gave me a boost of confidence that I took with me onto the playground at lunch recess.

"Hey, Vy!" Sara called after me as I ran toward the bars.

I slowed to a jog and turned around.

"Wanna play tetherball with us?"

Nelson walked up behind her and took her hand. He wove his fingers in between hers and then he smiled at me. Maybe it was my newfound interest in the idea of attraction, or maybe having three whole days without my best friend at my side was enough to wear me down and make me hear her out.

"Okay," I said. I walked with them toward the tetherball poles.

Usually, tetherball was a very competitive experience. Alice was known for being unstoppable at tetherball because she had an amazingly firm swatting hand. Some people, like me, would slap the ball as it swung around the pole and it wouldn't change direction; it would just stop, requiring another slap or serve to get it started again. Alice could hit a ball coming at her and it would not only change direction, but fly with such force that it was almost impossible to stop.

Luckily Sara's tetherball skills were on par with my own. For the first few minutes we played in silence. Nelson sat on the sawdust that surrounded the concrete tetherball "court." It was soothing to be playing with my best friend again—even if *he* was there. Sara spoke first.

"You ok?" she asked.

"Yeah," I replied with a grunt as I jumped to swat at the ball. "I'm just thinking about a lot of stuff."

"I'm sorry I haven't been around," Sara mumbled.

I looked at Nelson. His attention had drifted and he was staring over at some of the guys playing basketball on the blacktop.

"It's okay," I said.

"It is?" She caught the ball.

With a sigh, I walked to the pole.

"Yeah, it is," I said. "It's like—you remember when we had that that day in fourth grade when they split up our class and sent the boys to Mr. Esther's class and all the girls from his class came to ours?"

"Mm-hmm?" Sara sort of giggled.

I giggled too remembering how funny the word "penis" had been that day. It was still pretty hilarious. Penis.

"They said we're getting ready for *changes*," I said. "I'm still figuring it all out, y'know? All the changes? Maybe this—" I gestured toward Nelson "—is all just part of what they talked about that day."

Sara walked over and handed me the ball.

"I just don't want it to change *us*," she said.

I stepped back to serve.

"Me either, and I think that's why I was mad."

"You said you weren't mad."

"I was. But I didn't want to make it worse because I was pretty sure you already knew."

That's fair," she said, "now serve."

I shook my head and walked back over to the pole.

"Two things," I said. "I think part of my changing is that I'm discovering who I really want to be—like my future and all that. I mean, I was doing it all at first just to get back at you for spending all of your

54

time with—" I waved my arm at Nelson, who was still staring off toward the blacktop.

"You acted weird to get back at me?" Sara asked, quizzically.

"Well, at first, yeah. But now, I think it's really who I'm meant to be. I think you should probably know that."

"You want me to know you're meant to be weird?"

"No, I'm meant to be famous."

"Okay. That *is* weird," Sara laughed, but I knew she meant it in the best way. "So, what's the other thing?"

"I can't say it in front of *him*." I pointed at Nelson.

"Okay," Sara looked from side to side and over her shoulder before taking my hand and pulling me by the arm toward the school building. Nelson watched us with a confused look. We stopped just short of the line that separated the playground from the wall.

"What is it?" she asked.

I looked around, then leaned in to whisper.

"I think I have a crush. On a *boy*."

Sara's eyes lit up with elation.

"Who is it!?" She shrieked.

I quickly grabbed her shoulders and put my hand over her mouth.

"HANDS-ON! FWEEEEEEET!" The recess duty was charging at us, pointing at me. Nelson walked beside her. What was he doing with the recess duty? I dropped my hands to my sides.

"That rat!" I said under my breath.

"Wait! You don't know if he -" Sara grabbed my arm and tried to pull me back as I started to stomp toward Nelson.

"HANDS-ON! FWEEEEEEET!" The recess duty kept marching toward us, this time, she was pointing at Sara.

I jerked my arm away and balled my hand up into a fist shaking it in front of me in a *why-I-oughtta* gesture at Nelson. With a look of panic in his face, Nelson put his hand on the recess duty's arm, stopping her in her tracks. I slowed to a stop and watched. Sara ran up beside me.

"What is he saying to her?" I asked. My heart was pounding in my chest. I started to feel the old *I'm-in-trouble* tingly feeling go up the back of my neck. Sara and I stood beside each other, frozen. Nelson and the recess duty walked over to us.

"Did you flip him off?" The duty asked.

I looked at Sara.

"Who?" Sara asked.

"You," the woman said, pointing at me.

"Me?" I was mortified. I was also confused. "What's flipping off?"

The recess duty gave me a skeptical look.

"I saw you raise your hand to him, but I looked down at my clipboard," she explained. "He says you flipped him off. It's his word against yours."

I was still confused.

"Like this?" I asked, holding my fist up in the *why-I-oughtta* gesture again.

"Is your middle finger raised?" she asked me, still looking at her clipboard.

I studied my fist. My middle knuckle did look to be a little higher than the rest. I had always thought that was just because of the shape of my hand.

"I guess?"

The recess duty kept writing on her clipboard. Oh, this was bad. What did flipping off mean? All this time, I'd been shaking my fist at people and had no idea I was doing something horrible. At least I guessed it must have been horrible, considering I was getting a referral for doing it. Just as she finished writing the bell rang. Everyone raced toward their classroom door—everyone except me. I stood in front of the recess duty with fear tears in my eyes. She tore off the white copy of the office referral she had just written and handed it to me.

"Give this to your parents to sign and bring it back to Mrs. Saltor tomorrow, ok?" she said.

I nodded, knowing that Mrs. Saltor would see the yellow copy and Mr. Ritter, the school principal, would see the pink copy today. There was a good chance that my Mom would get a phone call about it even before I got home. My head fell and I fought back the tears as I trudged toward class. I had let my guard down about Nelson for two seconds and just look where it got me: busted. It appeared that sixth grade had me on a fast track in the wrong direction, no matter what I did.

For the rest of the day, I tried to lay low. The pursuit of fame and attention would have to wait until the heat blew over from the "flipping off" incident. I wasn't used to being in trouble. The last time I'd received an office referral on the playground was back in the first grade, when I bailed out of a swing at the wrong time and accidentally landed on Mya. Sure, landing on her was an accident, but bailing out of the swings had been against the rules for reasons the adults said were "obvious." In my six-year-old wisdom, I couldn't see the logic. Bailing out was fun and yes, it was a shame that Mya got hurt, but she shouldn't have been where she was when my buns left the swing. Once I was airborne I had no control over where I landed. Well, when that particular recess was over, I returned to my first grade classroom to find my teacher, Mrs. Halifax, at the front of the room writing on the chalkboard,

I am very sad today.

I was certain she was writing about me. I could see the yellow referral slip on her desk. I had never received a referral before, so I just assumed that public humiliation must have been part of the routine and that I was the first in my class to receive one that fall. I prepared myself for the worst. Tears and a knot welled up in my throat. Mrs. Halifax put the chalk down and walked over to the classroom door. She pulled a TV on a rolling cart in from the hallway, outstretched the rabbit-ear antennae and turned on the news. I was confused until we saw that the space shuttle Challenger, carrying astronauts and a teacher, had just exploded after takeoff. I can't say I was relieved, but I never bailed out of the swings again.

Back on the bus at the end of the day I got my sixth grade referral, I sat in the next-to-last row of seats. Jake bounded up the steps onto the bus. About halfway down the aisle he tripped over his size 10 basketball high-tops and landed flat on his face. He popped up quickly and smiled, pointing at me as he said,

"I'm a fallin' man, but I'm not a jerk."

I didn't get it, but it made me chuckle. I appreciated the laugh. Jake slid into the seat next to me.

"What's the matter?" he asked.

I handed him the referral.

"Oooh, tough break," he whistled, folding the paper in half and giving it back to me. "Hands-on and obscene gestures. I wouldn't have pegged you for those."

I nodded and leaned my forehead against the window, doing my best to look sullen. I knew from watching TV that you got just as much attention when people felt sorry for you as you did for doing something great, so I just stared out the window and imagined I was the star of a music video for a really sad song. Jake patted me on the knee and leaned his head on my shoulder.

"Thanks," I said.

"No problem. We still walking tonight?"

"I guess so," I was concentrating so hard on looking pathetic that I momentarily forgot about the referral.

"My cousins are coming over again," Jake volunteered.

"Really?" I lit up.

"No," Jake laughed, poking me in the side with his thumb, "but now I'm pretty much positive you have a crush on Dan!"

I poked him back.

"Do not!"

"Do too!"

"Shut up!"

"Hands-on!" He whisper-shouted.

I socked him in the upper thigh. Sara climbed onto the bus and sat down in the seat in front of us.

"Hey," she said, dropping her backpack to the floor.

"Hey yourself," I echoed. "Where's your boyfriend? No smooch goodbye today from Captain Tattler?"

"No," she said, "and he's not my boyfriend right now."

I was stunned.

"How come?" Jake asked.

"He ratted out my best friend for something she didn't do," Sara announced, matter-of-factly. "I told him that honesty is important to me, just like Vy is. So I dumped him."

I instantly got goose bumps. Never before had I experienced such a gesture of friendship. Sara and I had been friends forever and while we did great things for each other every now and then, I'd never felt as important as I did right then. I had nearly forgotten about the trouble I was going to be in when I got home. Oh yeah, the referral. I wondered what sort of punishment would be coming my way.

CHAPTER FIVE

My recess altercation led me to lose early morning latchkey privileges for two weeks. Starting on Monday, Mom would take me with Calvin to his babysitter's, where I'd spend the mornings doing homework and practicing piano to earn the use of a curling iron to style my bangs.

Calvin spent his days at Jean's house. Jean's mom had an in-home daycare and preschool. Their house was huge with hardwood floors and giant oriental rugs everywhere. They had toys that we didn't like a hobby horse on springs and unique features to the house like a breakfast nook and a basement. Sometimes I imagined what it would be like to live in a big old house like that.

In spite of being horribly boring, the next two weeks went by quickly. The worst part of it had been when the local paper came out on Tuesday and my face was there on the front page. In the picture, the two high school kids were "mid-crash" in their fake drunk-driving accident. My classmates looked on with delight. There I was, front and center in the photo, staring directly into the lens with a posed smile. I looked beyond stupid. But I *was* on the front page of the paper so I tried my best to own it.

"Nice smile, doofus," Tom said as I made my way to my desk Wednesday morning.

"Thanks," I replied.

"That wasn't a compliment," he clarified.

"I couldn't tell," I said, laying the sarcasm on as heavily as I could.

Comments like Tom's followed throughout the day and seemed to hit a peak during library time that afternoon. The local Tuesday newspaper hung from a big wooden stick like a flag just inside the door, next to the regional and metropolitan papers. My face smiled out in black and white at everyone who walked into the library. I was convinced that every whisper I heard was about me and my picture. Between the remarks at school and the trouble I was in at home, I was starting to think I should be on the lookout for a rock to crawl under. Maybe being famous wasn't all I had imagined it to be. It sure didn't feel like many people liked me.

Being grounded wasn't without benefits, though. My world didn't get too complicated with social calls or outings and I knew that if I got all of my homework and piano practicing done, I could work without interruption on the latest story project I had started. My grandfather's old typewriter sat on a blue, metal rolling cart in my room for a long time. That was replaced briefly by my mom's hand-me-down electric typewriter when dad got her the computer. After the master's thesis incident she took back the electric typewriter, but my grandfather's typewriter had already been passed along to the next recipient, so I used the computer instead.

There was a bright blue-screened word processing program on the computer. I saved the stories I wrote on a black 5¼ inch floppy disk with my name on the label. I kept that disk in a box on the desk in the living room. There were little alphabetical tabs in the box and I would have kept the disk filed under "V" for *Vy's disk* like it was labeled but instead, I kept it under "C," behind the *California Games* disk, just to throw off anyone who might try to go snooping through my stories. That computer game was my favorite, particularly the surfing and roller skating levels. I became quite adept at rhythmically tapping *up-down-up-down-up-down* on the keyboard to keep my surfer moving along the wave. Like most things, Victoria was better at it than I was.

We got a Nintendo game system the previous Christmas. Calvin called it the "Imbatendo." Victoria beat all of the single-player games that we had and together she and I beat *Bubble Bobble* after spending almost the entire summer working on it. She played it in single player mode for a month before she got to level 99 and realized it was impossible to finish without another player. There was no saving the game or switching to two-player mode, so she had to start from the beginning once she figured out she needed help. In the game, there was a breeze that prevented a single player from being able to "bubble up" and reach the magic potion that could turn all of the bad guys into ice cream sundaes before time ran out. We worked together to beat the game, taking far less time than she had originally put into it as a single player. I wondered if this realization might encourage her to invite me to play more often. It didn't.

After school on the last day of being in trouble for the referral, I was sitting at the computer, working on a new story. I had begun to make a reputation for myself as a writer in the third grade, when we read *James and the Giant Peach* by Roald Dahl and I started writing my own adaptation, wherein I played the role of James and set out on an orange with a bunch of bugs who wanted to see the beach. I wrote it all by hand on loose leaf paper and my teacher let me read my progress to the class every day at rug time after lunch recess. The school year ran out before I finished it. Besides, I was given grandpa's typewriter that summer, which changed my writing forever.

I loved the typewriter and its "ca-chuck-thwak" sound for each key I pressed, and the professional look of a typed page. I enjoyed using the Liquid Paper White-Out to correct my typing errors, taking a deep breath for each letter I painted over, savoring the chemical smell. The computer took my writing up yet another notch, as I could correct everything before printing it out on the dot-matrix printer. For all that I loved about the computer and printer—the ability to correct things, the strips of holed paper to tear off of the connected sheets that zigged and zagged up to the printer from a big box, the small, quick "clicks" of the keyboard—I was truly disappointed by the printer ink. It was almost entirely odorless.

Mom had to stop and get Calvin from the sitter, then drive all the way out to the middle school to pick up Victoria from a special band practice before coming home, which gave me a few extra minutes of quiet writing time on the computer after I finished my homework and piano practicing. I could hear Victoria talking a mile a minute as she, Mom, and Calvin walked into the courtyard toward the front door.

Then, suddenly, silence. Two or three seconds passed and Calvin began to wail. It was the kind of scream that either meant that he was really badly hurt or had just been told the word "no." There was a momentary scuffling at the door and I heard Mom's keys in the lock. I didn't move.

"Get a towel," Mom shouted as the door swung open. I heard Victoria struggling to take off her shoes. "Hurry!" Mom was pleading. I could hear how woozy Mom was just by the tone of her voice. Woozy only meant one thing: there was blood.

"Is a blue one okay?" Victoria called from the hall closet.

"No! An *old* towel!" Mom yelled back.

I heard Victoria racing back to the door. Calvin continued to scream. With a slam, the door closed. The sound of the screaming got farther and farther away. The car started and drove off. I wondered what had just happened. I wondered how long they would be gone. I wondered what I could do with these moments of freedom.

I looked at the clock. Dad wouldn't be home for at least another hour. If whatever happened to Calvin required a trip to the urgent care, Mom would have to drive two towns over. If Calvin needed to go to the emergency room, they could be gone well into the night. If he needed surgery, they could be gone for days. Either way, I figured I had time to make a phone call or two.

I called Sara. Since I hadn't been riding the usual bus in the mornings and we weren't walking in the evenings, our talk-time had been very limited over the past two weeks. I had started to question how much she liked me anymore.

"So, what exactly happened?" Sara asked once I got her on the phone.

"I'm not sure," I admitted. "I couldn't see the door from the desk. It just happened so fast."

"And how long are they going to be gone?"

"I dunno," I answered.

"Wanna go for a walk?"

"I'd better not," I said, pulling the phone down to the floor so I could lay with my legs against the wall. "If they came back or Dad came home and I was gone, I'd be in huge trouble."

"Ok," said Sara. "Are you still gonna be in trouble this weekend?"

"Nah," I replied. "My two weeks is officially up today. I should probably have a clean slate starting tomorrow morning."

"Good! Do you wanna spend the night?"

"Tonight?"

"No."

"Tomorrow?"

"Uh-huh."

"I'll ask."

I could hear Dad's keys in the front door.

"I gotta go," I told Sara, quickly hanging up and racing back to the computer desk. I saved my story just as Dad walked in.

"Vy?" He called out.

"Yeah, Dad?"

"Oh good, you're here. Mom stopped by my office on her way to take Calvin to the hospital and told me they left in such a hurry— anyway, it's just you and me for dinner tonight." Dad hung up his coat and put his hat on the top shelf in the closet. He wore a brown fedora and an overcoat every day, which made him look like a character in a comic strip. It was likely Dad wouldn't remember that today was the tail end of my being in trouble, so I decided to try my luck at getting him to agree to dinner out.

"What were you thinking to eat tonight?" I asked, taking the disk out of the computer and hiding it behind the California Games disk.

"I dunno," Dad said, walking into his room to change out of his business suit.

I loved Dad's suits. Especially on the nights when he and Mom would go out to dinner. They'd come back from Sapphire John's Steakhouse with the smell of gin and secondhand cigarette or cigar smoke in their clothes. The wool from Dad's overcoat combined with these elements was very memorable smell.

I wondered if I could convince Dad to take me out somewhere nice for dinner. I'd only been to Sapphire John's once and I remember they had a jar of fancy crisp bread sticks in the center of the table along with a bowl of butter spheres on ice. I ate the butter on the bread sticks, one ball per bite, filling up before my entree arrived. The chances were slim that Dad would take me out for steak, but I figured I might as well shoot for the moon since I might land someplace with milkshakes on the way down.

"Want to go out?" I asked.

"Sure," he said enthusiastically.

"How hungry are you?"

"Really hungry."

"Steak?" The moon was in my sights.

"What? Steak? Aren't you still grounded?" And then there was that.

I didn't want to get into the technicalities about it being the last day of my grounding and that at midnight, I really should be free to roam about my normal existence again. As Dad walked into the living room I flopped sullenly onto the couch.

"How about The Old Fashioned?" he suggested. The Old Fashioned was a drive-in burger joint with a drive-thru window, a walk-up window, and old wooden booths inside. Dad loved the burgers from The Old Fashioned and I don't think I'd ever heard him turn down the opportunity to get one. Mom worked there in high school. As an employee she got one free burger each shift and she would always save it for Dad, who stopped by every evening on his way home from basketball practice. They also had unbelievable milkshakes in flavors like marshmallow, peanut butter and root beer. I loved their tuna melts and fries.

"That sounds great, Dad." I said with a smile.

On the drive to get dinner Dad explained how Mom told him Calvin had been holding his green fuzzy blanket to his mouth while sucking his thumb as he walked up the steps to the door. He tripped over his blanket, landing face-first on the concrete step. He bit clean through his upper lip. Mom thought he needed stitches. Dad said he would have just put a Band-Aid on it.

"Get burgers for your mother, Calvin and Victoria, too," Dad said, handing me cash once we'd parked near the walk-up window at the Old Fashioned.

I loved these fleeting moments of adult-like independence. Ordering for the whole family and paying for it myself—with a big bill, no less—I felt like I could have been sixteen years old. I fantasized about what it would have been like to drive myself to The Old Fashioned. I imagined being behind the wheel of my dad's Buick, cruising with the windows rolled down and Debbie Gibson turned up on the radio. Everyone in town would watch me drive by in a kind of slow-motion, blurred-edge dream. I took a moment to soak up that fantasy and I leaned against the building after I paid for our order.

"HONK!" Dad laid on the horn and waved me back to the car.

"What?" I asked, walking over to his window.

71

"Get in," he said, "we can talk while we wait."

I was really enjoying my independence fantasy and the attention I would get for my taste in music and driving skills, but I never got one-on-one time with Dad, so I skipped back to the car.

"What's up?" I chirped, hopping into the passenger seat.

"Did you really beat somebody up and flip them off at school a couple weeks ago?" Dad asked.

"No! I covered Sara's mouth because she was yelling about me having a crush on a boy and then I shook my fist like this," I showed Dad the *why-I-oughtta* gesture, "and this tattle-tale kid told the recess duty—who didn't even see anything—he told her I flipped him off."

My Dad gave me a puzzled look.

"Really?" he asked in disbelief.

"Yeah!" I exclaimed with wide eyes. I really wanted someone to believe me. I never had the chance to explain myself after it happened; I just took the licks that were handed down and tried to move on.

Dad put his elbow out of his open window and looked off into the distance thoughtfully. A few moments passed. He reached into the backseat for a box of cassette tapes. He opened one and popped it into the tape deck. It was Creedence Clearwater Revival's *Green River*, side B.

"You know, when people pull that kinda crap, they deserve to be flipped off," Dad said, pushing the rewind button. Hold the phone. Had my dad just given me permission to flip people off? "Except you gotta do it right," he added.

Dad took my hand in his. Oh holy crap, Dad not only gave me permission to flip people off, but he was teaching me how to do it!

"Make a fist," he said.

I did.

"Now, hold up your middle finger."

I did that too, but my thumb was to the side of my fist. Dad helped guide it around to the back so it could hold down my index and ring fingers.

"Now point it at me."

"Like this?" I asked and pointed the tip of my middle finger at him.

"No, Vy!" He grabbed my hand and reoriented it so that my finger stood straight up with the knuckles pointing out. "Like this. Now that's how you do it if you really want to say 'eff you, buddy,'" he said. "But you have to be forceful about it and really jam your fist out there. And know that as soon as you do this, it's probably going to make somebody want to fight you, because that's really what you're saying to somebody when you make this gesture at them. You're saying, 'you're an idiot, and if I were closer to you, I'd punch you.' Got it?"

I nodded. The opening guitar riff to *Bad Moon Rising* started to play.

"What if I'm close enough to punch them?" I asked.

"Then they're close enough to punch *you*," he warned, "so think about that."

73

The lady at the walk-up counter put four white bags out, rang the little bell, and called my name. I jumped out of the car with a smile on my face, armed with a newfound sense of confidence and incendiary ability.

I WANT EVERYBODY TO LIKE ME

CHAPTER SIX

There's a big difference between a sleepover and a slumber party. First of all, a sleepover is one person sleeping at the house of another, whereas a slumber party involves several guests. Second, there are no organized events or games at a sleepover, while a slumber party may have games, organized hairstyle, makeup, nail, or fashion shows, and time set aside for prank phone calls. Finally, a sleepover is usually a spontaneously-occurring occasion, and slumber parties are planned with enough time in advance for everyone invited to get permission from their parents and, most importantly, for word to spread around school about it.

Alice was notorious for throwing the best slumber parties ever. She had them at least once a month and they were a real who's-who of girls from our school. Alice had horses, a pool, a hot tub, a sauna, a big-screen TV with a VCR, a 5-disc CD player, all the hairstyling appliances you could ever want or think of, enough makeup to cover a professional wrestler from head to toe in color, a trampoline in the yard, four-wheelers, and an indoor basketball court in the barn. Sara and I usually had *sleepovers*, mostly at her house.

I waited until Saturday morning to ask Mom if I could spend the night at Sara's. Mom, Victoria and Calvin didn't get home from the hospital until long after I had gone to bed the night before. There had been a big shooting in the city and a fifteen car pileup on the freeway that same day, so Mom, Calvin and Victoria waited almost five hours in the emergency room to get four stitches in Calvin's lip. During the wait Calvin drug his bloodied blanket around with him, tripping over it again and again. At one point, he landed on the broken leg of a man who'd just had his bone reset and was waiting for a cast. Needless to say, by the time they got home, Mom was fried.

Even though she had been the last one to get to bed the night before, she was still the first one up on Saturday morning. Not only did my mom keep our house super clean all of the time, she made a full, balanced breakfast for us every day. The commercials that showed cereal as "part of a balanced breakfast," including fruit, toast, pancakes, eggs, orange juice, and milk were exactly like what mom would fix for us, only the cereal *had* to be healthy. We weren't allowed to have "sugar-cereal" unless it was for a special occasion, like Victoria's 10th birthday slumber party when my mom made frozen yogurt smoothies and served hot chocolate and cereal shaped like chocolate chip cookies to my sister's guests. Mom made waffles with sausage and eggs the morning after Calvin got his stitches.

After breakfast I washed the dishes without being asked. I even gathered up the garbage from under the sink and took it out to the trash can behind the garage on my own. My mom started to suspect that I was up to something when I wiped down the dining room table.

"Is this going to become a habit?" she asked with hope in her voice.

"Good one, Mom," I scoffed. "Maybe?"

She smiled and kissed me on the cheek, taking her dust rag into the living room to start her Saturday morning chores.

"Want to dust with me?"

"Sure," I answered. I didn't really *want* to dust, but I was smart enough to know that if I was going to get her to even consider letting me spend the night at Sara's that night, I would have to play the game—I couldn't just ask right away. I started on the shelves in the living room, carefully moving every book and knickknack, dusting beneath them and then replacing them on the shelves. I dusted the piano, the coffee table, the end tables, the stereo cabinet and the speakers. Mom took a break from dusting to dish up oatmeal for Calvin when he woke up. His little eyes were still puffy from crying so much the night before. I had a feeling Mom would have her hands full with him for the rest of the day. He started to whimper as she handed him a plastic spoon.

"Hey, Mom?" I said.

"What is it, honey?"

"Do you want me to finish the rest of the house?" I offered, picking up her dust rag from the counter.

"Would you?" she sighed happily.

"Sure!" I exclaimed and skipped off, knowing that I'd just planted the seed for my sleepover request. All I had to do now was let it sit for a while and then ask at the perfect moment. After I finished dusting I heard Mom carrying Calvin back to bed.

"He fell asleep at the table," she said as we passed each other in the hallway. "Poor guy."

I made an exaggerated sad face and she turned back to give me a hug.

"What's that for?" I asked.

"Just because," Mom said, squeezing me tightly. She kissed my forehead. "Love you, sweetie."

That was the sign I had been waiting for. I just had to give it another few minutes to solidify before I made my move.

"Thanks, Mom. I love you, too." I hugged her back, and took the dirty dust rags to the washing machine. "Mom?" I called out in a whisper-shout from the laundry room.

"Yes, dear?"

"May I please spend the night at Sara's tonight?"

"Tonight?"

"Yeah, tonight," I said, sorting clothes from the basket into the washer.

Mom peeked her head around the corner and took notice of the extra chores I was doing.

"Oh, I suppose. Is it all right with her parents?"

"Of course!" I declared, adding, "But you can call them first if you want to."

"No, no," she said, smiling at me, "it should be fine. But see if your dad has any chores for you to do this afternoon before you go over there."

Dad-chores were always way better than Mom-chores. Dad-chores typically involved something dangerous or physically strenuous, whereas Mom-chores were almost always repetitive and detail-oriented. Mom would have me wash the floors, fold laundry, iron, or unload the dishwasher. Dad would have me wash the cars, mow the lawn, restack the wood pile or sweep out the garage. I especially enjoyed mowing the lawn. I liked the smell of the gas.

Dad had me wash his car. I called Sara as soon as I was done.

"What time do you want me to come over?" I asked.

"How about four o'clock?" Sara said, "we're having pizza delivered at five, so if you want to have dinner here—"

"Great. Four o'clock. See you then."

I put my nightgown and a clean outfit in my backpack and hopped on my bike just before four o'clock. My family was watching *Hee-*

80

Haw while Mom fixed dinner. Sara's family didn't watch a lot of TV. They only had one really small set and it was in the kitchen, which I thought was a weird place to keep it. I couldn't fathom not watching a lot of TV. I loved to imagine myself in the settings and scenarios I saw on the shows I watched. In my mind, I was a wounded soldier on *M*A*S*H*, an adopted daughter on *Growing Pains*, a classmate of Laura Ingalls Wilder on *Little House on the Prairie*, and Sam Malone's wealthy niece on *Cheers*.

After we ate pizza and made polite conversation with her parents, Sara and I retreated to her room. She turned on the radio and pointed it toward the door to mask our voices while we told secrets. We sat on Sara's bed among a pile of stuffed animals and leaned against the wall.

"So, who is it?" Sara asked.

"Who is what?"

"Your crush! You said on the playground two weeks ago that you had a crush on someone and you haven't said boo about it since!" She'd been asking me about that every day since the referral incident, but I hadn't felt like we were in a secure enough place to talk about it until that moment in her room.

"Promise never to tell anyone? Ever?" I held out my pinky.

She linked her pinky around mine and squeezed tightly.

"Promise."

"It's Jake's cousin."

"Dan?" Sara blurted out, a little too loud for my liking.

81

I reached for her face to cover her mouth, but she shoved a plush mallard at me before I could reach her.

"Shhhhh!" I hissed and swatted the duck aside.

"Sorry," she said, wincing.

"I'm not even sure it's a crush," I said quietly. "I'm still just feeling this all out."

It was my hope that by confiding in Sara, she could help me better understand what was going on. She was much more experienced than I was, after all.

"Do you like him?" she asked.

"Kind of?"

"Do you think he's cute?" she asked.

"I don't understand."

"Vy," Sara looked at me the same way my mom did when she was trying to get me to stop lying about something. Only this time, I wasn't lying. I truly didn't understand. I mean, I wanted Dan's attention and I didn't find him as gross as most boys. I didn't quite know how to say that to Sara, though.

"Vy, do you want to kiss him?" Sara asked.

I held a stuffed pink puppy dog up to my face. I closed my eyes tightly and held my breath.

"Vy!" Sara insisted.

"I don't know!" I shrieked. "I've never kissed anybody before!" I let my breath out and hung my head down.

Sara took my hand and wrapped both of hers around it the same way my grandma would whenever she said goodbye to me.

"Oh, Vy! That's okay," she reassured me. "Until this summer, I hadn't kissed anybody either!"

"You and Nelson," I paused to make a barfing gesture, "kissed?"

"Yep," she said as if it were no big deal, "all summer. Well, at least the whole week I was at Lake Minnifield."

Aside from what I'd seen on TV and in movies, I didn't quite understand kissing. My parents did it and I'd seen high school kids do it at football games, but other than that I was pretty clueless. In my family, we gave each other pecks on the cheek all the time, but *real* kissing—that was something entirely different.

"What was it like?" I asked, flopping over onto my stomach. I rested my chin in my palms.

"Well," she started, "it's hard to explain. It's like, you kind of have to just do it to know."

That made no sense to me.

"How do you 'just do it' if you don't know what you're doing? You kind of have to want to do it to get somebody to kiss you, right? But if you've never done it before, how do you even know that you want to do it?"

We heard the door creak. When we looked up we saw Sara's brother, Sam, poking his head in through the door.

"What do you want, Sam?" Sara asked.

"Mom and Dad are going bowling, so I'm in charge now," Sam announced. He looked over at me and asked, "Do you need to call your mom and dad or go home or something?"

"No," I said, "we're fine."

"Okay," Sam nodded, and he started to close the door.

"Wait! Sam!" Sara called out after him.

"What?"

"After Mom and Dad are gone, will you come back up here?" she asked, winking at me and then turning back to Sam. "We need your help with something."

"Sure, whatever," Sam said, closing the door behind him.

I hit Sara in the arm with the back of my hand.

"What's that all about? We don't need Sam for anything!"

"Trust me," she said, raising an eyebrow at me.

What was she planning? Sam Anderson was in the eighth grade and was a pretty popular guy. My sister's friend Carrie had gone with Sam to a school dance and I overheard Carrie telling Victoria how Sam kissed her behind the school by the theater door. I hadn't *planned* on snooping in on that conversation but I needed to use the phone and when I had picked it up, Victoria was already on the line. They didn't notice me picking up and their conversation sounded pretty juicy so I just listened in.

Sam was a little shorter than most boys his age. He had brown hair that was just long enough to curl up around the edges of his baseball cap, which he was rarely without. He had deep brown eyes and pretty grown-up features for an eighth-grader. He had long sideburns and a dark shadow on his chin and cheeks that looked the way my dad's face did when he didn't shave for a day. Sam was built like a soccer player, with strong calves and a tight butt—at least that's the way I heard Victoria's friends describe his body.

"You know that space behind the cafeteria by the theater door?" Carrie asked Victoria while I listened in from the phone in Mom and Dad's room.

"Yeah," Victoria replied, "by the dumpsters."

"That's it," said Carrie. "When Sam and I left the dance during the fast dancing, he walked me back there and kissed me."

"On the lips?" Victoria asked.

"On the lips."

"Tongue?"

"Yeah."

"Ew," I said under my breath, forgetting that I was snooping. I dropped the phone and ran. Victoria chased after me. I had to hide outside behind the wood pile until dinnertime to get away from her.

85

Back in Sara's room, I was still trying to figure out why she wanted Sam to come back upstairs after their parents left.

"I'm not sure if I can," I said to Sara.

"Not sure if you can what?" Sara asked.

"Trust you."

"Oh," she flopped back into the pile of pillows on her bed. "Are you still mad about Jason?"

"Nelson, right?"

"Yes, his name is Jason Nelson. Are you still mad about him?" Sara seemed annoyed. She was probably still irritated at him for ratting me out to the recess duty. They hadn't been talking much since then, at least from what I saw. I had to admit I was glad to have my best friend back from him, but I wished I could have swapped seats with Nelson in class so I could sit by Sara the way we had originally planned it before he came and ruined everything.

"He sure screwed things up," I said.

Sara stared out the window.

"I guess so," she sighed. "I *really* liked him, though, Vy. I mean, I *liked* him."

"Like a best friend?" I asked, hoping to imply my importance above any feelings she still had for Nelson.

"No, not like that," she picked up a hairbrush from the windowsill and handed it to me.

I sat up on the edge of the bed and she climbed down onto the floor so I could braid her hair.

"I mean I *liked* him," Sara went on, "and I wanted to be close to him all of the time. I wanted to listen to him talk and I wanted to tell him everything. I liked looking at him and I liked when he looked at me."

I couldn't see her face from where I sat, but I could tell by the sound of her voice that every word she was saying was coming from a place deep in her heart.

"When we were together, especially this summer, it was like everything except for him disappeared. Like this one time when we laid down in the tall grass next to the boat dock and we stared up at the stars together. We didn't say anything, we just laid there next to each other, holding hands and looking at the stars. It felt like ten minutes went by, but it was two hours. My gramma was so mad!" Sara chortled at her own story as she told it. "She was stomping all over the campground looking for us, shouting 'SarrrrrrrAAAA!'"

We both laughed at Sara's impression.

"So *that's* what you mean by *liking* someone?" I asked, putting the brush down on the bed beside me and separating her hair into sections.

"Yeah," she sighed, "it's just this feeling, y'know?"

"No," I said, "I really don't. I mean, I don't know."

"Do you think you feel like that when you think about Jake's cousin?" Sara asked.

"I dunno. Maybe? I like it when he looks at me," I shrugged.

"Well, that's a big part of it!"

I appreciated that Sara was sharing her experience. I was actually a little grateful for Nelson at that moment. If he and Sara hadn't had their little romance over the summer, how would I have learned so much about relationships? Plus, I think the experience was bringing Sara and me closer together, which was the whole plan to begin with. At that moment, it felt like our goals for sixth grade were falling right back to where they should've been.

I was wrapping a scrunchie around the end of Sara's finished French braid when Sam opened the door.

"Hey, Sar," Sam leaned into the room. "Whadja need?"

"Are Mom and Dad gone?" she asked.

"Yeah."

"Come in," Sara waved Sam into the room. She walked over to him and pushed him toward the bed, where I sat with my legs dangling over. Sam sat down at the opposite end from where I was. Sara plopped down between us and said, "Sam, Vy's never kissed anybody before."

Sam instantly started laughing.

"Pshhhht! So what!? You're in like, sixth grade? You got plenty of time!"

I was in shock. Why would Sara tell the most popular guy in the eighth grade that I've never kissed anybody? Did she want him to think

I was some kind of loser? I know he was her brother and all, but I was just blown away that she'd do that.

"Seriously, Sam!" Sara went on, "Vy kinda likes someone and she's never been kissed, and she doesn't want to be bad at it the first time, soooo..." Sara trailed off, standing up from her bed and backing toward the door.

"What are you doing!?" I whispered loudly at her.

"I'm leaving," she whispered back.

Sam was still laughing.

"Don't!" I hissed, but it was too late.

Sara slipped out the door. I looked over at Sam and awkwardly smiled. I tried to laugh but all that came out was a weird goose-like honking. He shook his head and stood up. I was sure that he'd just laugh the whole thing off and walk out of the room thinking Sara was a goof and that I was just one of her loser friends he could tell stories about to his buddies in the P.E. locker room. Much to my surprise, Sam offered me his hand. I looked at it and then up at his face.

"It's okay," he said sweetly, gesturing for me to take his hand.

I was terrified. Trembling, I put my hand in his. He pulled until I stood up. He was at least a whole foot taller than me.

"Well, this won't work," he said, looking around the room. "Ah-ha," he exclaimed, pulling Sara's suitcase out from under her bed. "Here, stand on this."

Was this really happening? Sara's brother, the most popular guy in the eighth grade, was going to teach me how to kiss; or, at least it seemed that way. With Sam's hand to help me balance, I stepped up on the suitcase. Sam looked me right in the eye and stood so close to me, I could feel his chest going up and down with each breath. Even though I was standing on a suitcase, he was still looking down at me.

The strangest feelings came over me. The fear and embarrassment I thought I was feeling was replaced by a new kind of excitement that I hadn't experienced before. My heart started racing. I could feel a tingling between my shoulders, working its way up my back and to my neck. My sides went weak. I suddenly felt like there was more spit in my mouth and it was extra watery. Sam put one arm around me and rested his hand on my lower back. His other hand cupped my jaw and ear. I had never thought anything of Sam other than that he was Sara's big brother, but at that moment, I felt everything Sara described of her feelings for Nelson wash over me and I wanted nothing more but to be with, listen to, touch, talk to, and above all, kiss Sam.

My eyes were open wide and my mouth had dropped open. If Sam hadn't told me to close them both, I probably would have started drooling like a bug-eyed idiot. Once I closed my eyes, I felt Sam move in closer. I could feel his warm breath on my cheek. I could smell his cologne, which I had never noticed before, but at that moment it became the sweetest scent on Earth—better than ditto ink, gasoline, and rubber cement combined. I wanted to bathe in it. Sam brushed his lips across mine, which made me gasp and hold my breath. This wasn't like the kissing I'd seen on TV—not even on the soap operas, and they did *a lot* of kissing on the soap operas. TV kissing involved a lot of mouths being pushed together and people "mawing" at each other.

"Just relax," Sam whispered, and I could feel his lips forming each word as he said it. "Breathe in and just let me do all the work."

I took a breath and he brought his mouth close to mine, separating my lips with his. He closed his lips around my lower lip, gently sucking on it. He pulled back and then brushed his lips over mine. I opened my eyes and saw that his were closed so I quickly shut mine again, too. He lightly pressed his lips against mine, turning his head a little bit to the side, which caused my mouth to open slightly. I felt his tongue move past my lips and lick across my teeth. Almost involuntarily I felt my tongue meet his, and like two dancers in the dark, our tongues gently explored the entryway to each other's mouths. I could feel Sam start to pull away, sort of sucking on my lower lip as he retreated.

I opened my eyes. Sam's were open, too. He was still standing close with his arm around my back. It was a good thing, because if he had let go, I probably would have collapsed.

"There," he said softly. "Think you've got it?"

I nodded with what I'm sure was a dopey look on my face.

"You gonna fall down?" he asked as he started to step away. I nodded again. Just then Sara pushed the door open.

"All done?" she asked.

Sam nonchalantly stepped away from me and headed for the door, wiping his lower lip with his fingers.

"Yep," he said. "I'm gonna be on the phone for a while, so don't make a lot of noise up here okay?"

"Sure," Sara agreed. "Thanks, Sam."

"No problem," he said, closing the door behind him as he left.

I was still standing on Sara's suitcase. My mouth had fallen open and my eyes were droopy.

"Hey!" Sara said, snapping her fingers in front of my eyes. "You survive?"

I let myself fall to the bed.

"I'll never be the same," I said, staring up at the ceiling.

Sara flopped down beside me.

"See? I told you it was easy," she said. "And now that you understand, is *that* what you want to do with Dan?"

I wanted to tell her that I no longer felt anything at all for Jake's cousin and that I felt everything for her brother, but I couldn't. I had to get my head on straight. I was spinning. I still smelled Sam's cologne. I wanted to smell it forever. But I had to keep things in perspective. Nelson nearly drove Sara and me apart. Sam would probably be the nail in the coffin of our friendship if I let it go that far. I was going to have to keep this feeling to myself.

"Sure," I said. "I'm actually getting kind of tired," I did my very best fake yawn.

Sara smiled at me and brushed my bangs to the side of my face.

"Okay, let's get some rest." She pulled the covers back on her bed and pushed the remaining pile of stuffed animals onto the floor. She flipped off the light and we both climbed under the blankets. "Thanks for being my best friend, Vy," she whispered.

"Thanks for being *my* best friend," I replied, and rolled over to face the wall. I stared at the shapes in the spackle and replayed every sensation of the kiss with Sam in my head until I fell asleep.

CHAPTER SEVEN

When I woke up the next morning, I felt different. Older. Calmer. I had a new perspective on the world. Sara was still asleep next to me so I stretched and stared out the window, thinking about what was next for me. The plans Sara and I made over the summer suddenly seemed so juvenile. I reflected on the conversation I'd had with Darci and how she said that maybe I should think about getting a boyfriend. It made so much more sense to me. Sixth grade *was* becoming the best year ever, but not in the way I'd originally hoped. I had clear goals for my future and felt so grown up since I'd had my first real kiss. I also felt like I had to pee really badly, so I climbed over Sara and snuck down the hall to the bathroom.

When I got there, the first thing I noticed was Sam's cologne on the counter. *Eternity for Men.* I locked the door behind me and brought the bottle to my nose to smell it. I took several deep breaths, inhaling as deeply as I could, trying to burn the scent into my brain in the hopes that the feelings and memory of the kiss would forever be associated with that smell. I really had to pee and I couldn't hold it for much longer, so I took the bottle with me over to the toilet. I continued to sniff the lid of the cologne bottle as I sat. But when I went to put the bottle back on the counter, I looked down at my underwear and saw something, well, *unusual.*

I snuck back into Sara's room as quickly and quietly as I could.

"Sara!" I whispered loudly, standing over her, pushing on her shoulders trying to wake her up. "Sara!"

"What is it, Vy?"

"Something *happened!*" I was so panicked. The day our classes were split up for the boys-only and girls-only health lessons I was a little too busy giggling at the words to really pay attention to details. *Blah, blah, blah,* bodies changing. *Blah, blah, blah,* hormones and attitudes. *Blah, blah, blah,* pregnancy.

"What?" Sara rubbed her eyes and sat up.

"Does kissing make you pregnant?" I asked with terror in my eyes.

"Are you kidding?"

"No! I have to know! Does kissing make you pregnant?"

Sara was still blinking the sleep out of her eyes.

"Vy! You're a crack-up," she said between yawns. "No, kissing doesn't make you pregnant." She shook her head and looked me in the eye. "Why?"

I didn't know how to say it, I was embarrassed and confused. I pulled Sara by the arm into the bathroom, locked the door and then showed her. With a sigh and a smile, Sara hugged me.

"What is that for?"

"You've had a big night, Vy," she said as she started to dig in the cabinet under the sink. She pulled out a big poofy pad and put it on the counter. "I'll be right back. I'm gonna grab you a pair of my underwear." Sara was really reassuring. She must have already been through this. What was this, anyway? While she was getting underwear, I picked up Sam's cologne from the floor where I'd dropped it and put it back on the counter where it was when I first walked into the bathroom that morning. Sara came back and tossed me a pair of white underwear with pink flowers around the waistband.

"So what is all this?" I asked.

"It's your period," Sara replied calmly, taking the wrapper off of the pad. She went on to explain what I probably would have learned if I had been paying attention that day in the girls-only health class. I faintly remembered overhearing my mom explain this to Victoria one night while she talked about wearing deodorant and shaving her legs, which were still way beyond me, so I just ignored it all. Sara was very kind and easy to understand. When I started to tear up she just leaned in and gave me a hug.

"Want me to walk you home?" she asked.

I couldn't have asked for a better best friend.

"Yeah," I said.

It was still early in the morning and everyone in the Anderson house was asleep, or so we thought. I kept my nightgown on but just slipped into my pants from the day before. She and I crept downstairs and slipped our shoes on. Before we could get out the door, we heard a creak in the floor from the kitchen. Sara hurried outside but I looked back. Sam was standing in the kitchen wearing a white t-shirt and a pair of boxer shorts. He was taking a sip from a mug when we made eye contact. He raised an eyebrow at me and I could see he was smiling as he brought the mug down. I blushed and raced to catch up with Sara.

When I left home the day before, I was just a girl. I was returning home a woman. A confused, scared, and uncomfortable almost-twelve year-old woman. Sara said she'd call me later on to see how I was doing. I hadn't figured out how to tell my mom about everything, or even if I should. I planned to keep the kissing part to myself but decided that for the sake of her next trip to the pharmacy, she might need to know that someone else in the house was going to be using the lady-products. Mom had just finished vacuuming when I got home.

"Why are you home so early?" she asked. "Is everything okay with you and Sara?"

I ran to her and hugged her. In spite of my new role as an experienced woman, I just wanted my mommy. I could feel tears welling up in my eyes.

"Sweetie?" She looked down at me as I pressed my face against her shoulder.

"I had to throw away my underwear," I said, sniffling.

"It's okay," Mom said, rubbing my back. "It's just an acc-" she stopped herself. "Oh, wait." She pulled me back and looked at my face. My eyes were puffy and tears were streaming down my cheeks. "Ohhhhhh," Mom smiled at me and walked me into the bathroom, where she ran some warm water over a washcloth and wiped my tears. Without saying a word she opened a cabinet under the sink and pointed inside at a basket holding a variety of different sized pads. She handed me the washcloth and kissed me on the forehead.

"I love you, Mom," I said. .

"I love you, too, young lady," she said with a smile and a nod.

Later in the afternoon after everyone's Sunday chores were done, I was digging around in the toy box in the garage. I didn't really feel like roller skating. Dad was at his workbench sanding something so I couldn't go rifle through his stuff, which was usually one of my favorite Sunday afternoon activities. At the bottom of the toy box, I found my dad's old baseball glove and my uncle's catcher's mitt. I pulled out both mitts and a baseball that had a Seattle Mariners logo on the side of it. I hadn't seen that ball before and it looked pretty new.

"That one's mine," Victoria said as she came up behind me with her arms folded.

I held the ball up to her. She snatched it out of my hand and then held her other hand out.

"What?" I asked.

"I'll play catch with you if you use the catcher's mitt," she said.

I hated using the catcher's mitt to play casual catch. We both did. But, if it meant Victoria would play with me then I'd use whatever mitt she wanted me to. I handed her the glove and we went out into the front yard. Tossing the ball back and forth was one of the few times when I could get Victoria to have a real conversation with me.

"Mom says you started," Victoria blurted out, pitching the ball my way.

"Yep," I said.

The ball landed in my mitt with a THWUP. "How old were you when you got yours?" We continued to play catch while we talked.

"Twelve."

"So I'm early?"

"Everybody's different."

"Victoria?"

"What."

"Have you ever kissed a boy?"

"None of your business."

"Oh." THWUP. She threw that one extra hard.

"You shouldn't be worried about boys, Vy. Mom says even I shouldn't be worried about them yet. Move back a ways, you're too close."

I took a few steps backwards and threw the baseball.

100

"Have *you* ever kissed a boy?" she inquired.

"Um, no," I answered quickly. I wasn't ready for the world to know about my womanhood.

"Do you want to?"

"What do you mean?" I asked, playing dumb. I could tell that Victoria was mining for information. She'd either tell Mom or somebody like Jean and soon enough I'd hear about it at school from someone who was never supposed to know.

"Do you like anyone?"

"Not really," I said. We tossed the ball in silence a few times before either of us spoke again.

"Jake came by last night," she said. "His cousins were over."

I threw the ball up and out of her reach.

"Hey!" she cried, jumping for it, but missing as the ball soared over her mitt.

"Sorry," I said.

Victoria dropped her glove and chased the ball into the bushes that separated our house from the next door neighbor's. She got down on her hands and knees and started to dig.

"What'd they want?" I asked

"Jake just asked if you were home. Mom told him you were at Sara's. Didn't they go over there?"

I froze. Jake knew how to climb up the woodpile in Sara's backyard to get on the garage roof so he could peek in through her window—he had snooped in on a slumber party the year before. What if he and Dan had gone over to Sara's last night to look for me and climbed up to the window? What if they saw me and Sam kissing? Any chance I may have had with Dan would be toast. Not that I really cared at that point, though. The only boy on my mind was Sam.

"No, we didn't see them." I said.

Victoria found the ball and threw it back. This time it went over my head and into the bushes between our property and the empty lot on the other side. I pushed my way through the bushes where I saw the owner of the lot lighting a pile of brush on fire in the far corner. He was a man in his seventies, wearing a Fiserv trucker hat and a sleeveless flannel shirt. When he saw me, he waved and I waved back. I saw the ball a few steps in front of me, picked it up, and took it back through the bushes only to find that Victoria had given up on our game of catch and was tossing the mitt back into the toy box in the garage.

Whenever the lot owner burned brush, he never really put the fire out all the way. He was pretty good about making a rock rim around the fire and keeping his burn controlled, but he always left a few embers burning when he left. I loved to find leftover brush and sneak a few pieces of wood from my parents' woodpile over to the lot and try to restart my own little campfire after he was gone.

It only took a few minutes after the old man drove away for me to find a good ember. I had just gotten a flame started on some blackberry brush that was left behind when I heard footsteps coming toward me in the grass. I looked up, fearing that it'd be Mom or Dad there to chew me out for playing with fire again. Instead, I saw Sam.

"Hey," he said, stopping just across the fire from me. His dark brown curls peeked out from beneath an old Boston Red Sox baseball cap. He wore a plain white t-shirt and jeans with hi-top black canvas sneakers. I noticed the muscles in his arms and the way that his t-shirt wrapped each of them tightly.

"Hey," I replied nervously.

"Whatcha doin'?" he asked, walking slowly around the fire toward me.

"Oh," I poked at my flame with a stick. "You know." I went to lay a big hunk of bark down on top of my burning brush and Sam grabbed my hand.

"Don't do that!" he said, kneeling down beside me. He took the bark out of my hand. "You're gonna smother it!" Gathering up his own handful of brush, Sam made a little tee-pee over the flame I had going. Then he bent down on all fours and started to blow on the base of the fire.

I leaned over just enough to get a whiff of his cologne. He wore so much of it, it almost overpowered the smell of smoke coming from the little fire in front of us. It was fabulous. He sat up and looked at the few pieces of wood I had next to me.

"Do you mind?" he asked, pointing at the wood.

I handed the sticks to him. He leaned them together over the top of the fire beneath and then sat down beside me. We watched as the little flame I'd started from the leftover burn pile built itself into a pretty nice little campfire.

"You like fire?" he asked.

"Sometimes," I mumbled. I was so nervous. I was wearing a pair of teal stirrup pants and an over-sized sweatshirt with a Koala bear iron-on on the front of it. He must have thought I looked so stupid. My hair still had bits of grass clippings in it from when I crawled through the bushes with the wood. I combed at it with my fingers. I hoped with all my heart that Sam liked me.

"You go camping?" he asked, tugging at leftover wildflower stems. "We go up to Lake Minnifield every summer and stay with our grandparents. They live right by a campground so I spend pretty much every night for like a week or so just making fires and hanging out."

"You're good at it," I said, instantly regretting it. Was he good at making fires? Was he good at hanging out? Was he good at staying with his grandparents? I felt so dumb. I'd never felt this way around Sam or anyone else before. I'd known Sam my entire life but we never really paid much attention to each other. Being a friend of his little sister, I figured I was thought of the same way my sister looked at me and my friends: as an annoying imposition.

"I mean, I know you go to your grandparents and you're good at the whole fire thing," I said, trying to clarify. It didn't feel any better.

"Yeah, I guess you knew that." Sam stirred at the fire and kept talking, "Sara sure was like a ghost at Gramma and Grandpa's this summer—up at the crack of dawn to go exploring by the lake with that kid."

"Nelson," I interjected.

"Whatever," Sam didn't really seem to care. "I get the feeling that she wised up a little bit after all of those make-out sessions with him."

The old Vy would have been furious that I was learning more about my best friend's make-out sessions from her brother. The new Vy understood perfectly why Sara might have wanted to keep those special moments to herself. As I sat there, watching the fire and trying to smell Sam's cologne through the smoke, my mind went back to Sam kissing me the night before. My heart picked up the pace and I got a shiver up my back. I looked at the space between us. He was sitting less than a foot away from me. I pulled my knees up to my chest and wrapped my arms around them, brushing his elbow with my own. For a brief moment we made eye contact again. I looked at his lips. He looked at mine. I quickly turned back to the fire.

"Wised up?" I asked.

He let out a sigh and looked down.

"You know," said Sam, "more mature or something."

That was a word that got thrown around a lot in my world. There always seemed to be someone telling me that I needed to be more mature, or that something was too mature for me. Something about becoming a woman overnight made me feel a lot more mature, like I'd be more responsible and thoughtful than before—like I'd make a better babysitter.

"Yeah, I get that," I said.

He laughed.

"So you get that?"

"Mmmhmm."

He snickered though I didn't understand why.

"Was that really your first kiss last night?" he asked.

"Yeah," I answered. "Why?"

"'Cause I've kissed a lot of girls, some a lot older than me even, and none of 'em were as good as you." The thrill that shot through my body when he said that could have been made of lightning. I looked at him and he was looking right at my lips again, with a smirk that I found so appealing. I watched him lean in toward me, slowly closing his eyes. He turned his baseball cap backwards, put his hand on the back of my neck and pulled my face toward his. I closed my eyes and only barely felt his lips touch mine when I heard my mom at the front door.

"Violet! Violet?" she called out.

I jumped up.

"I gotta go," I said. I waved my hand at the fire, "Put that out, ok?"

My mom called again.

"Violet?"

"Coming, Mom!" I looked over my shoulder at Sam, who was staring down at the fire. I yelled back to him, "I'll see you later!"

He just nodded.

CHAPTER EIGHT

My twelfth birthday meant more to me than any other birthday I'd ever had up to that point. I remember ten being a big deal because my mom finally let me get my ears pierced. I remember five because that was the last birthday party with more than just my family there. I knew I'd remember twelve for a long time because it came right after a major turning point in my life. Almost a teenager but already a woman, the high hopes I had for this year seemed to get higher by the minute.

There wasn't much of a big deal at school or at home that day. I had a bowl of cereal and did my homework at the table before school. I took a plastic container of no-bake cookies to class and everybody sang "Happy Birthday" after lunch recess. Grandpa came over for dinner and I unwrapped a new pair of black stirrup pants, a purple cropped sweatshirt, a four-pack of hair clips, and some new multi-colored scrunch-socks. Instead of squealing and gushing over each present like I used to do, I graciously said "thank you" and hugged my parents and Grandpa. I was such a young lady.

Mom was pouring cups of coffee for the adults while we all ate birthday cake. I sat on a barstool, looking over the kitchen counter.

"Mom," I asked, "may I have a cup?"

"You want a cup of coffee, Violet?" she sounded surprised.

"Yes please," I said.

Mom thought about it for a second.

"You know this stuff will stunt your growth," she warned. Mom must have had a lot of coffee very early in her life because she was barely five feet tall. Dad was nearly six-foot-four, which led me to believe he really didn't care much for coffee.

"I'm tall enough already," I said.

Mom shrugged and pulled another mug down from the cupboard.

"Want sugar and cream?" she asked.

I nodded. Black coffee would probably be taking things too far for one day. Mom poured coffee and cream into the cup and handed me the sugar bowl. How thoughtful of her to let me decide how much sugar was appropriate. I appreciated this display of trust. I added enough sugar to my coffee to make it taste almost like caramel. Sipping the warm, sweet, milky elixir, I watched Calvin and Victoria play a boxing video game called *Punch-Out*. Mom went over to sit on the couch with Grandpa, who was talking to Dad about a cord of wood they were going to split. I felt like one of the grownups, quietly surveying my surroundings and calmly taking everything in over a cup of coffee. It was the quietest birthday I'd ever had but probably the most meaningful.

The next day at school, Mrs. Saltor stood in front of the class, holding up a stack of papers.

"These are applications for the Odyssey of the Mind teams," She said. "On the back of the form is a description of the program and this year's problem you'll be solving. Each team is only seven students and applications are due by Wednesday." She walked down each aisle holding out the stack of papers. Only a handful of kids took applications, including me.

Odyssey of the Mind was an educational creative problem-solving competition where teams of seven kids were given a "problem" to solve with a limited budget. After a few weeks of work, they would present their "solution" at regional, state, and international level competitions. Last year there were two teams at our school. My team had to make a structure out of balsawood and glue that could hold more gym weights than any other team. We had to present our structure with a themed skit while placing weight after weight on top of it until it collapsed. Our skit couldn't have any talking in it; in fact, we couldn't talk at all during the presentation portion of the competition. They called it a "non-linguistic" problem. That whole nonverbal communication thing made me pay closer attention to body language and what people might be thinking, even if they didn't say it.

I read over the problems for this year's teams. There was a literary problem where you had to interpret Dante's inferno in a three minute skit that incorporated current events and music. I really wasn't too interested in that. The mechanical problem involved building a vehicle powered by either a mechanical or pneumatic jack. That sounded fun.

I didn't worry about whether or not my application would get me in. I had done Odyssey of the Mind since the fifth grade, which meant I was kind of a shoe-in. Sara's family was really into it, too. Victoria and Sam were going to be on the same team this year at the middle school and both of Sara's sisters were doing Odyssey of the Mind at the high school.

At recess Sara and I decided to skip the bars and just walk the perimeter of the playground. Nelson was sullenly sitting on the swings by himself. Jake and a group of boys tossed a baseball back and forth nearby.

"He looks bummed," I said when I noticed that Sara was staring at Nelson.

"Yeah," she said. She sounded sad as she went on, "since we spent so much time together right off the bat, he really didn't get much chance to make a lot of friends around here."

Nelson kicked at the sawdust under the swings. I don't know if it had anything to do with my new womanly perspective, but I felt sorry for him. I didn't really see what Sara saw in him. He was skinny and his stringy hair hung down in his eyes. He dressed differently from everyone else. He had perpetually red cheeks and kind of a baby face. He had earned the nickname "Applecheeks" from Cristina and Mya.

112

"You talk to him anymore?" I asked.

Sara kicked at the dandelions in the longer grass along the fence line.

"I called him last night," she said. "His mom picked up and said that she'd go get him when I asked if he was home, but she came back and said he was busy."

"I don't understand," I said, "how come he's mad? I mean, he's the one who ratted on me."

Sara sighed and ran her fingers along the chain link fence.

"Who knows? Maybe he's embarrassed or something."

"Do you still like him?" I asked.

Sara walked quietly looking at her feet. I could tell she still liked him. In my limited but very intense experience with men, I was finding that once you let one get into your head, it was really hard to get them out. I had Sam on the brain nonstop since that first kiss, and even more after the *almost*-second kiss. I wondered what his day was like. I knew that our class would be touring the middle school before the school year was over, and I wondered if I'd see him while we were there. I wondered what he'd do if he saw me. I wondered if he ever thought about our kiss. I wondered if he liked me.

All of the sudden a big cloud of dust flew up beside us as Jake slid up next to Sara like a runner from third stealing home plate.

"What's up?" he asked, standing and brushing the dirt off of his pants. Before we could answer he continued. "Hey, Sar, Jason just told me he wants to talk to you," Jake then turned to me and said dramatically with wide eyes, "*alone.*"

Sara's face lit up, but it quickly faded as she looked over at me.

"Is that okay?" she asked.

I shrugged my shoulders.

"You don't have to ask me," I said, pulling a dandelion seed out of her hair.

She smiled and gave me a huge hug.

"Thanks," she said, kissing me on the cheek. She patted Jake on the arm, saying, "thanks," before running off toward the swings.

"No kiss?" Jake called after her.

I punched him in the arm. He joined me and told me all about the new baseball mitt he was going to buy with the money he made mowing lawns. I daydreamed about Sam.

For weeks all I could think about was Sam. While I was wrote up my Odyssey of the Mind application, I was wondering what he would think of my ideas. Like I had suspected I would, I made the team. So did Sean Nealon, Dick Naughton, Sara, Lou Cane, Billy Rawlings, and Lonnie Bennett. Sean, Dick, Sara and I were sixth graders. Lou, Billy and Lonnie were all fifth graders. This was the first mechanical problem team that didn't have fourth graders on it as far as I could remember.

"Well, we probably won't have that bad of a shot to go to state this year since we don't have any *babies* on our team," Sean jeered at our first team meeting. He was the shortest and probably the smartest boy in our grade. He had a messy mop of blonde hair that always hung in his eyes and had a style that could only be described as "round."

Dick laughed along with Sean. They were best friends. They were like the boy equivalent to Sara and me. Dick was super-athletic and was probably the only kid in the sixth grade who could beat Jake in a foot race. He had jet black hair that was always cut in a military-style flattop. Dick and Sean were an odd couple when you saw them together. Actually, it was rare to see them apart.

Lou, Billy, and Lonnie all had several awards from years of spelling and geography bees and they'd been on Odyssey of the Mind teams together before. Lou was half Korean, half German and spoke three languages. He looked more German than he did Korean, but he had a distinctly Asian bowl-style haircut. Billy was tall, skinny and blonde, with eyes that were steely blue. If he had less of a "little-boy" haircut, he might look like somebody famous. He dressed like Zack from Saved by the Bell. Lonnie was a quiet, overweight and freckly redhead who wore a lot of corduroy. He was Sam's friend Mike Bennett's little brother and was super quick-witted. When Lonnie did talk, he always said something unexpected and hilarious.

This was the first time that all seven of us had been on a team together. Aside from pointing out the obvious age advantage that we might have over the other teams, Sean decided at the first meeting that he was going to be taking the role of team leader. Usually I'd want to have a say in something like that but I wasn't one hundred percent "in" that year. I was still pretty distracted by Sam. I wondered how things were going over at the middle school on Sam's team. I'd bet he was their leader. I'd bet he looked really good with his tight white t-shirt and a smudge of grease on his face like a mechanic. I wished I could see him leaning over a drafting table with a pencil behind his ear, studying the plan he just drew up for the vehicle. Just thinking about it made me shudder—in a good way.

From the time school got out until just after five in the evening, I was at Odyssey of the Mind. We all got rides home from Lou's mom, who drove a minivan. We thought it was pretty cool that her minivan was a Honda Odyssey. We considered it a good omen for our team. Sara would always get dropped off before me and I'd have the chance to stare at Sam's bedroom window from the van in the hopes that I'd catch of glimpse of him or that he might see me. After several weeks of his bedroom light being off and no sign of Sam at home, I decided to ask about it. I knew that his team only met until four o'clock because Victoria was on the middle school team with Sam and she was always home by the time I got there.

"Is your brother here?" I asked Sara as Lou's mom pulled into the Anderson's driveway.

"No," Sara said, gathering her backpack and a large canvas she was taking home to paint over the weekend. The presentation for our problem's solution was going to have a ballet-in-a-haunted-museum theme. Sara was the best artist on the team so she was going to recreate a Monet. "Sam usually goes over to the Bennetts' after practice."

116

"Oh," I tried to play it off casually. "That's cool. I was curious about what the middle school team is doing, 'cause you know, Victoria never talks to me."

Sara slid the door of the minivan open.

"Yeah, that sucks," she said, climbing out. "I'll ask him at dinner and call you later, 'kay?" Sara slammed the door and skipped away. I hoped she wouldn't go telling Sam that I was asking about him. Then again, it could get me back into his head, which wouldn't be a bad thing if I wasn't already in there. He was certainly in mine—I was pretty obsessed.

That night I went to bed imagining what it would be like if I was Sam's girlfriend. I thought about holding hands with him, kissing on long evening walks, hanging out after school, and all the stuff that goes along with being a girlfriend, like little 14k gold lockets from the mall and PeeChee folders with heart doodles around each other's names. It sure would make the start of middle school a lot easier if I had a boyfriend in high school. As I laid there staring out my window at the street light I decided that I needed a new plan for sixth grade, and it went beyond making everybody like me. I was going to make Sam Anderson my boyfriend.

CHAPTER NINE

It was Friday evening and my dad had been away on business the past few days. He was coming home that night and we were all excited to see him. Whenever Dad went on a business trip he always brought back souvenirs for us from the airport or hotel gift shops. I couldn't wait to find out what he was bringing. I wasn't sure where he had gone this time but it didn't really matter—unless it was Hollywood. I had been reading up in some of the popular magazines about famous people and I had decided that Hollywood was where I wanted to be. Everybody liked you if you were in Hollywood.

Victoria, Calvin and I had all taken baths and put on our pajamas by the time Dad got home. I was settling into a beanbag on the floor in my and Victoria's room to watch the ABC Friday night "TGIF" lineup when I heard Dad's car pull into the garage.

"Daddy!" we all shrieked, running for the front door. Calvin was still dragging his fuzzy blanket in front of him as he ran. His stitches had long since been removed but he had a pretty gnarly looking scar on his little upper lip. He was the first one of us to reach Dad, who had been in the rain just long enough for his wool overcoat to be cold and damp. When it was my turn to hug him I inhaled deeply. He smelled like he had been at a steakhouse. I loved that smell.

"All right you guys," Mom said, shuffling the three of us kids aside so she could welcome Dad home. He hugged her tight and gave her a movie-like kiss, bending her backwards at the waist. It was very romantic. He was still wearing his Indiana Jones hat and overcoat. Mom was wearing a blue, cotton nightgown that could have been a dress under the right circumstances. Her long hair was tied up in a single pink sponge curler like a topknot. I studied their kiss.

Dad had one arm around Mom's waist and another hand on the back of her neck. Their eyes were closed and the corners of their mouths seemed to smile as they pressed their lips together. Dad let out a quiet "Mmmmm," like he'd do when he was really enjoying his dinner. He tilted Mom back upright. They briefly looked into each other's eyes and smiled. Mom collected Dad's luggage and took it into the other room while he removed his coat and hat. There wasn't any heart-fluttering lead-in to their kiss like I had with Sam, or like I was used to seeing in the movies or on TV. Maybe kissing was something that got less exciting when you got older. For a moment I stood in the entryway just staring at the door, horrified at the thought that someday I could become bored with kissing.

"You coming, Vy?" Dad asked. "I brought home something for you!"

Victoria and Calvin ran behind Mom into my parents' bedroom. Mom opened Dad's suitcase and began hanging up his clothes. Dad pulled out a black plastic bag from underneath his shoes.

"Calvin," he said, presenting a flat, folded white thing to my little brother.

Calvin looked at it with disappointment. His chin began to quiver and tears welled up in his eyes. I could see Mom starting to get cross.

"Look," Dad said, putting his lips to the corner of the white thing and blowing it up.

The look of excitement on Calvin's face grew and grew until Dad had finished inflating a big white airplane.

"It's the Spruce Goose!" Dad exclaimed proudly, handing it to Calvin.

"What do you say?" Mom said, her face returning to her usual calm smile as Calvin ran out of the room making airplane noises.

"Neeerrrrrrrrrrrr! Thank you!" he shouted, disappearing down the hall.

Dad reached back into his bag and pulled out a brown package about the size of a shoebox.

"This is for you girls to share," he said.

Typical. Victoria and I had to share everything; a bedroom, curling irons, clothes—you name it, we shared it. When we did have the opportunity to have our *own* anything, we became rabid hoarders, protecting our possessions from each other like angry mother bears. We did this with our Barbies and Cabbage Patch Kids. Victoria had a Hawaiian Barbie doll with long, dark brown hair and several colorful floral skirts. Her Barbie had pointed toes and wore high-heeled sandals. I had a flat-footed, off-brand Skipper doll. She was too short to wear any of Victoria's Barbie clothes (not that Victoria would have shared them, anyway) and because she had flat feet, she could only wear the little white sneakers that she came with. Victoria's Cabbage Patch Kid doll was one of the corn silk kinds, with soft, long hair that you could brush with a real brush, instead of the standard yarn hair that most Cabbage Patch Kids had. I had a homemade knockoff that one of my mom's friends sewed for me. She had yarn hair tied in a rubber band. I tried to take the rubber band out once, but there was no hair at the crown; the yarn only came from the doll's hairline and was pulled back into a tight ponytail.

Victoria lunged for the brown box in Dad's hand and slowly picked at the tape that held it closed.

"Just rip it!" I chirped.

"Be patient," Victoria dismissed, still picking at the tape.

"Want the scissors?" I asked, leaping across Mom and Dad's bed toward the sewing machine.

"No," Victoria barked at me.

Mom put a hand in front of me before I could open the sewing cabinet.

"Don't," she hissed with a stern look. "Do *not* use my sewing scissors to cut anything but fabric."

I froze and slowly backed away. I could hear Calvin in the other room. He was still making airplane sounds. Victoria finally got the tape off of the box and began to remove the contents. Whatever it was, it was bubble-wrapped. I saw hints of yellow, white, and blue underneath. Victoria started in on the tape that held the bubble wrap closed.

"How was Southern California?" I heard Mom ask Dad.

"It was nice," he answered. "Our hotel was in Long Beach but we had meetings in downtown L.A. and near Burbank." Dad knelt down next to me. "I saw the Hollywood sign," he whispered in my ear.

My eyes widened and my mouth fell open.

"You did!?" I gasped. "Hurry up!" I pleaded with Victoria, jumping up and down. I realized that I was behaving like an impatient child and I didn't care. Even if Sam rode by on his bike at that moment and saw in through the window of my parents' room, it wouldn't matter. My dad brought back something from Hollywood and I was convinced it was going to change my life.

"A phone? This is a phone!" Victoria shrieked, tearing apart the bubble wrap hastily. "It's a phone! A phone!"

"What have you done?" Mom asked Dad in a low, somewhat disapproving voice.

"Come on, they're almost teenagers," Dad said, defensively.

"I'm *already* a teenager," Victoria corrected him with a snotty voice.

Dad gave Victoria a *watch-your-tone-young-lady* look. I dove for the phone, which Victoria held like a football under her arm. She stripped off the last bits of plastic and held it up for all of us to see. It was shaped like Bart Simpson in a squatting position. The FOX network logo was painted on the front of his orange shirt in white. The backside of his blue shorts opened up to reveal the keypad and the transmitter, strategically placed on his butt. The receiver was on the back of his head.

"We had a tour of their headquarters and they gave all of us one of these," Dad said, almost apologizing to Mom.

Mom's eyebrow was raised as high as it would go. She didn't like us watching The Simpsons because of the language. At one point, Calvin said "eat my shorts, man," around preschool and that quickly put an end to our viewing privileges.

"All right," Mom gave in, "but before you plug that in, I have a few ground rules."

Victoria and I were all ears, though we were vibrating with excitement.

"No phone calls before nine A.M., no phone calls after seven P.M. No phone calls to boys, no phone calls over fifteen minutes in length. Always use your very best phone manners and don't ever leave the phone off the hook. Got it?"

"Yes, Mom," Victoria and I said in unison.

"Okay," Mom said with a nod.

Victoria and I were off like a shot. We ran down the hall to our room and flew over the mattress on the bottom bunk and onto the floor in the corner where the telephone jack hid. Victoria unwound the yellow cord and plugged it in. We pressed our faces together next to the receiver and listened to the hum of the dial tone, which to us was a harmonious declaration of independence. Victoria's and my hands were wrapped tightly around Bart. We were both hoping to be the ones to make the inaugural call.

"I need to use the phone," I stated.

"It's in *my* hand," she argued. "Besides, who are you going to call?"

"Sara."

"Why?"

"None of your business," I said, maintaining my grip on Bart's butt. "Who are *you* going to call?"

"Ghostbusters," she said.

I sneered.

"Funny," I let a chuckle sneak through. Regaining my composure I asked, "Really, who are you going to call?"

"None of *your* business," she shot back.

"Let's have Mom decide who gets to go first," I suggested.

"No!" Victoria replied quickly. "No, don't get Mom involved. If she thinks we can't get along about this new phone she'll take it away. You don't want that *do you*, Vy?"

I made a face like I was considering it. After a few moments, I gave in.

"You're right," I said, releasing the phone. "But fifteen minutes and then it's my turn."

Victoria scooted herself back into the space between the bed and the wall—our own little semi-private phone booth.

Carefully watching the clock, I set out my clothes for the next day and thumbed through the TV Times to see if there were going to be any good movies on over the weekend. Exactly fifteen minutes after Victoria dialed the phone, I let her know that her time was up.

"My turn!" I chirped, crawling on my stomach under the bed with my face smiling up at her from just next to her feet.

"That wasn't fifteen minutes!" Victoria whined.

"Wanna bet? Now, hang up! My turn!"

Victoria put her foot on my forehead and pushed me backwards. I chose to ignore what I'd otherwise have considered a sign of aggression.

"I can go ask Mom to help," I threatened, shimmying myself backwards out from under the bed.

"I don't care," Victoria proclaimed, calling my bluff. She knew I didn't want Mom involved any more than she did. I stomped out of the room to the kitchen where the other phone sat on the counter. Mom was

126

carrying Calvin down the hall. He had fallen asleep in the living room, clutching his inflatable Spruce Goose. Dad was at the computer desk, eating his dinner while he typed something. Slowly and quietly, I lifted the receiver and put it to my ear.

"And then *he* said that he wasn't going to the dance with her because he had a girl he liked and she wasn't it," I could hear Jean gossiping on the other end of the line. They must have been on speaking terms again. Since their friendship ran so hot and cold, I could never tell if they were friends or enemies from day to day. By their tone during that conversation, I could assume that the pendulum had swung back over to the "friend side" for Jean and Victoria, at least for the time being.

"Wait, Sam said he didn't like Katy?" Victoria asked.

If they were talking about the Katy I knew then it was Katy Barnes, the Marilyn Monroe lookalike who was probably the eighth grade's equivalent to Darci Price.

"I don't know about *that*, but he said he wasn't going to the dance with her," Jean replied.

I was already nervous, trying to keep silent so Jean and Victoria wouldn't hear me as I listened in on their conversation but hearing them talk about Sam really got my heart racing. It was hard to keep everything under control. I pulled the phone away from my face for a minute and took a few deep breaths before putting the receiver back to my ear.

"When did he say that?" Victoria asked.

"After Odyssey practice," Jean answered in a know-it-all tone. "He walked home with Mike Bennett."

"Then how did *you* hear about it?"

"Mike asked me out today! I'm his girlfriend now, duh!" Jean said, snorting while she laughed.

Victoria clucked with disbelief.

"Why didn't you tell me that at Odyssey? Some best friend you are!"

"What, were we supposed to get up in front of everybody and make some big announcement? Whatever! Look, I gotta go. Don't tell Katy I told you what Sam said. I want Mike to think he can trust me."

"Okay, whatever," said Victoria. "Talk to you later."

"Bye."

I waited until I heard Victoria and Jean both hang up before I did. I sat on the kitchen floor and tried to catch my breath. Sam said he liked another girl? He actually told somebody? He *had* to mean me, even though I hadn't seen him since our last kiss by the fire in the vacant lot. But what if he didn't? Who else could he have meant? I ran through every possibility in my head and the only conclusion that made sense was that Sam must have been talking about me.

"I'm done," Victoria said, walking into the kitchen and opening the fridge. She poured herself a glass of milk and continued in a snarky tone, "but it's after eight o'clock, so really, you shouldn't be using the phone anyhow." She started her call after eight, though. Maybe we'd both be forgiven for bending the rule a little bit since it was our first night with the phone in our room. It was worth a shot.

I dialed Sara's number and playfully twirled the phone cord in my fingers like I'd seen teenagers do on TV. I hoped Sara would pick up and not her parents. I didn't want them telling my mom I was calling so late.

"Hello?"

It wasn't her parents. But it wasn't Sara, either. It was Sam.

"Um, hi," I said. My voice instantly began to shake.

"Who is this?" he asked. He was chewing on something.

"It's Vy," I said quietly, stretching my legs out underneath the bed.

Victoria came into the room and flopped down in the beanbag I'd set in front of the TV.

"Hey!" I hissed at her, waving my arm at her to shoo her out of the room. She stuck out her tongue and turned on the TV.

"Oh yeah, Vy! What's up?" Sam said, smoothly. His voice immediately dropped into a lower, breathier tone as soon as he knew it was me.

"Nothing," I said. I had originally called for Sara but I didn't want to get off the phone with Sam right away. I liked him, and now that I knew he was telling people he liked me too, maybe it'd be easier for me to get him to make me his girlfriend. How cool would that make me, if I had a boyfriend in the eighth grade? Not just any eighth-grader either—quite possibly the most popular and good-looking one there was.

129

"You wanna talk to Sara?" he asked.

I didn't know what to say. I wanted to talk to him, but was that weird? I decided to test it.

"What are you doing?"

"Just hangin' out," he replied. "You wanna come over?"

I laughed so hard I snorted. It was almost eight forty-five. I was already in my pajamas and Calvin was in bed. It was dark outside and raining.

"Nah, it's too late," I said.

"You sure?" he asked.

I was not sure. I started to think about all the possibilities. I couldn't ask to spend the night at Sara's this late because there was no way Mom and Dad would drive me over there and I'm sure Sara's parents wouldn't come pick me up, either. Also, if I went that route, I'd have to spend all my time with Sara and I really wanted to be with Sam. I could have pushed the screen out of my bedroom window and snuck out if it weren't for my having to share a room with Victoria. There was no way I could have gone out the front door without Mom or Dad noticing, and if I waited until they went to bed it would be after ten at least. Plus, if my parents ever caught me sneaking out I would be grounded until I was at least thirty. Nothing could describe how badly I wanted to go meet up with Sam. I sank when I realized how impossible it was.

"Yeah. What are you doing tomorrow?" I asked.

"I was gonna go down to the river over next to the golf course and pull a few balls out of the water," he said. "Wanna come?"

I couldn't believe it. Sam Anderson just invited me to spend one-on-one time with him. He would be my boyfriend in no time. I traced *Violet Alene Anderson* on the wall with my finger, drawing a heart around it when I was done.

"What about Sara?" I asked, watching Victoria closely to see if she'd notice that I wasn't talking to Sara. She was pretty well engrossed in an episode of *Just the Ten of Us* and didn't even flinch.

"I thought it could just be me and you," he said.

"Yeah, that's okay," I said, "but I meant, um, won't she think it's weird or get mad?"

"Why would she get mad? Because we're hanging out?" he asked. "She's having Jerry over tomorrow anyway."

"Jerry? Who's Jerry?"

"The kid from the lake this summer."

"Oh, Nelson," I corrected him.

"Okay, yeah, Nelson," Sam sounded distracted. "So I'm gonna go. I'll see you tomorrow, okay Vy?"

"Yeah, when?"

"Just come over after lunch."

"Okay," I said, hanging on the line until he hung up the phone. I completely forgot about talking to Sara. It wasn't until I had tucked myself into bed that I really thought about all Sam had said. Aside from inviting me down to the river, I nearly skimmed over the fact that Sara would be spending the day with Nelson. I'd never really given the guy a chance and part of me felt badly about that. I did want my best friend to be happy—it was just that every encounter I'd had with Nelson involved him ruining something. That was hard to forgive.

Sara had been talking more with Nelson in class during the past few weeks. I think it was hard for them to ignore each other, sitting together and always being paired up for in-class projects. She still spent most recesses with me though, which I thought was a pretty fair trade-off. I wondered if I would have felt the same way if I hadn't recently become a woman. I might have just gone down that selfish path and kept Sara from something that really made her happy. I started to feel glad that she'd be spending the day with Nelson. Not just because it meant that Sam and I could go to the river together alone, but because I genuinely wanted Sara to be happy and I knew Nelson made her happy.

CHAPTER TEN

I rode my bike to Sara's house just after lunch. A lot of thought went into what I was going to wear and how my hair looked. I put a ton of gel in my hair and scrunched it up so it looked curly and ratted my bangs up high with a superfine comb. I wore black stirrup pants and high-top lilac-purple converse, a hot pink tank top and one of my dad's old dress shirts with the sleeves rolled up and only three buttons buttoned so I could tie the bottom part of the shirt up at my waist. I remembered Cristina's number one fashion rule she told everyone about at one of Alice's sleepovers: *it shouldn't be on if it isn't neon*. She said she saw it on a t-shirt during her family's vacation to San Diego. I added a neon yellow scrunchie to my wrist for good measure.

Looking at myself in Mom and Dad's full-length mirror, I thought I looked like a dancer on MTV. My mom didn't want us to watch MTV, mostly because of the way people dressed in music videos. If I was going to get out of the house looking the way I did, I needed to do it quickly and without her seeing me. I bolted for the door.

"Bye, Mom!" I shouted.

She came around the corner from the living room.

"Did you get your chores done?" she asked, just before I could close the door.

"Bed, made. Bathroom, cleaned. Mirror, Windexed. Homework, done."

"Piano?"

"Can I pleeeeeeease practice tonight instead?" I begged.

She lowered her eyes. I gave her a pleading look. She looked me over from bangs to toes and scrunched up her face. She did not approve of my look. I tried my best to make sad-puppy eyes. With a sigh, Mom gave in and gestured for me to go. I shut the door and took off.

Sara's dad was in the garage with the door open when I rode up. He had a welding mask on and was connecting two large metal pipes together. He waved at me and tilted the giant mask up.

"Hi, Vy!" he shouted over the hiss of the torch. "Sara's inside with her little pal!"

How mortifying. Hearing her dad call Nelson her "little pal" made me thankful, for once, that my parents had strict no-boys-in-the-house rules for Victoria and me.

"Thanks!" I shouted on my way inside.

135

My heart started racing and I got a nervous tingle up the back of my neck. I could hear Sara and Nelson in the living room. They had moved the TV in there from the kitchen and were playing Frog Bog on the Atari. That was one of my favorite games. It was a two-player game where you were both frogs, hopping from lily pad to lily pad eating bugs and flies, trying to be the one to eat the most before the sun went down and the frogs fell asleep. While Sara was at her grandparents' place during the summer I played Frog Bog and ate Otter Pops over at Jake's house almost every day. The sound of the crickets and the frogs sticking out their tongues was unmistakable. *Boing. Bloop. Sproing.*

I walked into the kitchen slowly, where I found Sara's sisters. Judy was baking cookies and Julie was at the counter, flipping through a magazine. Judy was perky and sweet, while Julie was aloof and cool. Judy was the president of the Future Homemakers of America club and Julie hated clubs. She was on the Odyssey team, but that was it. They were both in high school and had the same long, beautiful blonde hair with pop can curls that Sara did.

"Hi Vy!" Judy smiled, pulling a pan of cookies out of the oven. Judy made the best chocolate chip cookies known to man. They were soft and buttery but never fell apart in your hands. Judy made her signature cookies at least twice a week and all of them were eaten within, at maximum, two days of her baking them (if they even made it off the cooling racks without being devoured). Julie looked up from her magazine and sneered at me. I'd known her long enough to know that this meant "hello." Julie was never one to engage in conversation with kids. During a sleepover once, I said,

136

"Good night, Julie," to which she replied,

"Get sick and die." It was just her way. I couldn't tell whether or not Julie liked me. I didn't think I'd ever know for sure.

"Want a cookie?" Judy held out a single, warm cookie on a spatula. I couldn't turn it down.

"Thanks," I said, blowing on the molten chocolate chips.

"Sara!" Judy called out. "Vy is here!"

I heard the distinct *bing* sound of the game being paused. Sara hopped over the couch and into the kitchen.

"Hey! What are you doing here?" she asked. I didn't know how to answer. I figured that Sam would probably tell her we were going to hang out, but I guess I was wrong. I shoved a bite of the hot cookie into my mouth. The chocolate immediately burned my tongue and the roof of my mouth. I started to do that reverse breathing thing to try and cool it down, but inhaled a chunk of the cookie. Suddenly I couldn't breathe. There was a big piece of cookie stuck in my windpipe.

"Vy?" Judy squeaked, walking slowly toward me with a worried look while I waved my arms wildly. My eyes were bugging out and I stomped my foot on the ground like a horse. Julie looked up from her magazine. She seemed annoyed.

"Oh Christ," Julie huffed, calmly moving up behind me and putting her arms around my chest. Just when I felt like I was going to lose consciousness, Julie jerked me backwards, forcing the piece of hot cookie to come flying out. It stuck to the wall right in front of Sam, who had just walked into the room. As Julie let me down my legs went weak and I slid to the hardwood floor in a heap. Tears streamed out of my eyes. I was so embarrassed.

"Vy?" Sara said, kneeling beside me.

I couldn't help but laugh a little as I looked up at her. My face was puffy and flushed and my white shirt had spots of chocolate drool that had dripped down while I was struggling to breathe. Sam stood over me. He had a look of confusion and mild disgust on his face.

"Erm, you still wanna go to the river?" he asked.

I looked over at Sara, who seemed to suddenly realize what was going on. She smiled and put her hands on either side of my face the way my grandma did when she asked how I was doing in school.

"You want to borrow a shirt?" Sara whispered at me.

I nodded. She took my hand and led me upstairs. Once I'd changed into a blue hoodie with a picture of some seed packets on the front of it, I met Sam on the front porch and we started toward the river. He had a five gallon bucket in his right hand and he swung it back and forth while we walked.

"How's your Odyssey team doing?" I asked, thinking a little small-talk could break the tension and ease the embarrassment I felt.

"Pretty cool," he said. "We're building our vehicle to be like an Imperial Walker."

"An Imperial Walker? Wow, that is cool," I said, and then stopped myself. "Wait – I know they're kind of the same thing, but do you mean an Imperial Walker or an AT-AT?"

Sam quickly threw his arm around my waist and swept me up off my feet. He planted a kiss on my lips and put me down.

"The fact that you'd ask that makes you so awesome!" he declared, and we walked on.

I couldn't keep myself from smiling and blushing. My knowledge of Star Wars was usually considered a nerdy quality, not an attractive one. I periodically glanced over at Sam, during the rest of the walk, hoping he might impulsively kiss me again. He didn't.

We crossed the river road and started climbing down the bank. The golf course was just across the way and people with a really bad hook shot usually lost their ball off the third tee box into the river. I could see at least a couple dozen balls in the water from the upper bank. The river had already gotten quite cold with the changing seasons and it was moving pretty briskly. Sam rolled up his jeans to his knees and walked out into the water with his shoes and socks still on. I sat on a rock not far from the water's edge.

"You coming in?" Sam called back to me.

"Um, no. Too cold," I shuddered.

I didn't really feel like getting all wet. I liked just watching Sam without feeling like anybody was judging me for staring at him.

"Suit yourself," he shrugged. "Grab that bucket, I'll toss 'em up to you."

I put the bucket in the mud in front of me, tilting it just enough so the balls didn't bounce out when he threw them in.

"Sam?"

"Yeah?"

"Why are you doing this?" I asked.

He was elbow deep in the river, peering down into the water with his face only inches from the surface.

"Because I can sell these back to the country club for a quarter each, or for seventy-five cents to golfers if I set up a stand on the corner."

"No," I said, "I mean, why are you talking to me?"

Sam stood up straight pulling a handful of golf balls up from the water. Instead of tossing them toward me like he had with the others, he waded over.

"Am I not supposed to talk to you? It'd be weird if you came down to the river with me and I just ignored you, wouldn't it?" He dropped the balls into the bucket and sat down on the rock next to me.

"That's not what I meant," I said.

He took my hand and started to trace the lines in my palm with his index finger. I shivered every time he touched me.

"I don't understand why you want to be around me," I whispered, just loud enough for him to hear over the rush of the river. "I'm just a sixth grader. I'm your baby sister's best friend. I don't wear makeup. I'm not super cute or anything. I'm probably the least popular person I know. I get made fun of a lot. To tell you the truth, I'm pretty embarrassing to be around—just ask Sara sometime."

"So you want me to know you think you're a loser, is that it?" he asked.

"I, um," I was all turned around and confused. "No, I just don't get it."

I wanted to have all of Darci's confidence. I wanted to have all of Alice's things and abilities. I wanted to be beautiful like Sara. I wanted to be girly like Mya, Cristina, Jennifer and Mindy. I wanted to be smart and aloof like Julie. I wanted to be all the things that I knew I wasn't, because I thought Sam was too cool to like just plain old me. I brought all of that up because I thought maybe if I could show him that I was realistic about the way I viewed myself, he might say or do something to make me feel better. Like tell me he liked me or make me his girlfriend.

"Oh, like, why don't I go out with somebody my own age?"

"Yeah," I said, "or somebody more popular like you."

Sam laughed and started wading back out into the river.

"Look, if you don't like it, I'll leave you alone," he said. "It's going to be hard, because I like you."

"I like you a lot, too," I said. I was immediately horrified at how quickly and honestly that came out. "I mean, you know," I let my voice trail off.

Sam laughed again. Part of me wanted to believe him because I really wanted him to like me. The other part of me didn't believe him because there was no logical reason for him to like me. But I wasn't exactly operating from a logical place. I was running on one hundred percent raw "tween" emotion.

"Wanna make out?" Sam asked, splashing water at me with his hand.

"Quit it!" I shrieked.

He ran at me and pushed me off the rock into the mud. We wrestled around for a while and he snuck kisses in whenever he could. We were covered in mud from head to toe when Officer Mike pulled over alongside the river road and shouted down to us from his patrol car.

"Hey! The water's pretty swift down there--it's too dangerous for you kids. Time to go on home," he shouted.

"Party's over," Sam said, gathering the bucket of golf balls and helping me stand up. He didn't seem fazed at all about the fact that Officer Mike saw us together. I took that as affirmation that he was ready for people to know about "us." Giving it more thought, I wondered if Sam was ever going to hold my hand or *really* tell anybody about us. I mean, Officer Mike was one thing—his friends were another. I had a feeling that I was going to end up being Sam's secret, and that's all.

A few days later, I finally talked to Sara about me and Sam while she and I worked on the set for our Odyssey presentation in the school cafeteria. I told her about the kisses and about how much easier my life would be if I could just make her brother my boyfriend.

"I know how you feel," she said, "It's the same way with me and my boyfriend too."

We were building giant easels for the artwork Sara had painted. The vehicle we'd built as part of our solution was made from two old bicycle frames with a platform connecting them. On the platform sat a mechanical jack. The jack was outfitted with foot pedals. Each time you stepped down on one, the jack pushed up a big lever, which pulled a long bike chain over a set of cogs and made the vehicle go. Since the vehicle had been completed all of our energies were going into the set and practicing our presentation.

"Your boyfriend?" I asked Sara.

"Oh, didn't I tell you? Jason and I are officially going out again."

I had heard that phrase used before but I always wondered why people said it. On *Happy Days*, they called it "going steady," which made far more sense to me. In my opinion, "going out" meant you were actually going somewhere. I didn't like to say it.

"It's great because it's like, I can relax and not worry about impressing him because he's committed to me," Sara said.

That made a lot of sense. Maybe Darci was right and having an actual boyfriend was the solution I needed. I spent a lot of time worrying about whether or not everybody liked me. If I had a boyfriend, then there would be this built-in person who always liked me. Sam liked me, I knew it. It only made sense that if he let Officer Mike see us together and really told Mike Bennett that he liked me like I thought he did, then maybe he'd actually consider making me his girlfriend—and not just a secret one. I had to find out.

"Anyway," Sara went on, "the whole time we were at the lake Jason never told his other friends about me. I was some big secret that he'd sneak out in the woods to be with. But then, when he moved here, he didn't have anybody but me, so it was okay for him to let people see us. He didn't have a reputation or anything."

"Sam has a reputation," I said, thinking aloud.

"Yes he does," Sara agreed. "There are a lot of stories about him and girls. I'd be careful if I were you. He may be my brother but I hear what people say about him. I love you both. I'll do what I can to help you, but Vy, just don't get hurt, mmkay?"

"I'll try."

CHAPTER ELEVEN

Every year on Halloween kids took their costumes to school in paper sacks so that after the last recess of the day they could change into them for a big hallway parade. With the exception of the kids who weren't allowed to celebrate for whatever religious or social reasons their parents gave, everybody in the whole school would line up in the hall and parade around so we could all see each other's costumes before returning to our classrooms for a party with cookies and juice.

Sara and I had decided way back in the summer what our costumes would be, and of course, they had to be identical. We wore green pants and sweatshirts, painted our faces yellow, and put pink tutus around our heads. We thought we looked like flowers, but people kept asking us what we were. There were a lot of store-bought costumes; we passed several Ninja Turtles, Mario and Luigi, and Batman outfits during the parade.

"Do you want to trick-or-treat together tonight?" Sara asked.

"I was thinking maybe we're a little old for that," I replied, only slightly considering how odd that was for me to say while wearing a tutu on my head. "Let's talk about it later."

After the Halloween parade but before we all went home, Mrs. Saltor handed out permission slips for the upcoming field trip. I was beyond excited. Field trips were always fun but this one was going to be especially awesome because we were going to be touring the middle school. Each class would be divided into four groups and led around by an eighth grade guide. Victoria told my family about it at the dinner table earlier that week—she was going to be one of the student guides.

"All the kids in the TAG program got picked to do it," Victoria proudly said.

TAG stood for *talented and gifted*. If you got a high enough score on the MAT-6 standardized test, they came and got you out of class once a week to go on a special field trip or do some really challenging and fun project with the rest of the TAG kids. Victoria got into TAG when she was in the fourth grade and my parents made a pretty big deal about it. I got into the program in the third grade but was told by my folks to be humble about it. Sara, Jake and Sam were in TAG too.

There was one field trip the TAG kids took the year before that I especially liked. It was to an old stone church just outside of the city, where we sat in the basement and listened to an old man play banjo and sing folk songs. His name was Pete Seeger and I knew all of the songs he was singing but I had no idea who he was. There was a photographer from the local paper who went with us on that field trip but I wasn't quite so worried about being seen back then and didn't end up in any of his pictures.

Darci noticed the numbers on the upper right corner of our permission slips, which were what divided us into our groups. I was in group 4-S (which stood for the fourth group in Mrs. Saltor's class) with Sara, Nelson, Jake, Cristina, Tom and Mindy. Our middle school guides were all waiting for their groups on the buses. We lined up by the playshed and waited for our teachers to assign us to a bus. I could see Victoria and Jean peering through the windows of one the buses. I waved enthusiastically at them. Victoria saw me and rolled her eyes. On another bus, I saw Sam sitting toward the front, talking with the driver. My group was lined up just between Victoria's and Sam's bus. I hoped and hoped that we'd end up on Sam's bus.

"Group four-S!" we heard, and then saw a teacher with a clipboard waiving his arm. "Bus ten!"

Our group was led away from Victoria's bus and toward Sam's. I felt my stomach start to flutter. I was next-to-last to climb aboard the bus, behind Sara and in front of Jake. Sam was sitting in the front seat. As I walked by him he slapped me on the left butt cheek and winked at me.

"Woah, buddy!" Jake said, quickly stepping between me and Sam. "Dude, Sara, you know your brother's a perv?"

Sam shook his head dismissively and looked out the window while Jake stared him down. I smiled shyly and walked on. Jake didn't want to let it go.

148

"Hey, man, you like putting your hands on little girls?" He was leaning over the seat trying to get in Sam's face.

Sam ignored him. Jake continued to move closer and closer to Sam.

"Keep moving," the teacher who had called us to the bus was standing behind Jake, trying to move him down the aisle.

Jake made a face at Sam and then stomped down the aisle to where Sara and I were sitting. He plopped down in the seat across the aisle from us. Even though Sam was two years older than Jake, he was no match for Jake's size or athleticism. For a brief moment I fantasized about Jake and Sam's little argument escalating into a major fight over me. I'd never thought about guys fighting over me before and I found it kind of thrilling to imagine. Still, I couldn't have Jake making Sam think I didn't like his attention.

Mike Bennett was introduced as our guide. While the other kids filed onto the buses he played "get-to-know-you" games with the six of us. I stared over the seat in front of me at Sam, who was getting acquainted with his own group. We made eye contact and he playfully raised an eyebrow at me. I blushed and looked away. Jake leaned across the aisle.

"Hey, what is up with that creep?" he asked, eyeballing Sam.

"He isn't a creep," I said. "He's nice to me."

Jake scoffed.

"Nice to you? You think smacking you on the butt and making googly-eyes at you is being nice to you?"

"Shhhh!" I hissed at Jake. "Shut up!"

Jake folded his arms and sat back in his seat, giving me a dirty look. Jake had been like a brother to me as long as I'd known him. I figured it was natural for him to want to protect me but I didn't want his "protection" right then.

"Look, Jake," I said, "if you want to be a good friend to me right now just leave Sam alone."

Jake squinted his eyes at me.

"I am *not* okay with anybody treating you like that," Jake said. He ground his fist into his palm.

"I know," I patted him on the knee. "But you have to trust me."

Jake sighed and nodded. If he was going to stay my friend he was going to have to let me fight my own battles. I knew that at some point I was going to have to tell Jake what was really going on between Sam and me. Just not yet.

Mike walked us around campus, showing us the different "pods" of classrooms—the seventh grade language arts pod, the math and science pod, the art, shop, and music pod, the gym, and the big building at the center of campus where the office, library, cafeteria and stage were located. As we walked into the cafeteria Sam's group was entering from the opposite side. He had three girls and three guys in his group: Darci, Mya, and Alice, along with Justin, Sean, and David Ritter, the principal's son. Mya didn't worry me that much but seeing Darci and Alice there, I was pretty concerned.

Darci exuded confidence, and why shouldn't she? She was probably the most famous kid in town. We all saw her commercials for grape juice and the local car dealership just about every morning on channel 12. After her appearance in *Kindergarten Cop*, she got another role as an extra in the *Teenage Mutant Ninja Turtles* sequel. Her agent must have been working overtime, because she was voicing a character for a locally-produced stop-motion animation series, too. It was singing and dancing fruit, and I think she played a pineapple.

That day on the tour she looked like she'd stepped out of a Motley Crüe music video. I remember seeing one when I snuck some MTV time while my parents had gone out to dinner. The girls had tight clothes with big, ratted hairstyles and really severe makeup. Darci's jeans were skin-tight and had little heart shapes cut out at the calves. She wore a tight white t-shirt with a black leather vest over it. She had a neon pink feather on a strand of leather clipped into her hair and wore expertly-applied liquid black eyeliner. Mom would only let Victoria and me wear blush and clear mascara if we got to wear any makeup at all.

Alice was wearing her soccer uniform because she had a game right after school that day. Her legs were long and muscular and her hair was tied up in an intricate wrap-around French braid. She was probably the only person in school who could braid hair better than I could. I loved to let her braid my hair because she always pulled it so tightly that the

151

braids would never fall out on their own. I'd have to put a lot of effort into taking them out.

I watched both Alice and Darci listening to Sam and saw him being just as nice to them as he was to me when we were in front of other people. If I was going to keep him interested I needed to boost my confidence, my look and probably my athleticism too. I made a mental note and moved along with my group.

When it came time for lunch all of the sixth graders met together on the field by the track at the top of the hill and ate sack lunches while our guides joined the rest of the seventh and eighth graders for their regular lunchtime. They didn't have recess but had a whole forty-five minutes for lunch. After eating in the cafeteria, most of them just walked the sidewalks around the pods. Some played basketball behind the gym. A few tossed a football in the grass that separated the soccer field from the track. Sara was having her lunch with Nelson. I sat with Jake, watching the seventh and eighth graders as they went about their business.

"Sorry about earlier on the bus," I said to Jake, nudging him with my shoulder.

He put his arm around me and squeezed.

"It's okay," he said. "Still best friends for always. Love you more than the mountains."

I smiled and leaned my head on his shoulder.

"Love you too, weirdo." It was probably as good a time as any to tell Jake about me and Sam. "So, do you wanna know why I'm not freaking out about Sara's brother?" I asked.

"Actually, yeah," he said between bites of his bologna sandwich, "why?"

I took a deep breath and stared at my feet.

"Because Sam and I have been, um," I tripped over the words a little bit. I wasn't sure how to describe what we'd been doing. "We've been doing stuff together," I said.

"Doing stuff? Like what do you mean?" Jake asked with a mouthful of bologna.

"Like kissing," I said quietly.

Jake's mouth dropped open. A piece of sandwich fell out.

"You little liar!" he shouted, shoving me with his free hand. Bits of bread and bologna flew everywhere. "You are so not kissing that guy!" Jake laughed uncomfortably. When he noticed that I wasn't laughing along he stopped. "You're not, right? You're not. Seriously? Oh, Vy, you are! You're making out with an eighth grader?" His voice got louder and louder.

I could tell by the look on his face and the tone in his voice that his feelings were hurt but I couldn't understand why. I just wanted him to be quiet.

"What's all this?" Mya slid up next to Jake as if he had suddenly turned on a flashing red gossip indicator light. "Who's making out with an eighth grader?" she asked. Mya was known for knowing all the dirt.

Somehow, when she spread something, it went faster and farther than any other rumor or truth that was told. When Darren Carson peed his pants in the library in the third grade he didn't even have time to get to the librarian to ask for help before Mya spread it all over the school. Somebody even said that Darren's mom knew before the office lady called home because Mya's gossip moved so quickly.

"Vy is," Jake said, crunching into an apple.

My jaw flew open. How could he? What a jerk!

"No way!" Mya exclaimed, looking at me and talking about me like I wasn't even there. "Violet thinks she's making out with an eighth grader? That's hard to believe. Well, who is the mystery man?"

I looked at Jake with pleading eyes.

"Sam Anderson," Jake mumbled, holding his apple in his mouth while he put the plastic sandwich bags and empty juice box into the brown paper sack from his lunch. He was avoiding eye contact with me and Mya both.

Just when I didn't think my eyes could get any wider, or that my expression couldn't show more hurt and shock, Jake dropped the big one.

"She's going out with Sara's brother, Sam," he said.

Mya's eyes lit up and her mouth curled into a snarky grin.

"Some friend," I muttered, slugging Jake in the arm.

"Reeeeeally!" Mya patted Jake on the head as if he were a puppy, then stood up and said, "Well, I doubt *that*, but it's interesting to know that those are the stories Vy is telling now!"

For some reason Mya didn't like me very much. She skipped back over to Cristina and Mindy. They all looked at me while Mya talked. And so it began.

Word spread quickly around both Sam's and my schools that I had claimed I was Sam's girlfriend. Jake was actually really nice in trying to stifle the rumors and apologizing for starting the whole thing. It still took at least a week of him giving me the dessert from his cold lunch before I could completely forgive him. I never did understand why *he* got so mad at *me* and he never completely explained it either.

Victoria came home laughing about the rumor, calling me an idiot for making up a story like that. I was pretty surprised that it got around the middle school so quickly, too.

"Way to go, Vy," she said while we were putting our folded clothes away. "Why would you make up a story like that? Everybody knows you're lying."

"I'm not lying!" I insisted. "Besides, I never said I was Sam's girlfriend."

"Then what *did* you say?"

"Nothing," I said. I didn't want to get into the details with Victoria. She already knew too much, or thought she did anyway.

Chances were she'd find any excuse to spill it all to Mom and then Mom would tell Dad and I'd never be allowed out of the house again.

"Well, you'll probably have some explaining to do if you ever run into Lacey Johnson," Victoria said, slamming a drawer shut.

"Why?" I asked.

"'Cause that's Sam's *real* girlfriend."

I froze.

"What?"

"Lacey Johnson. She's Sam's girlfriend—has been for like a month. He totally ditched Katy for Lacey. It was a pretty big deal in my grade. Everybody heard about it." Victoria shook her head and snorted. "I can't believe you'd think anybody would believe that you and Sam were going out. Ha! Where'd you come up with it?"

I knew of Lacey Johnson. She was tall, had long fiery red hair, and almost glowing green eyes. She was quiet and sweet and she came to my school once a week to read to third graders in the library. All of the boys in my class thought she was really pretty. I couldn't disagree. She was quite beautiful.

I wondered why Sam never told me about Lacey. If they'd been going out for a month, then they were going out when he and I went to the river. I wondered if Victoria was just making it all up. There was only one way to find out.

CHAPTER TWELVE

I called Sara on the Bartphone, at first hoping that Sam might pick up. He didn't.

"Hello?" answered Judy. I knew it was Judy, even though she and Julie had very similar voices, because I could hear she was smiling.

"Hi, Judy," I said. "Is Sara home?"

"Um, no, she's at the movies with Jason, can I take a message?"

"Oh, um, no, that's okay. Is Sam there?"

"No, he went with her," Judy said. "Double-date."

My heart felt like it dropped all the way down into my shoes.

"Oh," I said, my voice cracking from the big ball that was forming in my throat. "Do you know who he went with?"

"No," she said sweetly, "is this Vy?"

I sniffed. I didn't want her to hear that I was fighting back the urge to cry.

"I gotta go."

"Do you want me to tell them you called?" Judy asked as I hung up.

I couldn't decide if I was mad or sad. I wondered if Sara knew about Lacey. If she did, why hadn't she told me? If Sam was out at the movies on a double-date with Sara, then she just had to know about them. Questions swirled around in my head.

The newspaper was in the trash can in the laundry room. I fished it out from among the lint and used dryer sheets, and flipped to the movie listings. The local theater was playing *Young Guns II* in a little less than an hour. Sara and Sam were probably taking their dates to burgers first and then to the movie. I had to get to the theater.

If I wanted to go, I'd have to convince Victoria to come along with me—Mom and Dad would never drop me off at the movies alone. I knew Victoria would jump at the chance to get out of the house, and whenever we went anywhere together I generally left her alone so it was a win-win for both of us. I found her in the living room, shuffling through Mom and Dad's record collection.

"Hey, Victoria?"

"Not now, Vy," she said without even looking up. "I'm busy."

"Victoria, please?" I sat down next to her and leaned my face down between hers and the records. "Wanna go to the movies with me?"

159

"What? No. I said I'm busy. And it's almost five. Mom and Dad will never let you," Victoria said, pushing my face away with her palm.

"You mean *us*. Please? Seriously, I'll leave you alone and you can call any of your friends to meet you there. Please?"

Victoria stopped what she was doing. She thought about it.

"You'll leave me alone?"

"Totally."

"And Mom and Dad said 'yes?'"

I bit my lip and winced.

"Well," I shook my head. "I haven't asked yet."

"If you can get Mom and Dad to say it's okay, then I'll go with you," she said. "But good luck convincing them you're old enough to see *Young Guns II*. It's PG-13."

"Thanks!" I jumped up and ran into the kitchen.

Mom was putting away clean dishes. She knew right away that I was about to ask for something.

"Hello, Violet," she said.

I put on my best, well-behaved smile.

"Mom? Victoria and I really want to go to the movies. Can we go to the movies?"

Mom started to shake her head.

"I really don't feel like going to the movies," she said. "I have a ton of ironing to do and Calvin doesn't sit still enough to go to the movies yet."

"Oh, no, you can just drop us off!" I offered. "Sara's there, so we're going to meet her!" I saw Mom's face change expression as she started to consider my offer. "Dad could drive us and bring home burgers for you guys and Victoria and I could eat something there."

Mom thought about it and started to smile.

"I suppose if it's okay with your father. Do you have enough money to pay for a movie?" She asked.

I hadn't considered how I'd pay for it. All I had considered to that point was that maybe if Sam saw me while he was out with Lacey he would be able to directly compare us. Lacey was pretty but Sam said I was the best kisser he'd ever kissed. How could pretty Lacey compete with that? Kissing ability was far more important than looks, right? I wrinkled my nose.

"Maybe," I said, "I have to check my turtle-bank."

I ran to my bedroom and pulled the stopper out of the bottom of the ceramic turtle where I kept my money. I only needed two dollars for a ticket and I had more than five in quarters. I jammed my quarters in my pocket and ran back to the kitchen.

"I can pay for me and Victoria," I said proudly, "where's Dad?" Mom pointed at the garage. Dad was finishing a bookcase he'd built for Calvin's room.

"What do you think?" He asked, admiring his work.

"Looks great!" I said, checking my Kermit the Frog watch. The movie was going to start in just forty minutes and it was an eight minute drive to the theater. "Hey, Dad? Mom said that Victoria and I could go to the movies if you'd drive us and pick up burgers on your way back."

"When's the movie start?" he asked, putting the lid on a can of polyurethane.

"Forty minutes."

"What movie is it?"

"*Young Guns II*," I said, adding "it's a western."

My dad loved westerns. One of the first movies we recorded off the TV when we got the VCR was *Blazing Saddles*, which I don't think they would have let me watch if it hadn't been the *edited for TV* version.

"Sounds like fun!" Dad said, wiping his hands on a towel. "Sure, let me get cleaned up and I'll take you two downtown."

Dad drove Victoria and me to the theater, and as soon as we hopped out of the car in front of the theater she stepped in front of me with her finger pointing up at my chin.

"Okay, listen," she instructed. "You're going to the movie. I'm going to Dairy Queen up the street to meet up with a friend. If Mom and Dad ask, I sat next to you and covered your eyes during the bloody parts, got it?"

"There are bloody parts?"

162

"Quit it," she said. "I'll meet you out front by the payphone when the movie's over. Don't call Dad until I get here, okay?"

"Okay sure," I nodded.

Victoria waited for the stoplight at the end of the street to turn green and for Dad's car to round the corner before she took off. Bonus for me, I got to keep three of my five bucks in quarters since I didn't have to buy Victoria a ticket. Maybe I'd buy myself a snack.

I found a seat toward the rear left side of the theater where I had a pretty good view of everybody there. I saw this girl Rachel Harrison, who sat in front of me all year in the fifth grade, there with her mom, little brother, Scotty, and her step-dad. There were a few other people, mostly grownups that I didn't know.

I saw Sara, Nelson, Sam, and Lacey sitting mid-way to the front in the center seats. Lit by the projector behind them, I could only see the backs of their heads, but I could see very clearly that Sam had his arm around Lacey's shoulder. I stared at them for the whole first half of the movie. I couldn't tell you anything about the plot because I was so wrapped up in what Sam and Lacey were doing. She leaned her head on his shoulder three times. He nuzzled his nose behind her ear twice. They peck kissed enough times for me to lose count and really laid into a deep French kiss about forty-five minutes after the movie started. By that point I'd seen enough. I decided to go out into the lobby to get some licorice and stew some more about how I was probably a better kisser than Lacey.

Sitting on a purple velvet bench in the lobby, I looked around at movie posters and imagined all of the possible scenarios if Sam walked out to get popcorn or go to the bathroom. I could just picture it: he would walk out of the theater and see me sitting there.

"Vy!" he'd exclaim, happy at first but then looking nervous, glancing from side to side. "What are you doing here?"

"Oh, nothing," I would say, biting a red licorice whip in a way like I'd seen women do on TV. "This movie was kind of boring, don't you think?" I would use an aloof tone like the kind Julie always used.

He would look over his shoulder and stutter, "Yeah, I guess so," and then go on his way uncomfortably, having the memory of me stuck in his head while he went back into the theater. Maybe he'd get so nervous that he'd spill his soda or his popcorn in Lacey's lap, infuriating and disgusting her with him so much that she'd never want to see him again.

Jerking me back to reality, the door to the theater opened and my heart sped up as I hoped to see Sam walk out into the lobby. Instead it was Rachel's little brother.

"I gotta go potty!" he shouted back into the theater. He raced across the bright red carpet to the bathroom. Scotty looked to be about the same age as Calvin. He had a mop of white-blonde hair and skin that looked like it belonged on a porcelain doll.

A few moments after Scotty ran through the lobby, one of the grownups I didn't recognize left the theater and went into the men's room. After a minute or so passed, something felt weird. I couldn't put my finger on it but I got this sudden feeling that something bad either *had* happened or was about to. Before I could put too much thought into it, there was a scream from the men's room and the door crashed open.

"You're not my daddy!" Scotty screamed as the strange man carried him, kicking and screaming, out of the bathroom. "Help! Mommy!" Scotty shrieked. The stranger put his hand over Scotty's mouth. He hurried toward the exit. Rachel's step-dad burst out of the theater with a look of panic on his face. He looked at me and I pointed in the direction the stranger had gone with Rachel's brother. He ran after them. Rachel and her mother came out of the theater with a terrified look, quickly following Rachel's step-dad out the door.

Any thoughts of Sam were out of my head at that moment. I was so captivated by what was going on and my own fear that I hadn't noticed Sara, Nelson, Sam, and Lacey coming out of the theater.

"Vy? What are you doing here!?" Sara exclaimed, running over to me. She gave me a huge hug and took my face in her hands. "You're white as a ghost! What just happened?"

I told her what happened with the stranger and Rachel's brother with big gasps between each word. My voice was shaking and the fear tears were welling up. I heard police sirens outside.

"Victoria is up at Dairy Queen," I said breathlessly, "we have to go get her before Dad gets here!"

Lacey sat down on the other side of me and put her hand on my back. Her presence was very calming—like a mom.

"Sam, will you run up and get Victoria?" Lacey asked.

Sam had a look of pity on his face, like he felt really sorry for me for some reason and with a quick nod he took off to go get my sister.

"Just sit here," Lacey said, "we'll stay with you until your Dad comes." Lacey smelled really nice, like warm, sweet vanilla cream.

I knew that news traveled fast in our town and that as soon as my folks heard about a to-do going on at the movie theater they'd race downtown to get us.

It was a pretty bloody scene when my dad showed up. Rachel's brother had bitten the stranger on the arm, which slowed him down just enough for her step-dad to catch up with the guy and beat the tar out of him. My dad was friends with Rachel's step-dad. He was so occupied with his friend when he arrived that he didn't notice Sam and Victoria coming around the corner instead of out of the theater.

"Way to go," Victoria said to me. There was a tone of disgust and disappointment in her voice.

My jaw dropped. How was any of this my fault? I gave Victoria a dirty look and ran to my dad. I threw my arms around him and squeezed tightly. Sam followed behind me.

"Sir," he said to my dad, "I think Vy may have seen what happened. She's pretty well shook up."

My dad hugged me, putting his hand on the side of my head, partly covering my ear.

"Thank you, Son," Dad said to Sam, who joined Sara, Nelson and Lacey back by the payphone.

Victoria pried Dad's keys out of his hand and let herself into the car.

"Violet," Dad said, "why don't you go get in the car with your sister?" He gave me a reassuring smile and I ran to the car.

Victoria clicked the automatic locks just as I got there.

"Victoria!" I shouted, slapping at the window.

She unlocked it, then locked it again before I could get the door open.

"Come on!" I yelled, feeling the tears running down my face. I jerked the handle on the door just as she unlocked it again. The door flew open, knocking me to the ground. I leapt up and dove into the car, slamming the door behind me.

"WHAT IS WRONG WITH YOU?" I screamed at Victoria and she stared at me with a blank, somewhat cross expression.

"Geez," she said, "what's wrong with *you?*" I was sobbing and shaking in the back seat while she leaned over the front headrest.

"Oh, I don't know," I shouted with angry sarcasm, "it's not like I just watched a friend's brother get *stolen* from a movie theater bathroom by a *stranger!* Victoria! Why do you hate me so much?"

I sank back into my seat and stared out the window at the cop car that wasn't far from us. I could see the greasy black hair of the stranger in the back of the car. At one point he turned around and made eye contact with me. I quickly looked away and locked the door beside me.

167

Aside from going to school, I didn't really want to go much of anywhere for a while. I especially didn't want to go anywhere alone. The whole thing at the movies made me really revisit the idea of "stranger danger" we'd learned about way back in kindergarten.

Officer Mike came by my house the next day. Mom and Dad stood in the corner of the dining room while Officer Mike wrote down everything I told him about what I saw at the theater. Victoria was glaring at me from the hall doorway. When I got to the part about her being at Dairy Queen instead of at the theater, I saw Mom and Dad look at each other and then back at Victoria. Officer Mike had me, Mom, and Dad sign my statement. I worried that after he left, Victoria would pound me for getting her in trouble. Luckily, Mom and Dad were pretty concerned with me being traumatized so I got to stay close to them all day. Victoria warned me she wouldn't forget that she owed me a beat-down.

The Odyssey of the Mind regional tournament wasn't long after the movie theater incident. On Friday night before the competition my whole team got together at the downtown pizza parlor for dinner after practice. I still had a distaste for public places without my parents. I just wanted to go home, so I had Mom pick me up rather than getting a ride from Lou's mom. I had to be up early anyway. Going home early seemed smart. I was in my pajamas and washing my face when the doorbell rang. Dad answered it.

"Vy?" Dad called down the hall. "You have company."

I wasn't expecting anyone. I checked myself in the mirror—just in case—and made my way to the front door. There in the entryway stood

Sam. I stepped past him and onto the front porch. The last thing I wanted was anyone in my family to snoop in on our conversation. He followed.

"Hey," I said, closing the door behind me.

"Hey," he said, putting both of his hands into his pockets. "I just wanted to see how you were."

"I'm fine," I said, which wasn't entirely true but it wasn't entirely a fib either. I was paranoid and still pretty hurt about him and Lacey. It wasn't like he was my boyfriend or anything. I wondered if the rumor about me saying that had gotten to him. I hoped not.

"Sara said you've been kind of quiet lately, which isn't like you, so—"

"Did you really come over just to check up on me?" I asked flatly, interrupting him. My heart raced at my own boldness.

"Well, yeah," he said. "Is it okay for me to care about one of my friends?"

"Oh, I'm one of your *friends*, am I?"

"Since when are we not friends?"

I just stood there quietly and tried my best to look aloof. On the inside I wanted so badly to grin. I was a confirmed friend. He liked me. That was a fact. I was dying to be more.

"Anyway, I've been worried and thinking about you," he whispered, reaching up and tucking my hair behind one of my ears.

As confused as I was about "us," his touch was still electric. It made me inhale deeply and close my eyes for longer than I wanted him to see.

"You're going to be at regionals tomorrow, right?" Sam asked.

I nodded. He put his hands on both of my arms by my shoulders just like my grandma did when she was reminding me to "be safe." I figured it was an Anderson thing to hold me like my grandma.

"Good," he said. "Do you want to hang out with me when our teams aren't competing?"

I nodded again. For the first time since the night at the movie theater I felt safe. I let myself fall forward against him, throwing my arms around him in a tight embrace. He wrapped his arms around me and rested his chin on the top of my head. I smelled his cologne and was filled with the memory of our first kiss. Any trace of Lacey floated out of my mind and I was back in my happy little world where Sam was all mine. I looked up at him, hoping he would at least give me a little peck of a kiss, but instead I saw him looking at my bedroom window.

"Victoria is glaring at us through the blinds," he said.

I looked over my shoulder. I could see Victoria's finger and the courtyard lights reflecting off her beady dark eyes.

"Good," I said. "She thinks I have a crazy crush on you and that you couldn't care less who I am."

He laughed and hugged me tighter.

"Is that so?" he asked, looking down at my face. "Well, you can go right ahead and tell her that you're my little mistress."

I smiled. I had no idea what that meant but it sounded endearing so I accepted it as a complimentary role. Maybe it meant I was his secret girlfriend—I'd be okay with that. We separated and he stepped down off the porch.

"I'll see you tomorrow, okay, Vy?"

"Okay," I said. "Night, Sam."

"Good night, little mistress," whispered Sam.

I watched from Calvin's bedroom window as Sam walked down the hill. I was so excited for morning to come. I couldn't wait to spend the whole day with him—in front of other people, even. I hurried to bed and stared at the streetlight until I fell asleep.

CHAPTER THIRTEEN

There were two parts to an Odyssey of the Mind competition: "long-term" and "spontaneous." For my team, the "long-term" portion was the jack-powered vehicle and artistic presentation we'd been working on for the last few months. Five of our seven team members would be given three minutes to present to the judges and the crowd, showing that our vehicle could move forward for a given distance, in reverse, and could tow a certain amount of weight. The "spontaneous" part was when five of the seven of us would go into a room and be given a new problem, one minute to think about and discuss how we wanted to solve it, and then two minutes to respond with our solution. The two team members who sat out of the long-term presentation were required to participate in the spontaneous portion.

Teams from all over the county in three divisions—elementary, middle or junior high, and high school—came together at the high school in our town for the regional competition. Since my team was in division one we had to do our long-term presentation early in the morning, then wait until late in the afternoon for spontaneous. Victoria's team was in division two. They had spontaneous first, then presented their long-term solution last. There was going to be a big awards ceremony at the end of the day where everyone would meet up in the gym. My parents dropped me and Victoria off at the front of the school at seven o'clock in the morning.

"Victoria," Mom instructed, "try not to leave Violet alone for too long. She's still pretty easily spooked."

Victoria rolled her eyes but agreed.

"Okay, Mom," she huffed.

Since I'd be around my team all day I wasn't as afraid of the crowd as I might have been otherwise. Besides, I had plans to hang out with Sam. To be honest, I'd much rather Victoria left me alone—with him. I thought if I could be around Sam, I wouldn't have to be afraid of anything. He liked me, he said so. I'd been thinking about him non-stop since his visit the night before.

Sara and the rest of my team were already there, primping props and our vehicle in the staging area. We were so well-rehearsed and confident. Our design was impressive. Looking at our competition's stuff, we were pretty sure that if our presentation went well, we could easily win regionals and secure a spot at state.

Our performance was flawless. I could tell by the looks on the judges' faces that they were fascinated with what we had engineered. When they asked questions, Sean did most of the explaining about how

174

it worked and Dick described how we built it. Sara told them how and why we created our museum-themed presentation. After the long-term portion was over we sat in the gym watching our competitors and the other divisions do their thing.

"What's up, team?" Mike Bennett asked as he and the rest of the middle schoolers sat down behind us in the stands. "You guys looked good out there. Sweet ride!"

Sam sat down directly behind me, patting me on the shoulder. I looked back at him and he winked.

"How was spontaneous?" Sean asked Mike. The rules said that teams weren't supposed to talk to each other about the spontaneous experience, in case they were both given the same problem. They didn't want anybody to have an unfair advantage over anybody else.

"I think we rocked it," said Sam, adding, "Your team will do great."

Our teams hung out together almost all day. I stayed in the bleachers for most of the time, not wanting to get mixed up in the crowds. Sam stayed with me. At one point everyone else had gone to get lunch, leaving Sam and I alone together.

"Did Victoria say anything to you last night?" Sam asked, playfully punching me in the shoulder as he moved down to the seat next to me.

"No," I replied.

He put a hand on my lower back. Again, his touch took my breath away for a moment.

"What are you doing later tonight?" he asked.

"I dunno," I said, "probably going home."

"Well," he took my hand in his and wove his fingers between mine as he said, "our team is going to my house for pizza and a movie after. You wanna come?"

Sara sat on the other side of me with nachos she'd just bought from the concession stand.

"Wanna come where?" she asked, waving the chips at me. I took a bite. "What are you two planning?"

"Movies at home," he said, reaching over me to take one of Sara's nachos. "Mom and Dad said my team could come over. Your team should come too,"

Sara nodded.

"Good idea," she agreed. "Vy, can you come?"

"I have to ask my folks, but yeah, probably," I said. My parents wouldn't be there until the awards ceremony that evening and I doubted they would have a problem with it since Victoria had been invited too. "Is Lacey going to be there?" I asked, looking at Sam.

"Prolly not," said Sam, smirking. Perfect.

The spontaneous problem wasn't very tough for my team. We had to build something out of plastic straws and straight pins that could

176

hold a ten pound weight. Most of the people on my team were able to make it happen easily. I was a little distracted by the possibilities surrounding watching a movie in a dark room with Sam so it was probably a good thing that I sat out.

Sam and Victoria's team was the last division two team to present their long-term solution, and as it turned out, the last performance of the day. The awards ceremony would be held in the gym directly following their presentation so they had a huge audience watching them walk their Star Wars-inspired jack-powered vehicle around the course.

With only a few feet left to go before they reached the finish and thirty seconds on the clock, one of the bike chains that helped propel the vehicle snapped and the AT-AT Sam was driving came to a stop. He tried to fix it but ended up yanking on the chains with his bare hands to complete the course. There were audible gasps in the crowd as the chains cut into his hands but he didn't stop pulling. The walker took step after step and Sam's face winced with pain with each one. One of the judges put his clipboard down and started to slow-clap. The rest of the audience joined in.

"Time!" another judge shouted.

The walker stopped inches behind the finish line. Cheers and applause filled the gym as Sam, Victoria, and the rest of their team ran together into a group hug. They were all in tears and Sam's hands were well torn up by the chains.

For not finishing the course and for their vehicle being powered by something other than the mechanical jack for part of the presentation, their team was disqualified and wasn't eligible to move on to the state semi-finals. They left their walker where it stopped and the master of ceremonies began recognizing teams and handing out awards.

It was no surprise that Sam was given a "most inspirational" award and his team was given an honorable mention for their design and presentation. Unfortunately it was the execution of that design that failed them. The MC began to announce the division one team awards and Sara gripped my hand.

"I hope we go to state," she whispered.

"Me too!" I whispered back, giving her a squeeze.

Sam came up behind me and put one of his bandaged hands on my arm.

"You got this," he said, leaning between Sara and me.

Sure enough, our team took first place and would advance to the semi-finals. We leapt from our seats, hugging each other and running to the stage to receive our trophy. When we returned to the bleachers I was greeted by Sam with a big hug and a kiss on the cheek. A kiss in public seemed like such a big step. I took careful notice of everyone around who saw it. Luckily, my parents didn't. Too bad Lacey wasn't there to see it. I wanted her out of the picture all together so he could be mine. All mine.

My parents were fine with me going over to Sara's for movies that night, mostly because Victoria already had permission to go. There were twelve kids strewn around the Anderson's living room, passing bowls of popcorn and two liters of soda around while we watched *Back to the Future*.

"That's what we should've built," said Mike Bennett, "a DeLorean!"

"What were we thinking building a walker?" Jean laughed.

"It was *his* idea," Victoria smirked, pointing up at Sam, who was sitting next to me on the couch.

Sam shrugged.

"Yeah, but it was a *cool* idea," he said.

Sam, Dick, Lou, and Billy all nodded in agreement.

"A cool idea that'll probably keep you off the baseball team this year," Victoria shot back, pointing at Sam's hands. They were both wrapped in bandages, making him look like a patient on an episode of *M*A*S*H*. I had heard of the Florence Nightingale effect before and I assumed that was what I was experiencing when I realized how much more seeing Sam all bandaged up made me care for him. As gross as it sounded I wanted to hold his poor, battered hands and kiss them.

A little further into the movie Sam pulled a fleece blanket off of the back of the couch and gestured for me to scoot in closer to him. I obliged and he draped the blanket over the front of us both. I felt his hand sneak up over my leg and grab my hand. Gently, so as not to upset his bandages, he held my hand. I leaned my head on his shoulder and he wrapped an arm around me. I fell asleep this way, with my head on his chest. I woke up with a snort toward the end of the movie when Doc

179

shouted "The Libyans!" and everyone in the room shouted it back at him. I couldn't tell if anybody heard me or not. It didn't matter anyway. They liked me.

CHAPTER FOURTEEN

I had my picture in the paper for Odyssey of the Mind. Sara figured out how to perfectly balance boyfriend and best friend time. On top of that, even though he wasn't my boyfriend (yet), I was getting occasional attention from Sam. Things were looking up.

Just after Thanksgiving, my parents announced our family holiday plans. We would be spending Christmas and New Year's at the beach. My uncle was in commercial real estate and had helped a large hotel chain build its flagship lodge on the Oregon coast. They invited him to spend the holidays at the lodge at no charge, but my aunt's mother passed away so they weren't able to go. Dad volunteered our family to go in their place.

I always loved Christmas. Once the tree was up I would spend my mornings sitting behind it atop the heat register with my nightgown filling up with hot air like a big balloon. I wasn't big into present-shaking but I always carefully surveyed their shapes. Soft gifts were usually clothes. Boxes were often misleading and contained something that had a complex shape of plastic packaging within. As I sat on the heat register one morning, looking at my presents, I noticed something that was shaped like a wedge. I poked at it and found it to be a mostly solid, hard shape with odd contours in some places. I hypothesized that this was either several curling irons or a remote-controlled car. I hoped for the latter.

When it came time to unwrap gifts on Christmas Eve I saved the wedge shaped one for last. I always saved the most highly sought-after thing for last. When I ate waffles I would cut them into squares and the center, edgeless piece was the one I saved for last because it would usually get the most butter, soak up the most syrup and be the softest bite. The same bite was present in French toast or pancakes. I called it the "favorite bite." On occasion, Dad would swoop in over me at the breakfast table, stealing a bite under the guise of "Dad tax." There was a good chance that he'd take the favorite bite, which would always be met with intense whining and complaining on my part.

There was a card attached to the wedge gift. Usually Christmas gifts didn't come with cards if they were from Mom and Dad. The handwriting on the envelope was definitely Mom's, so this gift must have been truly special. I opened the card first. In it there was a gift certificate for twenty-five dollars to Fred Meyer, the big box store two towns over. Twenty-five dollars was a lot of money to me. When I'd go on field trips with my class or the TAG program, my parents would give me five dollars to cover lunch and possibly souvenirs. I could buy just about anything in the store with twenty-five dollars, I thought.

"That's for you to get something to fill what's in your present," Dad said. Mom quickly shushed him.

I pulled the wrapping paper off of the wedge. It was one of those impossible-to-open plastic containers with a portable CD player and a pair of headphones inside.

"We'll stop by Freddie's on the way to the beach," Mom said. "Then you can pick out a CD to listen to."

I was beyond excited. This must have cost a fortune. My parents had a CD player but we used it far less frequently than we used the cassette deck or the record player on the stereo console in the living room. Dad bought Mom a copy of the *Pretty Woman* soundtrack right after it came out along with a Bonnie Raitt and Nitty Gritty Dirt Band CD. The player held five discs. Since we only had three we just never took any of them out.

I couldn't wait to go to Fred Meyer to pick out something new. I got a Michael Jackson cassette in my stocking, which was exciting, but didn't have the same feeling that I knew I was going to get from a brand new, shiny, round, perfect CD of my own choosing.

I was so impatient the next morning when we loaded up the car to head for the beach. I had woken up in the middle of the night and snuck into the living room to watch MTV, just to get an idea of what kind of music I should buy. I saw Motley Crüe, Poison, The Cure, and Modern English videos. They were all cool but none of them really spoke to me. Just before I turned off the TV there was this video that had a man wearing a king's crown and big red velvet cape with a white fur border. He was carrying a lawn chair up a hill and he sang while he walked. I was mesmerized, both by the song and the video. The man was so handsome and his voice was so clear and unique. I had never heard anything like it. As the video came to an end I decided exactly which CD I wanted to buy: *Violator* by Depeche Mode.

Mom had a collection of Del Shannon records, which she listened to all the time. She was such a super fan that when she bought a new car she got a vanity plate that read *RUNAWAY* after his song of the same name. Until I discovered Depeche Mode my musical tastes had only ever been influenced by what my parents, sister, or friends were listening to. My sister listened to Paula Abdul. My friends listened to Poison and Weird Al. With the exception of Billy Joel, most of what my parents listened to was old. Nobody I knew liked Depeche Mode so I felt like I was building stock in my uniqueness by getting into their music. I raced for the section of CDs in the music department at Fred Meyer, avoiding my usual stop at the cassette singles rack. It was right there, at the front of the "D" section. The cover was black with a big red rose on it. I hugged the cellophane-wrapped, long, thin, white cardboard packaging to my chest and raced to the cashier.

On top of feeling independent and unique, I also felt incredibly wealthy as I pulled out my twenty-five dollar gift certificate to pay for my CD. I even got five dollars in change, which I pocketed in case I ran across a must-have souvenir at the beach. There was usually some trinket I'd find that I just had to have but my folks wouldn't want to spend money on. I wouldn't even have to ask them this time, since I had five dollars of my very own, to do with whatever I pleased. Ice cream? Done.

Googly-eyed clam shell? Done. Novelty t-shirt? Done. I was on top of the world.

I listened to all nine tracks on repeat at least three times during the drive to the beach. When we arrived at the lodge our rooms weren't quite ready so the bellhop told us he'd hold our bags. Mom and Dad suggested Victoria and I pull our swimsuits out and hit the indoor heated pool while we waited. We thought this was a tremendous idea and I shoved my CD player into my suitcase after I took out my swimsuit. Victoria and I changed, stashing our clothes in the cubbies that were provided in the women's locker room.

We played in the pool for an hour or so before Mom knocked on the window from the lobby to let us know the room was ready. She both mouthed and signed the room number at us through the window. We climbed out of the water and headed back to the locker room to dry off and change.

"Where's your stuff?" Victoria asked as she pulled her clothes from a cubby.

I was at the shelves of towels with my face covered in a fluffy, white one that smelled strongly of bleach.

"Right next to yours, dummy!" I shot back at her, playfully.

"No it isn't," she said. Her tone was sort of snarky so I blew it off.

"Ha ha," I said, still under the towel, "very funny."

186

"I'm not joking, Vy!" she said, raising her voice and pointing at the cubbies. "Look!"

Sure enough, when I pulled the towel off of my head I saw that the cubby where I'd put my clothes was empty. My navy blue polo shirt, my shoes, and my favorite jeans that had the five bucks in the pocket were nowhere in sight.

"Where's my stuff?" I shouted.

"Like I know," Victoria said sarcastically, pulling her jeans on. She slid into her shoes and tossed her towel into a blue canvas bin in the corner of the room. "Maybe Mom came in and grabbed it," she suggested.

It sounded believable but I couldn't understand why Mom would take my clothes and not Victoria's. I wrapped up in a towel and was determined to find out.

It was a very cold walk from the pool to our room, especially since I was still pretty much soaked to the bone. When we got there, Mom and Dad had already arranged all of the suitcases along the wall. As a family, we never unpacked our stuff into the provided drawers or closets in hotels. Mom said there was too much risk of leaving something behind. I frequently lost things on family trips anyway though, so I doubted that not using the drawers or closets made any difference.

"Mom, did you come and take my clothes from the pool?" I asked, kicking the door to the room closed.

She looked puzzled.

"No," Mom replied, "we took Calvin to the gift shop. He picked out a squirt gun shaped like a fish."

"Look!" shouted Calvin, proudly holding up his fish.

"Not now, Calvin," I said, looking around the room for my suitcase. "My stuff wasn't in the cubby after we swam," I said. "Where's my suitcase?"

Mom looked around the room.

"One, two, three, four," she counted. "Hmm. I thought we only had four?"

I dropped my arms to my sides dramatically.

"There are only three in here!" I shouted, pointing at each one. "You're counting the big one twice!"

"Look!" shouted Calvin, waving the squirt gun at me.

"Not now, Calvin," I said, annoyed. "So, my clothes get stolen from the locker room *and* my suitcase goes missing? What the hell kind of place is this?"

Mom and Dad froze, looking at me with wide eyes and open mouths. Calvin was still swinging his fish gun around in the air.

"What did you just say?" Dad asked, narrowing his eyes.

"I said, 'what the hell kind of place is this?'" I repeated, slightly more frustrated than the first time I'd said it.

"Watch your language, young lady," Dad warned sternly.

I stomped my feet. I had no clothes to wear other than a wet swimsuit. All of my money was gone. I had no shoes. My Christmas CD player and my brand new Depeche Mode CD were gone. The knot formed quickly in my throat. Rage boiled behind my eyes.

"This will all be fine," Mom reassured me. "We'll just go to the front desk and see if they're still holding one of our bags. They probably have it at the bellhop's station."

"Oh, sure," I started laying on the sarcasm, "I'll just cruise on back to the lobby in my bare feet and my wet swimsuit."

"Young lady, watch your tone," Dad warned. "You're already on thin ice with that language, and you don't ever speak to your mother that way. There's no need to be so dramatic. How about you just call the front desk?"

I wrinkled up my face and stomped over to the phone. I dialed "0" and waited for someone to pick up.

"Front desk," said a sweet female voice.

"Hi," I said, shivering. "We're in room four-oh-three, and we had four bags held at the bellhop's but only three of them are here. And my clothes got stolen from the locker room." There was silence on the other end of the line for at least ten seconds. "Hello?" I said.

"Yes," she said, "this is the front desk, how can we help you?" Could she not hear me? I tried speaking slower.

"Hi," I said. "This is room four-oh-three. We left four bags with the bellhop and only have three in our room. Also, I was just in the pool and had my clothes stolen from the locker room."

"We don't have any bags in the lost and found right now, would you like me to transfer you to the local police to report this theft?" Talk about dramatic. I was freezing and just wanted clothes to put on. Calvin shoved his squirt gun in my face again.

"VY! LOOK!" he shouted. I took a deep breath.

"Very nice, Calvin," I said dismissively, holding the phone out for my Mom. "They want to talk to you," I lied.

She rolled her eyes at me and took the receiver. I went into the bathroom to get a dry towel to wrap around myself. Hanging on the back of the door was a fluffy white robe. Awesome.

The front desk lady was just as rude to my mom as she was to me and my suitcase never turned up. My stuff from the locker room was also a lost cause. Being twelve years old I only had one thing I could do about it and I decided I was going to do it with an unmatched vengeance and fervor—I was going to pout.

While my family went out to dinner I stayed in the hotel room, watching TV on the bed in my robe, pouting. At one point while they were out I filled up Calvin's fish gun with water and did a little target-practice with the teal and pink diamond shapes on the curtains. I watched mostly channels that Mom and Dad didn't usually let me—MTV, VH1, the Comedy Channel, and the movie channels—but I was watching the news when I saw all of the preparation for *Dick Clark's New Year's Rockin' Eve.*

I was glad this year was coming to an end because it had gotten really complicated. I thought back to when my life was really simple and wondered why it had to change. I looked at Calvin's fish gun. He was so lucky. Sure, he had absolutely no independence and was shushed or redirected at every turn it seemed, but I don't think he really knew how good he had it. He didn't have many expectations of him. To be liked when you were five years old you just had to keep from taking other people's toys and try not to bite anyone.

I felt stuck in a weird in-between stage, where I wasn't quite sure how to deal with the world around me. My relationship with my best friend got weird. Boys came into the picture. I had begun to define my life's goal to become famous. I'd witnessed a pretty major crime being attempted and became part of a sneaky second-banana relationship with my best friend's brother. It was a lot for one girl to handle.

My family brought back a doggy bag with some halibut and fries for me. I remained in my spot on the bed to eat, guarding the TV remote with Calvin's gun until Dad gave the executive order to turn the channel to the Portland Trailblazer game and leave it alone. Mom and Victoria were going to the outlet stores the next day and said they'd pick me up a couple of outfits. I told them they didn't have to and that I'd be just fine in my robe for the rest of the vacation. I kind of liked the idea of being a hotel room hermit, just pouting in bed all week. Unfortunately my parents weren't on board with my plans.

The next evening I was at dinner in the hotel restaurant with my family, wearing a new dress. My guess was that Mom thought it was cute, like something she'd have made me wear when I was six, and because she knew I'd look like a goober in it Victoria totally championed for it. The dress was made of ivory flannel with little blue whales on it. It had long poofy sleeves and a Peter Pan-style collar, which along with the fact that it had no waist, made it look like a nightgown from *Little House on the Prairie*. I really didn't have much choice in the matter so I put on the dress, thanked my mother, and went to dinner. At least nobody I knew would see me in that God-awful thing.

There were a few other families there but just one with a kid my age. At least I thought he was my age; it was hard to tell because he had a long, thick ponytail. He had on dark blue jeans, a white, long-sleeved collared shirt and a vest—the kind you'd see someone wear with a suit. Our eyes met from across the room and I smiled at him, a little ashamed of the way I looked. He smiled back at me, raising both of his eyebrows and mouthing the word, "hello."

It was a buffet dinner and Mom let Victoria and I dish ourselves up. Usually she hovered somewhere behind us to make sure we made healthy choices but on this night we had more independence. Knowing I could still receive Mom's signature judgmental gaze when I returned to the table, I made sure to balance the enormous mound of mashed potatoes with at least a few greens. I was reaching for the tongs in the green beans when I noticed the boy with the ponytail standing across from me.

"Oh, I'm sorry," I said, pulling my hand back as he went for the beans, too.

"No, please," he said, handing the tongs over to me. "You go first."

I blushed.

"Are you sure?"

"Yes, I insist." He sounded very suave and mature. Most boys my age didn't use words like "insist."

"Thank you," I said.

"What's your name?" he asked.

"Violet, what's yours?"

"Bobby," he answered. "Are you staying through New Year's?"

"Yeah, are you?"

"We are," he moved along the other side of the buffet, keeping pace with me.

Already feeling pretty silly about the way I looked, I carefully considered my expression and posture. But then, as I reached for the asparagus I thought, *Why do I care what this kid thinks?* I released the tongs back into the warming tray and cut over to the carving station. Bobby followed me.

"One, please," I said to the man at the prime rib. He slid a thin slice of meat onto my plate. "And horseradish," I requested. "A lot."

"Will I see you at the party down here on New Year's Eve?" Bobby asked.

"Maybe?" I said, smiling kindly. "I don't know what my parents have planned."

"Well I hope to, Violet," he said and walked away.

Bobby and I glanced at each other several times throughout dinner that night. He was kind of good-looking and seemed interested in me. I figured that at the very least I could probably get a pen pal out of this horrible trip. Sure, a pen pal really didn't hold a candle to the CD player and Depeche Mode album I had lost, but it was something, anyway. I let my imagination wander. I daydreamed about walks in the surf and flying kites from the sand with Bobby. At one point in my fantasy, Bobby turned into Sam. We were just getting ready to make out by a sand dune when Dad asked,

"Vy? Are you not hungry?"

I looked at my plate. I was so busy fantasizing about Sam that I hadn't touched my food. I was hungry but my entire family was done eating and looked ready to leave. Calvin was whining for dessert and Mom was trying to shush him, wiping his mouth with a cloth napkin she'd dipped in her ice water. Luckily for him, this time it wasn't the licked-thumb-face-wipe. He wriggled and writhed around, making sounds that drew a lot of attention to our table. I set my silverware on my plate the way Mom had taught me to at the end of a meal, with my fork and knife together like the big hand on a clock that read twenty-after.

"No," I said, wiping the corners of my mouth with a napkin, "I'm done."

There would be no walks on the beach or kite-flying in the sand, as the weather was bad the whole time we were there. The Oregon Coast is pretty well-known for being wet, grey, and cold in the winter. Aside from a couple of trips to souvenir, book and antique shops, we generally stayed in. I spent a lot of time sitting on the bed with Calvin's fish gun, imagining how things would have been if Sam were there.

Bobby also popped into my mind. I saw him in passing in the lobby twice. The first time we smiled and went about our business. The second time he walked right up to me and handed me a folded piece of paper before walking away.

"Make a new friend?" Dad asked, walking beside me.

"From the buffet line," I said, shoving the piece of paper into my pocket before anyone in my family could see it.

"Odd of him to just shake your hand and not say anything," Dad remarked.

I nodded.

"Yep."

We were waiting for the valet to bring the car around. It was taking an exceptionally long time because the cast of *Wings* was at the hotel shooting a scene and between the camera crew and the autograph-seekers, the hotel had a good-sized swarm of people buzzing around and slowing things down. I heard *Wings* was a pretty popular TV show, but I

195

didn't watch it. Rumor had it that the cast and crew would be staying for the New Year's Eve dinner and dancing that night.

After my uncle heard about the loss of my luggage and personal belongings, he called up the hotel to give them a piece of his mind. Then they were really nice to us. They gave us free tickets to the New Year's Eve dinner.

When I heard that the film crew would be at dinner I begged my mom to get me a dress that didn't look like a nightgown. It took quite a bit of pleading but it eventually worked. In the car on the way to the outlet stores, I took Bobby's note out of my pocket. I unfolded it to find the words *Swim tonight at 8* written on a torn corner of hotel stationary in messy boy handwriting.

"Mom," I asked, "what time is dinner?"

"Six," she answered, "why?"

"What time is it over?"

"It's a New Year's Eve party, honey, so it ends after midnight. Why?"

"Do we have to stay until it's over?"

"No, Vy."

"Can I go swimming at eight?"

"We'll see," Mom said. When she gave that answer instead of a solid "yes" or "no" I knew it was time to back off. "We'll see" typically meant "probably not" or "pipe down." I had learned not to push it any further because the next step was a definite (and likely angry) "no."

196

I waited to ask again until Mom was doing her makeup for dinner. She had big, white, hot rollers in her hair. She let me borrow one to curl my bangs, since my curling iron had been in my suitcase when it was stolen and Victoria wouldn't share hers.

"Mom," I asked as she opened her mouth and clamped an eyelash curler down over her left eye. "Can I go swimming tonight?"

"By yourself?" she asked. I could tell by her tone that if my answer was "yes," hers would be "no."

"With Victoria?" I suggested. I didn't want her to come along at first, but considering this Bobby kid was technically a stranger, it would probably be a good idea for her to be there – for safety's sake.

"If Victoria goes with you, you can," she nodded, still holding the eyelash curler tightly against her eye.

I had little trouble convincing Victoria to go swimming with me. She couldn't have cared less about the cast and crew of *Wings*, and had no interest in hanging around the restaurant with my parents. It was more challenging convincing myself that this was truly a good idea. I wasn't sure I really wanted to go swimming with Bobby. I wasn't sure I liked him. All I knew was that I liked the attention.

Dinner was the fancy kind where there were only a few options on the menu: chicken, beef, or fish. Everybody got the same side dishes, salads, soups and bread, and there wasn't any kind of a kids' menu. Calvin was the pickiest eater on earth, so the lack of options could potentially be a big problem for our family. Victoria had pretty limited tastes too. When she was younger, my parents tried to feed her Brussels sprouts.

197

The rule at the dinner table was that you ate least ate one of each thing on your plate and you stayed at the table until you did. Victoria held firmly against the vegetables, refusing to even touch them. She sat at the table, staring at her plate while Mom did the dishes. She sat there while I took a bath. She sat there while Dad watched *M*A*S*H* and *Jeopardy*. She sat there while Mom read me a story and tucked me into bed. I never knew how long she actually held out but she said Mom and Dad caved around one in the morning, letting her go to bed without touching the greens. I didn't entirely believe her because I could swear I heard gagging and retching sounds coming from the dining room as I nodded off that night. Plus, Mom and Dad *never* caved.

At the big New Year's Eve dinner, Bobby and his family were sitting at a table on the opposite side of the room from ours. His mother looked like a librarian with her gray hair pulled back into a ponytail and a long, flowing Santa Fe patterned skirt and sweater. His father looked like the spitting image of Radar O'Reilly, the company clerk character from *M*A*S*H*, who was short, roundish and wore circular wire glasses. Bobby's dad wore a perfectly pressed tuxedo. Bobby had on a vest and a bolo tie. He looked much older than before.

I had a hard time identifying the cast and crew of *Wings* since I didn't watch the show. I recognized the guy with the flowy hair from the NBC promos but that was about it. He wasn't anywhere to be seen that night. I saw a blonde lady wearing a teal, sequined dress sign an autograph for someone and assumed that she must've been somebody famous. I made sure whenever she or anyone else from her table was nearby I looked as poised and interesting as possible.

I worked hard to make my hair eye-catching that night. My bangs were styled to look like a cascading waterfall that led into teased-out ringlets on the side of my face. The rest of my hair was stick-straight. The dress I'd picked out was drop-waisted, had a black velour top with puffed sleeves and a short, poofy hot pink skirt with little black velvet hearts all over it. Mom let me get sheer black nylons to wear with it—not the opaque tights that she usually made me wear. With my outfit and hair I felt like I could have been on the cover of Teen magazine instead of in the dining room at an Oregonian coastal hotel. I hoped someone with clout in Hollywood would notice.

The only person who noticed me that night was Bobby. Every time we made eye contact he made swimming gestures with his arms, puffing up his cheeks and holding his breath. My dad caught me chuckling at it while we ate. After that, I kept my behavior and manners in check for the rest of the meal. When my Kermit the Frog watch read seven-fifty, I nudged Victoria under the table.

"Wanna go?" I asked.

"Yeah," she said, folding her napkin and tossing it on her plate. "Can we go?" she asked Mom and Dad.

"Where are you going?" Dad asked. Apparently, he hadn't heard Mom give us permission earlier.

"Swimming," I said.

"Can they take him?" he asked Mom, pointing at Calvin, who was fishing ice cubes out of his water glass with a butter knife.

Mom furrowed her brow.

"Not to the pool," she said. "They're not quite old enough for babysitting in the water yet."

Dad leaned over and whispered something in Mom's ear, then kissed her on the cheek.

"Okay, girls," Mom said, turning to Victoria and me, "you can swim for forty-five minutes. Then I want you to come back here, get Calvin and take him back to the room so your father and I can enjoy ourselves alone tonight."

That seemed reasonable enough. But Victoria switched the deal when we got back to the room. I put on my swimsuit and noticed Victoria wasn't changing.

"What are you doing?" I asked.

"Not going swimming," she replied.

"Why not?"

"I'm going to stay here and make a phone call."

Mom said that I could only go swimming if Victoria went too. I had a tough decision to make. I could still go swimming and just hope that Mom and Dad never found out, or I could stay in the room and pretend I wasn't listening to Victoria's phone conversation. Before I could weigh the risks or benefits to either choice, Victoria put her foot down.

"You can't stay here," she warned.

"What if Mom finds out I went swimming without you? I don't want to be there all alone! Somebody already stole all my stuff! What if they try to steal me?" I whined.

"That's your problem, scaredy-cat."

Really, Victoria was leaving me with no choice. She gave me a get-lost-or-I'll-pound-you look. I gathered up my courage and went to the pool all by myself.

When I got there, Bobby was already in the water, sitting cross-legged on the bottom in the deep end. When I stepped in, he bobbed up to the surface.

"I thought you weren't coming," he said, swimming around me as I slowly lowered myself into the water.

"I can't stay long," I said, watching the windows between the pool and the lobby. I had a weird sinking feeling.

"You're really interesting," Bobby said before he dove underwater.

"Thanks," I said when he came up. Though it took a second or two to sink in, it was a compliment that felt pretty good to receive.

"I mean, you're not just a pretty girl. You're confident. You're like royalty," he said in a very sweeping and mature tone.

I soaked up the attention and was starting to get that flutter in my chest that I felt when I was around Sam. Bobby dove down underwater again, and swam up right in front of me. In one smooth motion he came up out of the water, took me by the shoulders, and kissed me. His kiss

201

was different from Sam's. He wasn't as forceful, and he either had a lot more spit in his mouth or he'd taken in a lot of pool water. I closed my eyes and considered the moment. I felt pretty. I felt grown up. I felt someone watching me.

I opened my eyes to see Dad looking in through the window from the lobby. The fluttering in my chest turned immediately into a knot of fear in my throat. Dad's eyes were huge. He looked so angry that he could've burst through the glass at any moment like *He-Man* or *The Incredible Hulk*. Dad pointed at me and then pointed at the floor next to himself. I lowered my head and started to walk toward the pool steps. Bobby grabbed my hand and tried to pull me back.

"Where are you going?" he asked with a laugh.

Dad slapped the window. It made a deep sound that resonated around the room and made both Bobby and me jump. Dad's face was dark red.

"I gotta go," I mumbled. I ran toward the locker room.

So much for having a pen pal. I didn't even know Bobby's last name.

CHAPTER FIFTEEN

Dad was pretty angry about the pool incident. I lost just about every possible privilege for the next two and a half months. I lost the Bartphone, I lost any freedom to go on walks or over to friends' houses and I even lost Odyssey of the Mind privileges, which meant the team would have to go to the state semifinals without me. I was embarrassed and heartbroken. I couldn't wait to get to school and tell Sara all about the horrors of my winter vacation.

Due to my grounding, I was back with Calvin's babysitter in the mornings which meant I didn't get to see Sara until we got to our classroom. Even then I didn't get to talk to her until morning recess. There was so much to share—we both raced for the fence line to start walking and talking.

"I missed you so much! How was your vacation?" Sara asked once she caught her breath.

"Only like the most horrible and mortifying thing ever," I said, adding as much drama to my voice as I could.

"Yeah, mine was pretty rough too," she admitted.

I wanted to hear about her stuff, but I really thought my story was a super big deal. I wanted to talk first.

"So I got a CD player for Christmas and bought this really cool CD, have you ever heard of Depeche Mode?"

"We're moving," Sara said.

Talk about dropping a bomb. It was so huge, I barely heard it.

"Anyway, it's this really cool band and this CD is like the greatest thing I've ever heard, but as soon as we got to the hotel, Victoria and I went swimming and—" Sara stopped walking and I got a couple of steps ahead of her before I turned around. "What?"

"Did you hear me?" she asked.

"Hear you?"

"Violet," she said, stepping toward me, "we're *moving*."

I froze. Moving. What did this mean?

"Moving? To a new house?"

"To California."

This was the greatest news ever. If my best friend lived in California I could visit her all the time and we could go to Hollywood together and get discovered.

"That's great!" I said.

205

She looked confused.

"What? No, Vy! This is horrible! We leave as soon as school is out for the summer. I'm supposed to pack up all my stuff between now and then," Sara started walking again with her head down.

I walked alongside her, thinking more about the situation. The chances that my parents would actually let me go to California by myself were probably pretty slim. Then it dawned on me that if Sara was moving, Sam would be going away too. I was only five months from losing my best friend of all time and my first not-quite-yet-boyfriend. I stared at my feet and half-listened while Sara kept talking. She said something about her new city and the new school where she'd go for seventh grade while I imagined being alone for the rest of my days. Sixth grade was halfway over and was officially now the weirdest and worst year ever.

"So we can probably make our plans for the rest of the year at Odyssey state next week, right Vy?" Sara said.

"Not exactly," I said. "But I'll tell you about that later."

The bell rang and everyone ran for the doors. I didn't feel like running. Everything was sinking in slowly and it felt an awful lot like my whole life was going down like a ship into the ocean.

Since its discovery a few years ago my mom had become fascinated by the shipwreck of the Titanic. We watched a lot of PBS shows about it. At first I thought the photographs made the ship look monstrous, with big brown tentacles of rust. Later, I started to understand the beauty my mom saw in it. It was something elegant that

206

was broken and forgotten. When it was later found with all of its scars, everyone looked beyond its ugliness and saw the classic beauty and charm that it once had. I loved that idea. Broken and forgotten were two things that I felt a lot lately. I was still waiting for someone to discover me. I wondered how much longer I'd have to lay on the sea floor before they did. It would have to take at least ten weeks, since that's how long I was grounded.

CHAPTER SIXTEEN

The Odyssey team came back from state with silver medals. I saw the team's picture in the big city paper on the same Sunday morning that marked the last day of my grounding. They'd lost to a private school team that used a pneumatic jack instead of a mechanical one and had a vehicle that looked a lot like a Japanese bullet train. They had some sort of Kabuki-style presentation and it all looked really polished, Sara told me later. I didn't like losing, so it was probably good that I couldn't go. It was pretty embarrassing to have to tell the team why I had to quit, especially since, technically, it was Victoria and that stupid boy Bobby's fault, not mine. But as much as I tried to explain that to my parents they wouldn't hear it.

"You're responsible for your own actions," Mom had said, "and you should take care to never allow yourself to get into situations that even *look* bad, let alone *get* bad."

I think Dad was just mad because one of his greatest fears was his daughters growing up and becoming interested in boys. Victoria was too into herself and her schoolwork to pay that much attention to anything else. Dad must have thought that since Victoria didn't have trouble with boys, I would be OK too. Dad really moped around for a long time after we got back from the beach. It seemed like he was just starting to come out of it as my grounding wound down.

Dad started working on a model ship just after Calvin was born. It was extremely detailed and on a very small scale. He worked on it pretty infrequently and kept his progress on a shelf just above the computer desk. The model ship made it easy to know when Dad was stressed, because it seemed like he worked on it to calm himself down. He had put in a lot of hours on it over the past month. The hull was almost fully built along with the rudder and pieces of the masts. I loved the smell of the glues, stains and varnishes that he used on his models. He built a model B-17 once and I used to sneak smells of the army-green paint. Dad was working on the ship that Sunday morning.

"Whatcha gonna do today, Daddy?" I asked, hoping that a family trip to somewhere like the mall was in order. I loved going to the mall with my parents.

There was a habitual order of events for family visits to the mall. First we'd do the department store thing—Meier & Frank, Penny's or Mervyn's. Then we'd visit McDonald's. We didn't have one in our town so getting chicken nuggets or a McDLT sandwich was a real treat. After that we'd go to the B.Dalton bookstore or Waldenbooks and if we were *really* good, Mom would let us each pick out a book to take home.

Victoria was into *The Babysitter's Club* and *Sweet Valley High*. She did a good job of keeping up with the series so as soon as we made a trip to the mall, she'd be ready to buy the most recently released one. I preferred the *Sleepover Friends* series but was hardly as committed to them as Victoria was to her books. I read mine out of order and only had books 1, 3, 4, 5, and 7. Being that I cared so much about what other people might think of me, I wanted to make sure that whatever I was reading was something I wanted to be *seen* reading.

Last summer I rode my bike to the downtown library and checked out *War and Peace* by Leo Tolstoy. I had seen *Bon Voyage, Charlie Brown (and don't come back!)* on a *CBS Special* and I became enamored with the intensity with which Linus talked about the story. It must have been something really important if he felt the need to shout at Charlie Brown in the chateau about Tolstoy having written all of *War and Peace* "WITH A DIP PEN!" When I found the book at the library, it was huge. It looked long and complicated. I took it up to the counter and handed it to the librarian, Ms. Sandy.

"Oh my," she said, looking over the counter at me. "Are you *sure* this is what you want to check out?"

I nodded, giving her my most serious, adult expression.

"It's due back in two weeks, are you going to be able to get through it?"

I nodded again. She didn't really need to know how long it would take me to read it—if I actually read it at all. I just really wanted to be seen reading it. I carried it around with me for the full two weeks. I tried to read it on the shore of the river while people I knew splashed around in the water. I tried to read it in a golf cart when my Dad took me along with him for eighteen holes with one of his colleagues. I took it to the neighboring city pool. I sat on the curb of our house reading it, just hoping that someone would drive by and take notice. I never really read past the first ten pages, and I lied to Ms. Sandy about it when I returned the book.

"Well, there," she said, stamping and returning the card to the inside sleeve, "what did you think?"

"I can see why people say it's such an important story," I said, quickly turning to leave.

She called after me as I pushed open the glass door.

"How about the ending?" she asked.

I had to think quickly.

"It took a long time to get to it," I smiled.

She laughed and I ran out to my bike.

Back to the final day of my grounding: Dad was hunched over, filing a tiny piece of wood under a magnifying glass for the model boat's deck. He didn't respond right away, so I bounced up beside him and asked again.

"Whatcha gonna do today, Daddy?"

"This," he said. He was concentrating hard on what he was doing. He seemed a little mopey. I had overheard something about his sister, my aunt Clarice, being sick again, but it was more likely that he was still bummed out about his baby girl growing up before his eyes.

"Oh," I said, shuffling my feet around next to the desk. "Did you, um, have any chores you needed me to do?" I asked.

Dad waved me away.

"Go ask your mother," he said.

I found Mom folding clothes in the laundry room. My hope was that neither she nor Dad would remember that this was the official last day of my grounding and perhaps they might allow me an early release based on good behavior. I did every chore I was assigned with no complaints for as long as I'd been grounded. I practiced my piano without lying about how many times I played each song. I refrained from engaging in back-talk or whining and I volunteered to help with Calvin whenever I sensed Mom's nerves were getting a little fried. I leaned up against the door frame in the laundry room.

"Mom?"

"Yes, Violet?"

"Do you have anything you'd like me to do?"

"Not right now," she said, folding the last towel from the dryer.

My timing was perfect. If I had been there even a moment before, she probably would have made me fold clothes. I picked at my fingernails while she transferred the load from the washer into the dryer. After she started the dryer, she put her hand on my shoulder and smiled at me.

"Do you *need* something to do?"

"Well," I said, trailing off. I really just wanted her to tell me I could do whatever I wanted, but I didn't want to ruin my chances by being too overt about it.

"Grandpa's coming over after lunch with a cake for Calvin's birthday," she said. "If you go organize your closet this morning, you can finish up being grounded after Grandpa leaves, okay?"

It wasn't perfect, but it was still a good deal.

"Okay!" I chirped, darting to my room.

Cleaning out my closet was a favorite chore of mine, mostly because it was like opening a time-capsule. In it were toys, a box that contained my baby book, old projects and assignments, and of course, my clothes. I loved to organize and reorganize my closet, throwing away tattered memories and the occasional candy wrapper. I threw open the doors and started in. I could hear Victoria's voice from behind the bed,

"No, she got busted for sucking face with some kid in the pool at the beach so she couldn't go."

"I'm right here," I said.

"Doyee," Victoria rudely remarked. She went on, "Not like they would have won with her there anyway." She was probably talking to Jean, who I would guess was looking at the picture of my former Odyssey team in that morning's paper. Calvin wandered in.

214

"Vy? Can you play Imbatendo with me?" he asked.

"Buddy," I said sweetly, "I wish I could right now but I have to clean my closet because I'm still in trouble. Maybe after lunch?"

He wasn't satisfied.

"But I want to play Imbatendo NOW!" he whined.

It was the poor kid's birthday, for Pete's sake. I walked him into the living room to turn on the TV and the Nintendo.

"There pal," I said, patting him on the head. "I'll come play after my jobs are done."

He didn't hear a word I said. He was instantly transfixed by the 8-bit glow from the TV. When I walked back into the bedroom I caught the tail end of Victoria's conversation.

"Somewhere in California," she said. "Ask Lacey, she'll know. Anyway, yeah, if you wanna go see Dan and Chris, I'll walk over with you."

Dan? Chris? Was she talking about Jake's cousins? What did Jean want with Jake's cousins? Was that even Jean? Not that I was interested in Dan anymore—I just wondered. I mean, he was still cute, but if I was going to do anything with my reclaimed freedom that afternoon it was going to be a visit to Sara's house with a pop-in on Sam. I went back to cleaning the closet. Victoria shimmied out from behind the bed.

"What are you going to do this afternoon?" I asked.

"None of your beeswax," she said, walking out of the room with a flip of her hair.

215

I finished cleaning the closet just before lunch. Grandpa arrived not long after. He was Mom's dad and he always brought over the cake for our birthdays. My favorite was the Boston Strawberry Cream cake. Victoria liked German Chocolate. Calvin liked yellow cake with multi-colored frosting and sprinkles.

Calvin was far less interested in his cake than he was in his presents, which Mom pulled out of the hall closet and put on the kitchen counter. One at a time he opened them, squealing as he threw paper all over the dining room. His excitement was contagious and I smiled the whole time while he shouted,

"THANK YOU!" after each present.

There was a boomerang, a sweatshirt with Super Mario on it, a red Sony "My First Walkman," and a pair of blue and black roller blades. He was most excited for the boomerang, but I was eyeballing his roller blades. Calvin and I had the same sized feet. That meant that I could possibly fit into his roller blades. I had never rollerbladed before. I had heard it was like ice skating. I loved my skates and had always been much better at skating on four wheels than ice skates, but that didn't mean I wasn't interested in trying. I waited until Grandpa left and Calvin had taken his boomerang out to the back yard to ask.

"Hey, Calvin? Is it okay if I borrow your new roller blades?" He was throwing the boomerang vertically, dodging it as it flew down towards him and stuck into the lawn like a dart. I couldn't remember him ever really caring about roller skating before.

216

"Go ahead," he said with a grunt, flinging the boomerang toward the sky.

"Thanks!" I said, bolting back into the house. I scooped up the roller blades under my arm. Mom called after me as I opened the front door.

"Vy, what are you doing with Calvin's new skates?"

"He said I could try them," I said. "I wanted to try in-lines. I asked him first."

"Okay," she said in a warning tone, "just be careful. Remember, those were your brother's birthday present. Don't ruin them before he gets to enjoy them."

"I know," I said, closing the door behind me.

My four-wheeled skates were great for the garage and the driveway but were pretty lousy on the graveled streets. The big wheels on Calvin's roller blades seemed like they'd be perfect for skating down the hill. I'd only ever walked or ridden my bike down the hill, so my perception of how steep it was had been limited by my experience.

Sitting on the curb, I strapped on the roller blades. My skates had long, purple laces. These had plastic straps like zip-ties that clamped down across my ankles. It took quite a bit of effort to get them on and secure without making them too tight. I stood up and found them to feel a lot like ice skates. I had gone ice skating several times at the mall in the city nearby. Sara had her birthday party there the year before and we got to watch Tonya Harding practice just a few days before she took third place in the U.S. Figure Skating Championships.

"I'm gonna be just like her someday," Sara said, watching Tonya pivot and glide gracefully around the rink. Sara liked to skate but she wasn't very good. Watching Tonya, I took careful mental notes as to how she did things so I could attempt her moves on my roller skates later. She did this thing where she'd jump up and spin around three times in the air. I'd seen her do it at least twice. I overheard someone saying that she'd never done that move in competition but that if she did, she would be a sure thing for a gold medal at the Olympics. I wished they had four-wheeled roller skating in the Olympics.

As I stood by the curb in Calvin's skates, it took me a few moments to steady myself. I decided to do a few laps around the driveway just to make sure I was fully prepared to go down the hill. I was pretty sure trying the hill on roller blades was a good idea. Not positive, but pretty sure. I rounded my third lap and was building my courage when Jake and Dan rode up on their bikes and stopped at the base of the driveway.

"What's up, dork?" greeted Jake.

"Hey there, Captain Excite Bike," I shot back, still skating around in a circle. "What are you guys up to?"

"Nuthin' much," Jake leaned back and pulled on his handlebars, lifting his front tire off the ground. Balancing on the rear wheel, he spun his handlebars and front tire around in the air. "We just got done over at

Tom's house. We were playing football in his backyard until he lost his retainer and started crying. Hey! You got new blades?"

"No, they're Calvin's."

"You can fit into your five year-old brother's roller skates?"

"He's six now."

"Still," Jake said, dropping out of the wheelie position he was in, letting his bike bounce beneath him. "You must have tiny feet."

"Better than walking around on those loaves of bread you've got!" I pointed at him and tried a crossover move with my feet, stumbling a little but regaining my composure quickly. I looked over at Jake's cousin Dan, who was kicking at the pedals on his bike, making them spin around. Dan laughed at my comment about Jake's feet. I started to get a little more confident. "I thought my sister and Jean were supposed to be hanging out over at your house today," I said.

"They are," Jake said.

"So why aren't you guys there?" I asked.

"Last time Victoria and Jean came over they just wanted to hang around Chris and they made fun of me for sweating. I didn't want to let that happen again so me and Dan are just riding around."

"Where are you guys planning on going?" I asked.

"Prolly to the Minute-Mart by the railroad tracks," Dan answered. He rode his bike up into my driveway and started following me around in a circle as I skated.

"Yeah? When?" I asked.

"Now, 'cause I'm thirsty," Dan said. "Wanna go?"

Since I had considered going down the hill anyway it might be nice to show someone like Dan exactly how brave I could be. I imagined myself zooming behind their bikes on my skates with my arms tucked at my sides like a downhill skier. I pictured Sam seeing me whiz down the hill from his bedroom window, wishing he was by my side instead of hanging out with dumb old Lacey like I figured he was that day. With that, I had convinced myself that skating down the hill was the best idea I'd ever had.

"Yes," I said firmly. "Yes I do."

I tucked a dollar I'd found on the floor in the coat closet the day before into my left sock. That was all I needed to get a Coke or maybe a Grape Crush when we got there.

The road was bumpier than I'd anticipated as I rolled from the driveway onto the street. It took a lot more effort to keep pace with Jake and Dan than I'd thought. By the time I reached the crest of the hill, I was huffing and puffing. Jake and Dan were almost halfway down the hill already when I first started down. My feet bumped and vibrated as the wheels of Calvin's skates rolled over the gravel-covered road.

Twice a year the big tar trucks would drive through the neighborhood, painting the streets with the black sticky stuff. Gravel trucks would follow behind, dropping loose rocks onto the tar. The covering would start to even out as the cars drove over it but it never really got to be completely flat. I felt every little lump and bump as I rolled down the hill.

My feet were going numb from the vibration and I started to panic. Jake and Dan made it to the bottom of the hill and rounded the corner without me. I still had my arms tucked close to my sides and my knees bent like I'd seen the Olympic skiers do. I must have been going at least ten miles an hour, but it felt more like fifty. I was a little more than halfway down the hill when my ankles started to wobble. I lifted my foot to try and steady myself but it just made everything worse. My legs were stomping and my arms were flailing all over the place. The moment I knew that a crash was inevitable was the same moment everything went black.

CHAPTER SEVENTEEN

There was a TV. An episode of *Cheers* was on. I was alone. My head hurt. My side stung. My palms were covered in cuts and scrapes, some of which still had little pieces of gravel lodged in them. I saw through the window blinds that it was a bright sunny day outside. I gathered that I was in a hospital pediatric ward from the bed and the little yellow ducks that were painted around the border of the room near the ceiling. Several nurses came and went over the next few hours, and all of them asked me the same questions.

"What's your name, honey?"

"Violet."

"And what day is it?"

"Ummmmmm…" I had no idea what day it was. "Sunday, maybe? Is that right?"

Calvin's birthday had been on a Sunday and it didn't feel like much time had passed since then so that was my guess. I must have been wrong because every time I answered, the nurse would shake her head, write something on a metal clipboard, then walk out of the room. I had a hard time remembering what I'd answered when the last nurse asked, so I always guessed Sunday. Finally, a doctor came in to look me over and ask me questions. He seemed to be willing to help me out a little.

"Well, hello there," said Dr. Herzog, a tall, round man with a large gray mustache. He was my regular pediatrician and I was a little surprised to see him in a hospital setting. I had never been hospitalized, as far as I could remember. "Take a little spill, didja?" He asked, sitting on the bed beside me.

Ah-ha! I must have fallen down on the roller blades. Oh no—the roller blades! My mom was going to kill me. If I crashed, that means I probably messed up Calvin's roller blades even before he ever had the chance to use them.

"How are you feeling?" asked Dr. Herzog.

"Sore," I complained. "A little tired, too."

Dr. Herzog laughed.

"That's because no one around here is going to let you sleep very well!"

I didn't understand and my face must have shown it.

"When you konk your noggin, we like to wake you up a lot to make sure you *can* still wake up," he explained.

224

I guess I must have hit my head when I crashed.

"I see that you know your name now," he said.

Had I not known it earlier?

"Can you tell me what year it is?" he asked.

I knew this one.

"Nineteen ninety-one," I said.

"Attagirl," he was making marks and flipping pages on the big metal clipboard. "How about the day?"

"I'm not sure, but I don't think it's Sunday," I admitted. "How long have I been here?"

"Four days."

Holy crap! I was missing four days of my memory? This was the kind of thing that happened on TV or in a movie. I thought back to the *Muppets Take Manhattan*, which was the first movie I ever saw in a theater. I remembered the part when Kermit was hit by a taxi. The doctor in the movie called it "amnesia." Kermit didn't come out of it until Miss Piggy socked him in the gut and sent him flying across the room where he landed upside down on his head in a chair. Nobody had to sock me in the gut to get me out of the fog I must have been in, though. I just kind of slowly drifted out of it.

"So that makes today Wednesday?" I asked. "Wait, no," I corrected myself. The closing credits to *Cheers* were on TV. *Cheers* ran on Thursdays. I should have put that together sooner! "It's Thursday," I said proudly.

225

"Okay! Hey! She's back!" Dr. Herzog exclaimed, coming at me with his hand raised for a high five. I slowly raised my hand but instead of slapping it, he gently took hold of my wrist and looked at the scrapes on my palm. He scrunched up his face.

"That's no good. Four days and you still have road bits in your hand? We'll take care of that. You rest—I think we'll keep you here for one more night just to make sure the memory sticks. Anything coming back to you about your little accident?" Dr. Herzog asked.

I shook my head but then winced. It felt like my brain was rattling around in my skull.

"Yeah, don't do *that*, okay?" Dr. Herzog said, shining a pen light in my eyes. "Just keep resting and we'll talk more tomorrow morning, okay? I'll see if the nurses will only wake you up every two hours now, how about that?"

"Okay," I said, smiling. My face stung when I smiled. There wasn't a mirror in the room so I really didn't know how bad I looked.

Just as Dr. Herzog reached the door my mom walked in. They spoke in really low voices, looking over their shoulders at me every so often. When Dr. Herzog left Mom closed the door and came to my bedside. She bent over and kissed me on the temple.

"Hey, sweetie," she whispered, brushing my hair to the side. "How are you feeling?"

"Fine," I said. "I mean, kind of fine?" I was still pretty confused. "What happened?" I asked. "Did I break Calvin's skates?"

Mom laughed and sat down in the chair next to me.

"Yes, you broke Calvin's skates," she said. "You almost broke yourself, too." She started to dig into her purse. "It's good to talk to you, finally! Vy, I've been trying to talk to you for the past four days and you've been pretty out of it. You told me you couldn't remember anything and you hardly knew me. You only remembered your name two days ago! The doctor said you had a concussion and temporary amnesia."

I knew it! Just like Kermit the Frog. Luckily for me, I wasn't trying to get a show on Broadway or reunite with all of my friends from across the country.

Mom pulled a compact out of her purse, opened it and handed it to me. Oh yikes. When I looked in the mirror I saw not only a very dirty face and greasy hair that hadn't been washed in at least four days, but scrapes, bruises, and crusted blood both on my skin and in my hair.

"Gross!" I exclaimed, putting the mirror down for only a second before bringing it back up to further survey the damage. "Geezus," I said under my breath.

"Violet!"

My mother didn't like swearing. She snatched the compact out of my hand, snapped it shut and tucked it back into her purse. She took a deep breath and sighed.

"I'm sorry, sweetie," Mom said. "I'm glad you're okay, that's all." She leaned over and gave me a kiss.

"Will you tell me what happened?" I asked. Mom put her purse down and leaned back in her chair, folding her hands in her lap.

"Well honey," she started, "I can only tell you as much as I know. How much do you remember?"

"Um, Calvin said I could try out his roller blades, and I remember skating around the driveway in them. I remember Jake and Dan came over and invited me to go with them to the Minute-Mart. That's all I've got," I said.

Mom nodded along slowly.

"Well, that definitely helps piece this back together a little more," said Mom. "The last I had seen of you was when you took Calvin's skates out to the driveway. Just about a half hour later, Sara came running up to our door, crying and telling us to 'come quick.' Well, we didn't get much further than the end of the driveway when we saw her brother carrying Calvin's roller blades in one hand and helping you to walk barefoot on the gravel. Oh, Violet, there was so much blood," I saw Mom swallow hard to fight off the woozies she usually got around blood. "You had this glassy-eyed look and you wouldn't talk. We asked you 'what happened?' so many times, but you just sort of stared blankly."

"Wait, Sam walked me home?" I asked, hopefully.

How did Sam come into this? Had he come along with Jake and Dan and I and I'd forgotten about it? Was all of that "little mistress" stuff a dream? Was Sam really my boyfriend and my amnesia had been going on for far longer than it seemed? Victoria had clonked me on the front of the head with one of Dad's golf clubs during the summer, so maybe

228

that triggered the real amnesia and all of this was just bringing things back to me. I could only hope.

"Sam, yes," Mom went on, "that's his name. I can never remember. Sam walked you home. You were slumped over his arm, moving really slowly. He said that he and Sara were helping their parents set up a garage sale and they saw you fly down the hill and crash headfirst into the curb. Oh, Violet, why didn't you wear a helmet?"

"I don't have a helmet," I said matter-of-factly.

"Well, we need to get you one," Mom said. "This is one too many of these."

I couldn't remember any other head injuries aside from the incident with Victoria using Dad's driver, though Mom made it sound like there had been several more.

"Sara told us that after you crashed, you just laid there and didn't move. She thought you were dead. And by the looks of what you'd done to your head, well, I could understand why. Anyway, she and her brother ran over to you and just when Sara screamed 'Somebody call nine-one-one!' you sat up, took off the roller blades, and started walking home. You just left the skates there in the road and started walking like a zombie." I could hear Mom's voice start to shake. Tears were welling up in her eyes and she swallowed hard, like she had a knot building up in her throat. "Violet, baby, I was so scared! You didn't talk! You looked right past all of us!"

"What did Sam say?" I asked. I knew Mom and Dad were worried, but I was more interested in what Sam thought.

"He handed the roller blades to me and helped Daddy get you inside. He only stayed for a little while to help Sara tell us what happened. The whole time they told the story, you just sat on the edge of your bed and stared at the wall. There was blood dripping down from your head and you had road rash all up and down your side, your hands, your face, just everywhere."

While Mom described the scene for me, I fought to find any memory of these events in my brain. There wasn't a single bit. I imagined myself sitting on my bed, staring at the yellow walls of my room while Sam stood in the doorway, looking at me with pity and adoration in his eyes. I tried to imagine his arm around me while my bare feet walked along the jagged gravel. I tried to hear him call my dad "Sir" and my mom "Ma'am." I wanted to remember him kissing my bloody forehead over my blank stare, vowing in a whisper to never forget me, like a nurse over a dying soldier in the war. But none of it was real. I didn't have any real memory of it. It was deliciously dramatic.

"So if Sam and Sara took me home, how did I get to the hospital?" I asked. I had never been in an ambulance. I hoped that my parents, worried about my zombie-like behavior and what sounded like a massive head wound, would have called for an ambulance to whisk me off to the emergency room where some sort of neurosurgeon, probably one who was young and handsome like Hawkeye Pierce on *M*A*S*H*, would do emergency surgery to bring me out from the grasp of amnesia.

"Your father and I drove you here," she said.

230

Well, there went that fantasy. So much for flashing red and white lights, a blaring siren, attractive EMTs administering IVs and bandaging my wounds. Instead it was a navy blue Buick, going the speed limit with no lights on. Well, maybe at least headlights.

"They said you had hit your head pretty hard," Mom continued, "that you had a concussion and they were worried about serious damage since you couldn't tell anybody your name or what day it was. But you started talking more a couple of days ago and finally remembered your name. Dr. Herzog just told me you know what day it is now, so after one more night of observation, they'll let us take you home."

I was starting to get a headache so I closed my eyes, thinking I could just listen to Mom. I must have fallen asleep because the next thing I remember, the room was dark and a nurse was waking me up to shine a pen light in my eyes again.

Since Sam had come to my rescue, I hoped maybe he'd get a little of that Florence Nightingale thing going for me and I would be stuck in his head. I wondered if he had called to ask about me while I was in the hospital. There were no flowers or cards or teddy bears in my hospital room. Just the yellow painted ducks on the wall. I wondered if Dan and Jake felt bad at all for leaving me in the dust to crash and burn, or if they knew what happened at all. I wish I could remember the walk from the bottom of the hill back up to the house. I at least wanted to remember Sam's arm around me and the smell of his cologne. It had been so long since I'd been close enough to him to smell it, I was starting to forget his scent.

I WANT EVERYBODY TO LIKE ME

At seven o'clock the next morning, the phone on the table next to my hospital bed rang. There were no adults around so I ignored it. After the sixth ring a nurse popped her head through the door and said,

"That's for you, sweetie. Go ahead." I picked up the receiver and held it to my ear but quickly pulled it away because the scrape on the side of my face was still sensitive and holding the phone up against it really stung.

"Hello?" I said, wincing.

"Vy!" a voice shrieked on the other end.

"Sara?"

"Yes! Oh, I am so glad you're okay!" She shouted.

"Sara, this is a long-distance call," I said, pulling the receiver even further from my ear. I was still a little drowsy. The lack of consistent sleep combined with the pain had me feeling really tired. One of the night nurses had mumbled something about wanting to give me different pain medication for what I was going through but that they couldn't for some reason since my head was all messed up.

"Shut up, Vy!" Sara squealed at top volume. "I know! You think I'm going to let a little thing like a phone bill keep me from checking up on my best friend after something like this?"

I loved how worried she sounded. I'd always thought that a major medical emergency would get me lots of attention but having not received any flowers, cards, gifts, or visitors had me thinking otherwise. Sara's call restored some of my faith.

232

"You're so sweet," I said, adding an extra layer of pathetic to my voice. I considered coughing but decided against it.

"I thought you were dead!"

"That's what Mom told me."

"When are you coming home?"

"Today, I think."

"Well, when you get home, call me. I have all your homework for the past few days and me and Sam want to come over and see you. Did you get any stitches?" On top of being extremely loud, Sara was talking a mile a minute.

Homework? Why did I have homework? I thought when you had a major medical emergency like I just did, they forgave the assignments you missed. After all, I was in the hospital and would probably require a little more time to recover after I got home. And Sam wanted to come see me? This was great news. Perhaps my Florence Nightingale hopes were being realized. At that moment a nurse and my dad walked into the room together.

"Sara, I gotta go," I said.

"Okay, feel better! And call me later," she instructed before we both hung up.

Whenever I got sick or hurt, I got popsicles. Sure enough, after Dad checked me out of the hospital, we drove to the grocery store and picked up popsicles on our way home. It was almost lunchtime so we drove through The Old Fashioned to get Dad a burger. I wasn't really all that hungry. More than anything I wanted to sleep uninterrupted for a whole night. I wanted to take a bath and do my bangs. Then I wanted to call Sara so she and Sam could come over. They would be in school until after three so I'd have plenty of time for a bath and a nap first.

Dad knocked on the bathroom door in the middle of my bath. I had already washed and was just soaking in the warm water.

"You awake?" he asked from the hallway.

"Yes, I'm awake," I replied.

"I'm not supposed to let you fall asleep in there," he said.

"I'm fine," I said.

"You seemed kind of tired in the car, that's all."

"I'm okay, Dad." I sighed and pulled out the stopper.

I decided that my chances for an uninterrupted nap would be better if I was within Dad's line of sight. After my bath I laid down on the couch near the armchair from where Dad was watching *Perry Mason* and sipping what remained of his peanut butter milkshake from The Old Fashioned.

"You want one of your popsicles?" he asked.

"Maybe later," I said. I pulled the big, fuzzy throw blanket off of the back of the couch and covered myself with it. I didn't even make it through Perry's cross-examination before I fell asleep.

CHAPTER EIGHTEEN

I woke up to the smell of bacon and waffles. I was still on the couch in the living room where I had fallen asleep during *Perry Mason* the day before. I slept through Victoria coming home from school. I slept through Mom and Calvin coming home. I slept through dinner and all through the night. I felt rested but still sore. My skin felt tight around the scabs and scrapes all over my body.

"Well, good morning!" said Mom from the kitchen when she saw I had opened my eyes. "I don't think I've ever seen you sleep that much. Well, maybe when you were an infant, but not since then." She walked over and looked carefully at my eyes, then went back to fixing breakfast.

"What time is it?" I asked.

"Six-thirty."

"On Saturday?"

"That's right."

"I have to call Sara," I said, pulling the blanket off of myself and sitting up slowly.

"Why don't you wait until after nine so her family has a chance to wake up," Mom suggested. "She came over after school last night but you were sleeping so she said she'd talk to you today."

"Did Sam come with her?"

"No, just Sara," she answered.

My face must have shown my obvious disappointment.

"Did you want to say 'thank you' to Sam?" Mom asked.

"Yeah," I said, trying to nod. "That's it, I wanted to say thanks."

Any time I moved, it felt like my skin was tearing a little, so even nodding hurt. It seemed like kind of a double-edged sword to be hurt like this. I wanted the attention that came along with it but I didn't like the reality of being uncomfortable. I took another bath and slid into a loose shirt and some overalls so my clothes wouldn't rub against my cuts. My hands were healing pretty quickly, which I especially appreciated when it came time to style my hair. The hair gel I used stung my palms a little but it wasn't nearly as bad as it could have been. Victoria came into the bathroom while I was trying to curl my bangs.

"How are you doing?" she asked.

"I'm okay," I said. I knew better than to try and use my injury to get attention or pity from Victoria. She'd been hospitalized at least fifteen times in her lifetime and was the queen of getting attention from it. Whenever she got the flu she refused to drink the Pedialyte that mom gave her and would dehydrate really quickly. It got to the point where any time Victoria threw up, Mom would automatically start packing an overnight bag for the hospital. She'd barf up something yellow and Mom would drive her into the city and they'd spend the night with an IV in Victoria's arm. Victoria always got flowers, teddy bears, cards and visitors when she went to the hospital. One time, she got a stuffed pink bunny that was taller than she was from Dad's parents. They brought it to her in the hospital and came to the house every day after she got home to check on her. She never appreciated that kind of attention—at least not the way I would have.

"You look awful," she said.

"Thanks," I accepted the compliment, although it sounded a bit backhanded. "That's the look I was going for." I moved slowly with the curling iron, not wanting to bump the cuts on my forehead with the hot metal barrel.

"Thought you might wanna know that Sam and Lacey broke up," Victoria told me.

I tried to turn toward her quickly and the curling iron fell out of my hand. The hair it held unraveled and the curling iron swung back against my face, hitting me in the temple. It made a sizzling sound before I could unclamp it from my bangs.

"Ow!" I yelped, dropping the curling iron into the sink. Now, on top of having road rash all over my face, I had a big, rectangular burn mark right next to my left eye. "Great," I said in a frustrated tone as the tears welled up in my eyes. "That's just great."

"I thought you'd be happy to hear that," Victoria remarked, picking up the curling iron, which belonged to her anyway, and reaching for my hair. I sat down on the edge of the bathtub. Victoria carefully started to comb through my bangs with her fingers.

"Why?" I asked, sniffling and trying to blot at my tears with my sleeve.

"Because you like him, don't you?" Victoria re-curled my bangs, taking care not to pull my hair or touch my face.

"Kinda," I said.

Victoria raised her eyebrow at me.

"Oh come on," she said, unrolling the curling iron and setting it on the counter. "He told our Odyssey team that he made out with you."

"He did?"

"Yep. He told Mike Bennett that you were a good kisser." Victoria fluffed at my bangs with a comb.

I was surprised, both by Victoria's kindness and what she was saying.

"Anyway, he broke up with Lacey the day after you dove into the curb with your face. I just thought you'd want to know that." She reached for the bottle of hairspray on the counter. With one hand shielding my face, she spritzed at my hair with the hairspray.

I looked in the mirror to see that she'd made my bangs look really cute. They were much more evenly distributed than they were when I styled them. She also used a lot more hairspray than I usually did.

"Thanks, Victoria," I said. I tried to hug her but she pulled back and gave me a look that said *no way, weirdo.*

"Yeah, you're welcome," she turned and walked away. My sister had her own ways of showing she cared and I loved her for it.

CHAPTER NINETEEN

The smell of lukewarm institutional chili wafted down the hall and into my classroom from the cafeteria. I couldn't have been more grateful that Mom packed me a lunch that day. It was gray and rainy out and I was looking forward to the thermos of warm bean and bacon soup before the inevitable indoor recess we'd be having. I couldn't be sure, because I didn't see her pack the rest of my lunch, but I would bet that Mom included a hostess cupcake and maybe even a pop. Ever since my accident, my whole family had been extra nice to me.

That morning Mrs. Saltor divided us into groups of three for our big geography and history projects. Every year the sixth graders had to do reports in groups about different countries. They presented them at an "international fair" in the cafeteria where all of the younger classes and parents would walk around and see them. You were just supposed to write a report and put together a big board with pictures and facts, but it seemed like every year it got a little more competitive. Teams would dress up in the historic clothes of their chosen country and serve some sort of traditional food. I especially liked the team that presented on Mexico

242

when I was in the third grade, because they handed out little bags of tortilla chips that we got to take back to class. I was really excited about this assignment, because I was grouped together with Sara and Nelson.

Over the past few months, Sara and Nelson had become probably the best-known couple around school. It was almost like the teachers were on board with their relationship because they held hands all the time and never got in trouble for hands-on. They peck kissed goodbye at the bus lines every day and people just turned a blind eye. Maybe it was that I was noticing it more since I'd become a woman, but as the school year went on it seemed like relationships were blooming left and right amongst the sixth graders. You could always tell who the newer pairings were because they would get their faces all mashed together in these wet, weird kissing sessions in front of everyone. Sloppy kissing had become kind of an expected ritual announcing to the school that you were going out with someone. I thought it was tacky and gross. I'd seen far too many of my classmates' tongues in the last few months, most of which were pretty oddly shaped, if you asked my opinion.

For the international fair project, our group had been assigned Germany, both East and West combined. East Germany and West Germany had been separate for the classes that came before us. I was pretty happy about it because we had kind of a built-in story to tell, what with the Berlin Wall coming down last year. That also meant we would have to do our research at the library, instead of using the encyclopedias I had at home. Those encyclopedias were where I typically got most of the information for my reports. Sara, Nelson and I made plans to meet at the library downtown that afternoon to get some books. After that, we'd meet at Sara's in the evenings for the rest of the week to work on our project.

Mom made a huge deal about me needing to wear a helmet when I told her that Sara and I were going to ride our bikes to the library. It had rained for most of the day but the sun came out right after school.

"The pavement's still wet," Mom said. "It's pretty slick out there and I don't want you having another accident."

"We'll go slowly I promise," Sara reassured her. "Especially on the way home, since our backpacks will be so heavy with all of the books."

"Yeah!" I chimed in, "Besides, I don't even have a helmet, remember Mom?"

Mom wrinkled up her face. I could tell she didn't want to let me go but good grades meant everything to her so there was no way she was going get in the way of my homework. The worst thing that could happen in this situation was that she'd drive us to the library instead, which truly wouldn't be so bad, since the road rash on my hip was still healing and riding my bike was probably going to hurt.

"Okay," Mom said. "But Violet? Go slow. And come straight home. No fooling around." She pointed at me, and then at Sara, just to drive home the point.

We nodded and hopped out the door, calling over our shoulders in unison,

"Yes Ma'am!"

Steam rose up from the wet streets as Sara and I rode side-by-side on our bikes. We were quiet for the first few blocks. Neither one of us wanted to talk about her moving away, but we were both thinking about it. At least for me, I had this feeling like if I didn't talk about it maybe it wouldn't happen, so I avoided the subject for months. Still, I knew that was just fantasy and sooner or later I'd have to face the music: I was going to be starting middle school without a best friend.

"So," I started, "California. Wow."

"Yeah," Sara seemed just as disinterested in talking about it as I did. The conversation really felt like a chore.

"Are you and Nelson going to try to be long-distance boyfriend and girlfriend?" I asked.

"Nah," she replied.

I was actually surprised by her answer. They seemed inseparable and probably more mature than any other sixth grade couple out there.

"If we were going to see each other during the summers or something, then maybe. But I have to break it off because when we leave, we aren't coming back," Sara said, blinking hard like she had tears coming in.

"Not ever?" I asked. I could feel my own tears welling up. If this was going where I felt like it was going then I wasn't just losing my best friend for a little while. I was losing my best friend permanently.

"Probably not," she said. "But you and I will write each other all the time, promise?" She knew how much I loved pen pals.

"Promise, for sure." I said, riding through a shallow puddle, watching the water separate and spray from the sides of my front bike tire. "But you're still here for another couple months, right?"

"Right," Sara balanced her bike on the curb as she rode. "Mom's going down there next week and Dad's going to ship boxes of stuff to her one at a time. She'll have the whole house unpacked and put away by the time we leave. We'll just have to fly down there with one suitcase on our last day here."

It sounded like a real adventure. I loved to fly. My parents took me on an airplane to Disneyland once and to Hawaii another time. Airplanes were the only places that I ever drank tomato juice or ginger ale. I loved the hollow cylindrical ice they served in their drinks. I liked the smell of the airport, too. Something about the forced air, strong coffee and jet exhaust was just delicious. I imagined traveling by plane, just me and Sara. I pictured us moving to Hollywood together, living in a little apartment and working as characters at Disneyland while we waited to be discovered by big-time agents who would sign us to multi-million-dollar contracts. While I was fantasizing about it, I imagined Sam living there too.

"Vy?" Sara stopped her bike. I almost ran into her and it jerked me back to reality.

"Yeah?"

"I'm scared."

"Scared?"

"To move."

I didn't know what to tell her. I'd never moved before. We'd lived in the same house all my life. My parents grew up here, and their parents grew up here too. Sara was born here but her parents grew up in California. For them, this was going home. For Sara, it was leaving home.

"Don't be scared," I said. "Your whole family is going with you, so you won't be alone."

I thought about how limited my chances to spend time with Sam were. Was it even worth it anymore to consider making him my boyfriend? I hadn't talked to him since the accident. I thought about how he had broken up with Lacey for me. If he went to all that length, I had to at least give it one more chance. I just needed to figure out how to approach it.

Sara seemed to be having kind of an emotional moment as we stood there and I didn't want to come off as totally insensitive, so I put my bike down and gave her a hug.

"You'll be fine. I know you will." I said, stroking her blonde hair with my ragged-looking hands. She hugged me back, a little tighter than I found comfortable in my condition but I wasn't going to let a little pain ruin a best friend moment like that. What did ruin it, though, was Nelson. He rode up beside us and skidded to a stop.

"We're losing daylight, ladies," he said.

Sara wiped a tear from her eye and climbed back up on her bike. I rode behind the two of them the rest of the way to the library. Watching

Sara and Nelson ride together and listening to them talk, I wondered if Nelson knew about her plans to break things off before she moved away. The idea that he might be in for a big, disappointing surprise was somehow satisfying. He was nice enough to me and he made Sara happy. I should have felt a little bad about knowing what he was in for but I still held him responsible for my turbulent start to the sixth grade.

Thinking about Nelson and Sara's impending breakup brought Sam and Lacey's breakup back to mind. I wondered why I hadn't heard anything from him since my accident. Could it be possible that his crush on me had made him too shy or nervous to see me? The clock was ticking and there wasn't much time left for shyness if he and I were going to be together. It became clear that I was going to have to make a move.

As we rode along I tried to come up with a plan. I needed to find a way to leave a lasting impression on Sam—one that would have him pining away for me well after his family had left for California. I imagined the long, poetic handwritten love letters he would send me. They'd be haphazardly folded pieces of college-ruled paper, maybe even torn from a spiral notebook, placed in legal envelopes with hearts drawn around my name.

Dear Violet,

How is seventh grade? High school is okay. I spend all day thinking about you so it's really hard to pay attention in class. I couldn't bring myself to ask any other girl to the homecoming dance because none of them are anything like you. Your face is all I want to look at. Your eyes are all I want to see. Your body is all I want to touch. Your lips

are all I want to kiss. Nobody could ever excite me like you do. Please wait for me.
Let's plan to go to the same college so we can be together again someday. We can live
in the dorms by each other and get an apartment our senior year after I propose. I
miss you. I love you.

XOXOXO

With all my undying affection and attention,

Sam

P.S. Don't go out with anybody else, ever. I won't if you won't.

Sara, Nelson and I locked our bikes together outside the library. We asked Ms. Sandy for help finding information about Germany for our report. She gave us some books about German history and then used the microfiche machine to find newspaper and magazine articles. We had more information than we knew what to do with and our backpacks must have weighed fifty pounds each by the time we were ready to go. Sara had been right when she told my mom that it would be slow going on the way home. We were only halfway to our neighborhood when the streetlights came on.

"So Violet," Nelson began "I heard you read *War and Peace* last summer."

"Where'd you hear that?" I asked.

"My grandpa hangs out at the senior center next to the library. I think he has a crush on Ms. Sandy. She told him there was this super-smart fifth grade girl who read all of *War and Peace* in like two weeks."

249

"What makes you think that was me?"

"Who else could it be?" he asked. He had a good point. "That's pretty awesome, Vy."

I didn't want Nelson to know it, but that was probably the coolest thing he could have said to me. I tried to hide a proud smile but it crept through.

"Thanks," I blushed.

"So are you and Sam still going to hang out?" he asked.

Really, it was none of Nelson's business if Sam and I were hanging out, but since Nelson was such a staple in Sara's house he probably knew more about what was up with Sam than I did. I decided to play along with Nelson's friendliness and hopefully use it to my advantage.

"I haven't seen him since I had my temporary amnesia," I said.

"Yeah, I heard you couldn't remember your name for three days."

"Almost a week," I exaggeratedly corrected him.

"That's pretty insane," he said. Sara had dropped in behind Nelson and me and was riding along quietly.

"Hey, I have a question for you," I told Nelson, sort of changing the subject. I figured he might be able to lend some perspective about my plan to reconnect with Sam. "How do most guys feel about a girl making the first move?"

"You mean like leaning in for the kiss?" he asked.

"Kind of. Or like asking you out. Is it weird for a girl to ask a guy out?

"Oh," he thought about it for a moment. "Hmm. Well, I think most guys would think it's kind of weird. But, I mean, there's nothing wrong with a girl showing a guy she's interested. Like, giving him a present or something. That's kind of along the same lines but without being pushy about commitment and stuff. Most of the guys I know don't like the idea of commitment. They think it holds them back from experiencing other stuff. Make sense?"

It totally made sense. I could make Sam feel welcome to have his crush on me and reinforce his decision to break up with Lacey by giving him some kind of present. Only I didn't have any money. I couldn't exactly cut and paste something for him out of construction paper—I wasn't in kindergarten—so I'd have to carefully think about this. Sara, Nelson and I would be working on our project over at Sara's the next night, which would be a great time to set this plan in motion. Whatever I came up with, I'd have to make it happen quickly.

Inspiration came from my clock radio. Two Christmases ago I got my very own clock radio. Victoria had one when I moved into her room and I think Mom and Dad just figured we'd share. Since the radio was technically hers, I was never allowed to change the station or use the alarm. She picked the time for the alarm to go off. She picked the station. When I got my very own clock radio it was as if I had finally been granted my freedom from a prison where the iron bars were made out of the greatest hits of Michael Bolton. Not only did my clock radio provide me with the ability to listen to whatever station I wanted and wake up at a time of my own choosing, but my clock radio had a tape deck. I could listen to and record songs from the radio onto cassettes to my heart's delight. As I lay in bed that night, the flashing blue ALARM ON light seemed to be calling me. I had to make Sam a mix tape.

My parents had already shut off the TV and gone to bed so I snuck out into the living room, got a blank tape and Dad's headphones. Back in my room, Victoria was fast asleep on the top bunk. I plugged the headphones into my clock radio and tuned to Z100, the popular music station. I put the tape into the deck and held down the pause button while I pressed play and record at the same time. All I had to do was wait for the perfect songs to come up and I'd release the pause button to record them off the radio.

I recorded *It Must Have Been Love* by Roxette, *Nothing Compares 2 U* by Sinead O'Connor, *Close to You* by Maxi Priest, all because they expressed my desire to be with him. I recorded *Rock the Cradle of Love* by Billy Idol to show I could laugh about our age difference. Those were on the "A" side of the tape.

On the "B" side I put *If Wishes Came True* by Sweet Sensation and *I Wish it Would Rain* by Phil Collins, then finished it off with *Enjoy the Silence* by Depeche Mode, just because I liked those songs. It was almost 1:30 am when I rewound the tape and drew a little purple violet on the label. I loved being named after a flower.

My plan was to slip the tape under the door of Sam's room the next day while Sara, Nelson and I were working on our group project. I kept it in my coat pocket all day at school. I had to stop myself from holding it too often so I wouldn't rub my drawing off of the label. I was a bit of a zombie all day. Between staying up late and fantasizing about how I'd give him the tape, I got next to no sleep. I had imagined Sam, in his room, glancing up from his homework to see an unfamiliar cassette tape on the floor.

"I wonder what this could be?" he'd mutter, picking up the tape to inspect it. "Violet," he would whisper, tracing his fingers along the tape's label. He would then rush over to his boombox to play it. With each song he'd become more and more overwhelmed by the need to be with me. Finally, at the very tail end of the Depeche Mode song, just after the last "Enjoy the Silence…" and before the "ding" sound (which I had to cut off a little bit on the tape because a really loud and annoying used car commercial started up before the song was totally over) he'd leap up and burst out of his room like a hungry animal. He'd race around the house until he found me working on my international fair project at their dining room table, scoop me up into his arms, and demand right then and there that I become his girlfriend. Of course I'd accept and he would kiss me before calling all of his friends to let them know that we were going out. He may or may not have to shout something about it into the night sky from the front porch. I'd have to wait and see about that.

I was vibrating with excitement as I walked from my house toward Sara's after school. In spite of the fact that my backpack was heavier than ever, it felt like I was flying down the hill. My hand clutched the tape in my pocket and the butterflies in my stomach seemed to be multiplying as I got closer to their house. The sun was out and spring was

253

showing. Flowers were everywhere in the neighbors' yards and the trees were filling out again. I felt like I was at the edge, standing just on the other side of something new, exciting and wonderful. I could smell change in the air. It smelled like a combination of lawn clippings, diesel exhaust, and lilacs.

Nelson's bike was leaning up against the garage door at Sara's house when I arrived. I noticed that the seasonal decorative flags and ceramic figures that Sara's mom usually put out were missing when I stepped up onto the front porch. I knocked softly while I pushed open the door.

"Hellooo?" I called out, stepping into the house. There were boxes everywhere. Some of them already had shipping labels on them while others sat open, half-packed. Judy poked her head out from the hallway at the top of the stairs.

"Oh hey, Vy!" she waved at me with a grin. "Sara and Jason are in the kitchen. Go on in!"

I waved back and started walking to the kitchen. *Tonight* by New Kids On The Block was playing on the radio from the living room. As I passed the downstairs bathroom door I nearly collided with Julie as she was coming around the corner.

"Woah, hey," she exclaimed in a surprised but flat tone. "Oh, Vy – oh! Geez, you look awful," she said, examining my face.

The scabs from my road rash were starting to flake and leave white and pink scars. Part of me was sad that the reminders of my accident were becoming less visible. My appearance was changing from

254

that of someone who'd been through something terrible to someone whose skin was just kind of weird.

"I don't mean awful like you have any control over it or anything," Julie added, probably because she noticed my expression flashed to look a little hurt at what she'd said. "We're all glad you're okay, though. You got pretty messed up." Julie patted my shoulder and walked away. That was probably more than she'd ever said to me. She plodded up the stairs and I made my way into the kitchen where Sara and Nelson had already spread out papers everywhere.

The report was actually going to be pretty easy. It only had to have three pages to it and half of the first page would be taken up by the German flag. Once we got all of the facts down about the population and size of the country we just had to write two paragraphs about the history, which came together relatively quickly. With my writing, Sara's eye for design, and Nelson's knack for keeping things organized, we worked really well as a team. Once the report was done we started drawing the maps and flag for the presentation board.

"You're pretty lucky that you know so much about the move before you go," Nelson said to Sara. "When my parents decided to move us here, we had no time at all to prepare. It seemed like, 'c'mon, let's get outta here,' and the next day we were loading up a U-Haul and hitting the road. I didn't really get to say goodbye to anybody."

"That sounds awful," Sara said.

I nodded along.

"Yeah, I had to leave all my friends behind. All my pets, too."

"You had to leave your pets behind?" I asked. "Like at your old house? Or did you let them loose or something?"

Nelson laughed.

"No, no, we couldn't let them loose. We took them to a reptile rescue."

"Reptiles?" I asked.

"Yeah, I had a monitor lizard and a bearded dragon."

It made sense that Nelson was into lizards. In my mind, he seemed like kind of a slimy guy.

"My brother had a bearded dragon once," Sara said.

Sam! How could I possibly have forgotten about Sam? The tape was still in my coat pocket. Slyly I pulled it out and wriggled it into the back pocket of my jeans. I probably should have been wearing more loose-fitting pants, considering how much it hurt when the rivets rubbed against my still-healing scrapes, but these were really cute jeans. They were stone-washed and had little bows on the backs of the ankles. I tucked my hot pink tie-dyed t-shirt into my jeans and bloused it out a little. My sneakers were oversized high-tops that were hot pink, just like my shirt. I was glad Sara's family didn't have the same "no shoes in the house" rule that mine did, because the combination of my shirt and my shoes really brought my whole outfit together. I looked like I could have been one of those girls sitting in the bleachers overlooking an outdoor basketball court in a magazine ad for super high-fashion jeans where everything except for the hot pink stuff was black and white.

I needed an excuse to go upstairs. There was a bathroom in the hall right by the kitchen and it was unoccupied so I couldn't say I had to pee. I really liked my outfit, so it wasn't like I could spill something on myself and ask for replacement clothes from Sara's room. I didn't want Sara to go with me so I couldn't ask to talk to her privately in her room either. Just when it seemed completely hopeless, Judy came through the kitchen and went into the bathroom. I jumped up from the table.

"I gotta pee," I announced just as Judy closed the bathroom door. "Oh, wait," I said, faking a little disappointment.

"Just go upstairs," Sara suggested.

Perfect. The butterflies returned to my chest as I skipped up the stairs. I stopped at the top one and held tightly to the railing, taking a deep breath in. I let it out slowly and stepped toward Sam's room. I could see light shining out from underneath the door. He was home. My hand shook as I reached into my pocket and pulled out the tape. I looked at the label. My little violet drawing still looked perfect. I knelt down. Just when I was about to slide the tape under the door I heard a giggle. A *girl's* giggle.

"Sam, stop it!" the girly voice squealed. There were a couple of wet smacking sounds. "You're an animal!" She laughed. It became obvious that the wet smacking noises were kisses. I stood up quickly, causing the hardwood floor beneath me to squeak. My eyes widened and I froze. All of the sounds from inside the room stopped.

"Probably just one of my sisters," I heard Sam say.

"Go check!" The girl insisted. Then I heard footsteps walking toward the door. I couldn't move. I tried so hard to make my feet walk away but they wouldn't even lift off of the ground.

"Look away, Violet! Just leave!" I heard my own voice say inside my head but I was paralyzed on the spot. Everything was happening in slow motion. First the doorknob turned. Then the soft glow of light from under the door turned into a sharp beam as the door opened. Then the beam stretched wider and wider. The shadow of a figure appeared on the floor. The shadow moved forward. Sam stepped out of the room and stopped right in front of me. The butterflies in my stomach were now playing bass drums. Everything went muffled. A girl I'd never seen before stepped up behind Sam. I could see her lips move but I couldn't hear anything.

"Who's that?" I saw her say.

"Just one of my sister's friends," Sam smiled.

I heard it clear as day. My eyes welled up with tears faster than they ever had before. I dropped the tape on the floor and it bounced against the door. The girl bent down and picked it up.

"What's this?" she asked, holding the tape up to Sam, who took it from her hand and gave it back to me.

"Are you okay, Vy?" he asked me. Turning back to the girl Sam said, "This was that girl I told you about--Sara's friend, who ate it into the curb on the corner, remember?"

"Oh yeah!" She said, smiling at me like I was an infant. "How are you now, sweetie?"

My feet still wouldn't go anywhere. I started to silently pray that if I couldn't walk away I could at least lose consciousness or something dramatic like that.

"Did she get brain damage?" the girl whispered, glancing at Sam. I stood there, paralyzed and horrified as Sam laughed.

"God, I didn't think so," he squinted at me, "but I dunno. Hey Violet, you in there?" he asked, pretending to knock on my skull.

Like a sudden bolt of lightning had zapped down through my body, I jerked to life and ran down the stairs. I went straight out the front door and down the street. I just ran and kept running. My legs felt like they'd never get tired, and my eyes had been leaking tears nonstop since I crossed Sara's front porch. I could feel my lungs drying out and my chest burning while I ran, just like in P.E. class when we had to run a whole mile around the track. But that didn't stop me. I couldn't hear anything over the wet sobs that poured out of my throat along with heaving breaths. My feet started to ache because my sneakers were really more for looks than they were for running. I slowed my run to a walking pace when I reached the river.

CHAPTER TWENTY

I had never been more embarrassed in my life. I had never been so hurt. The time Victoria hit me in the head with Dad's golf club didn't hurt nearly as bad as this did. I don't know how I got it so wrong. It just didn't make sense. Sam acted like I was just some kid at his house for a playdate with his baby sister. Who was that girl? Why didn't he like me anymore? What happened to the guy who cared so much about me after my accident? What happened to the guy who broke up with Lacey because he liked me so much? I sat down next to a rock and pulled my knees up to my chest, burying my face behind them. What an idiot I was. I chucked the mix tape down into the river.

The ground was cold and damp but I didn't care. The sun was going down but I didn't care. Nobody knew where I was but I just didn't care. I closed my eyes tight, hoping if I kept them closed tightly enough I could force the tears to stop coming out. It didn't work. I was breathing through my mouth the whole time and my lips had gone dry. With my eyes still closed, I leaned my head back and tried to breathe deeply. I felt a hand on my shoulder.

Nelson.

"Violet?" he said, slowly sitting down beside me. He put his arm around me and I instinctively leaned over into his embrace. He hugged me and let his chin rest on the back of my head. I started to sob again. My shoulders shook and even though I didn't think it was possible for me to cry any more, tears poured down my face like rain. Nelson held me tight. I don't know exactly for how long but he stayed there until I didn't have anything left. When I finally lifted my head I saw I had left the biggest wet spot of all time on his shirt. It was sort of shaped like my face.

"I'm sorry," I said.

Nelson brushed my hair back from my eyes, shook his head and smiled.

"Don't," he said. "Don't be sorry."

Nelson and I sat quietly for a long time, just staring at the river and listening to the water run over the rocks. I imagined that darn tape floating downstream, smashing over rocks and eventually being crushed to tiny bits. The streetlights had come on at some point while Nelson was hugging me. My parents thought I was still at Sara's working on homework. I wondered if Sara knew Nelson was here with me.

"Did Sara send you?" I asked.

"Sort of, yeah, but I was going to have to go home anyway," he said.

I looked over my shoulder and saw his bike laying in the gravel between the curb and the road, not far from where we sat. I picked up small rocks and threw them down toward the river, hoping that if the tape was still down there I could possibly break it with one of them.

"Wanna hear a story?" Nelson asked.

At that point, so long as it wasn't about Sam, I was willing to hear anything.

"Sure," I said.

"At my last school, on the last day, we had an assembly. The whole school was there, every grade—the kindergarteners all the way up to the eighth graders—there were even some high schoolers in the gym. The principal was giving out awards for the year and doing a little graduation thing for the eighth graders. Anyway, I got called up to get an award for having perfect attendance and as soon as I got up on the stage, my stomach started to rumble and my throat clenched up. The principal went to hand me a certificate and you know what I did?"

"What?" I asked, shaking my head. I wiped my eyes and sniffed.

"I puked. All over the principal. In front of everybody."

I laughed. Nelson smiled and shrugged.

"Are you serious?"

"Yep. I barfed, big time. They called my parents and I had to wait in the office for them to pick me up. There was this girl in the office who saw the whole thing and made up this rhyme about me. Wanna hear it?" he asked.

I nodded.

"It goes, 'Jay-son Nel-son barfin' on your shoes. Jay-son Nel-son's tummy's got the blues. Jay-son Nel-son never skipped a day. Jay-son Nel-son's pukin' all the way!'"

I laughed out loud. I snorted trying to keep it in.

"You could jump rope to that," I said, laughing even harder.

He laughed along with me.

"Yeah, you could, couldn't you?" He chuckled. "You know what? I think they did, too!"

I imagined little fifth grade Nelson, looking all pathetic, puking his guts out on the stage at school. I felt a little bad for him but it was still pretty funny.

"Sing it again," I said, throwing another rock down the ravine.

"Jay-son Nel-son barfin' on your shoes. Jay-son Nel-son's tummy's got the blues. Jay-son Nel-son never skipped a day. Jay-son Nel-son's pukin' all the way!"

By the time he was done with the rhyme we were both laughing hysterically. With a big sigh I calmed my laughter.

"Hey, Nelson?"

"Yeah?"

"I'm really sorry."

"You don't have to be."

"I know," I said, "but I am. I never really gave you a chance. I've been kind of a jerk. I don't blame you if you don't like me."

"I know," he said back to me. "But it's okay. You didn't have to. And I like you just fine." He stood up and offered me his hand. I took it, and he pulled me up. "C'mon, Vy, let's get you home."

I don't think I'd ever been out that late before. I'd been up that late, but never *out* that late without my parents. The streetlights were on and cars were whizzing by with their headlights on. There wasn't any trace of daylight left in the sky and when we were between lightposts I could see the moon and the stars above us. The whole way home Nelson and I talked about everything—things we liked, things we didn't like, our families, and even Sara. Just before we got to my driveway he stopped.

"Hey, Vy? You didn't *really* wanna be Sam's girlfriend, did you?" he asked.

"I dunno," I said. I thought about it for a few seconds. "Maybe?"

"He's kind of a jerk, don't you think?" Nelson said, kicking at the pedals on his bike.

"I don't want to talk about it right now."

"Okay, okay, that's fair." Nelson put out his hand like he wanted me to shake it. I bypassed his hand and gave him a hug.

"Friends?" I said, still hugging him.

"Yep. Friends."

CHAPTER TWENTY-ONE

It didn't take long for "the mix tape" story to get around school. It was the first thing I heard about when I got off the bus the next day. I could tell that Jake wanted to ask me about it, but being such a good friend he didn't. In fact, he almost socked Mindy Wilson in the nose when we heard her giggling and pointing at me in the hall. Everywhere I went I thought I heard whispers. It was way worse than my *D.A.R.E.* picture on the front page of the paper.

I spent most of the day staring at my feet, trying to become invisible. Even in the bathroom I could swear I heard people talking about how I mistakenly thought Sam Anderson would be my boyfriend if I gave him a mix tape. I sat in the stall, counting the mint green tiles on the floor, waiting for the room to clear out before I came out to wash my hands. When I finally did I saw Darci at the mirror, applying bright purple lipstick.

"Hey," she said, glancing in the mirror's reflection at me.

"Hey," I parroted back. I stepped on the foot-pedal that turned on the crescent shaped spray of the sink.

"Don't listen to any of them," Darci said, smacking her lips and inspecting her work.

"What?"

"Don't listen to any of them," she repeated. "Only you know what was really going on there, right? You have nothing to be embarrassed about, Violet."

I was surprised that Darci even cared. I was also surprised that she knew so much about my personal life.

"What do you mean?" I asked.

"Well," she said, clicking the cap down on her lipstick and sliding it into her pocket, "here's what I know about boys: you want to make them happy, because if they're happy you think you'll be happy, right? You do all this stuff to get them to like you and to promise they'll like you forever, but you forget that whether or not they like you there are other things that make you happy still. Yeah? It's like, if you care too much about what everybody else thinks of you, you forget what you think of you."

"Wow," I said. "You sound like a grownup."

Darci smiled and laughed a little.

"Cool. Anyway, listen Vy, not that I'm a stalker or anything, but I've been watching you all year."

I shook the water off of my hands.

"Okay," I said, only slightly creeped out--mostly, I was just interested in what she thought. If Darci thought I was interesting then surely that meant that anybody less important would have to think I was, too.

"You want people to like you."

"Yeah," I said, wiping my hands on a paper towel. "So what?"

"No, I mean you want *everyone* to like you."

"Sure."

"I don't think *you* like you." Darci said, patting me on the back. "You might want to think about that."

I stood, still wiping my hands on the paper towel while Darci walked out of the room. I didn't really get it. I shrugged my shoulders and followed her into the hall.

Back in our classroom, we were supposed to be having SSR or "sustained silent reading" time. I saw notes being passed back and forth across the aisles in my peripheral vision. I imagined that on the inside of each intricately folded piece of paper was something equally as embarrassing as Nelson's little puke rhyme, only about me instead. Looking back over my shoulder I saw Nelson resting his head on his desk, holding his copy of *White Fang* sideways a few inches away from his face. Sara was reading *Jurassic Park*, a book she promised to let me borrow when she finished it. For the first time in a long time I noticed that Sara and Nelson didn't have their feet sticking out into the aisle between their desks.

At lunch recess, Sara asked if I wouldn't mind letting her and Nelson have some time alone so she could let him down easy. She walked around the perimeter of the playground with him while I sat on a swing. Jake came over and joined me, sitting in the swing next to me.

"Whatcha lookin' at?" he asked.

"Them," I said, pointing across the way to Sara and Nelson.

"Breaking up?"

"Probably," I said. "How did you guess that?"

"Just look at 'em," he said. "They aren't holding hands anymore and they *always* hold hands. They didn't kiss at the busses yesterday, and during library, she sat in the beanbags while he sat under the magazine racks. These are classic signs of things being over, Vy."

I guessed he was right. I knew Sara was eventually going to break it off with Nelson, but I didn't think she'd do it with so much time left in the school year. Ever since my talk with him down by the river, I'd been thinking about Nelson a little differently.

"Yeah, and she's moving away, so it's probably better for him if she does it now, like a Band-Aid," I explained.

Jake put his feet down and stopped swinging abruptly.

"Better for him? I don't think I've ever heard you say a single nice thing about that guy," Jake said. "Suddenly you care about what's good for him? Geez, Vy, what changed?"

"I dunno," I said dismissively, watching Sara wave her hands around as she talked. I could tell she was talking about the distance that

270

was going to be between them by the way she pointed into the air in front of her. She always did that when she gave directions. "We worked on our country report together, the three of us, and I just think I got to know him better doing that."

"Oh," Jake said, accepting my explanation. "My group hasn't even met yet. I'll probably end up doing the whole report myself. Idiots. Morons. All of them. Without question."

"What country did you get?"

"Haiti," he replied, "which is fitting because I 'hate-ee' the group I'm in. Lazy bums."

Jake and I continued to swing back and forth while we watched Sara and Nelson walk around. Part of me expected Nelson to have some sort of emotional reaction but he never did. I wished I could be more detached from emotional things like that. I must have seemed like an idiot, crying about the whole Sam situation the way that I did. The bell rang and everyone on the playground ran for the door, with the exception of Sara and Nelson. They hugged and then walked back slowly.

Later, Sara and I sat next to each other on the bus. There was no kiss between her and Nelson—no goodbye at all, in fact. She stared out the bus window with a glazed-over look in her eye.

"Hey," I said, "you okay?"

"Yeah," she nodded, still staring out the window. "That was really hard. But I had to do it. If I waited too long I wouldn't do it, or I might miss him so much that I'd drive myself crazy."

Sara reached into the front pocket of her backpack.

"Here. Jason wanted you to have this," She said, handing me a folded piece of loose leaf paper. It was plainly folded over three times, with my name written on one side. You could always tell girl notes from boy notes based on the way they were folded. Girl notes had fancy folds with pull-tabs, flaps and designs. Boy notes, if they folded them at all, were just plain. Sometimes boy notes were even wadded up like garbage.

I took the note and started to unfold it, then stopped.

"Do you want me to open it?" I asked. Sara nodded.

"Yep," she said. "I already read it." Part of being a best friend meant special privileges, like reading your best friend's notes. I unfolded the paper.

Dear Violet,

I know you and I haven't always seen eye to eye.

I hope you'll still be my friend after Sara is gone.

Here is my phone number, please call me tonight. I could use a friend right now.

Your pal,

Jason Nelson (206) 555-8891

"Are you gonna call him?" Sara asked.

"Do you want me to?"

"I didn't ask that," she said, putting her hand on my knee and looking me in the eye. "You and I both are going to have to get used to the fact that I'm not going to be around here forever. If you and Jason want to be friends that's cool with me. I like him a whole lot. And I love you. It'd make me feel better about abandoning you both if I knew you had each other to fall back on. I think you'd get along with him if you gave him a chance. Vy, I know you've had a hard time with me and Jason being together but I really hope you'll give him a chance." It looked like Sara was on the verge of crying.

"Are you gonna cry? Are you okay?" I asked.

"No, I'm not okay!" she said. The frog in her throat made it pretty obvious that she really was about to start crying. "I'm leaving forever in like, a month, and I have to leave my house, my boyfriend and everybody I've known as long as I've been alive and we're not coming back! This sucks!"

The bus driver looked in his rearview mirror and shushed at us. Sara lowered her voice and scowled at him.

"I hate him," she said. "He's the worst substitute bus driver on the planet. He has a stupid face and dumb blue striped coveralls." Sara started laughing at herself.

"Let's just take it all out on him," I jokingly suggested. "Throw stuff and make noises and pick on the little kids or something. Do whatever you have to do to get your feelings out. Only I can't get a referral. I've had way too much trouble this year already."

Sara chuckled and gave me a big hug. Jake popped his head up over the back of our seat.

"Hands on!" he called out, jokingly.

Sara and I both quickly shushed him. I pulled my fist back like I was about to sock him, which elicited a warning look from the bus driver, who reached up and turned up the volume on the radio, which was playing MC Hammer's *U Can't Touch This.* The three of us slunk down into our seats where we couldn't be seen.

CHAPTER TWENTY-TWO

When I arrived at home I raced to my room to stake my claim on the Bartphone before Victoria could. She had recently started going to a church youth group with Jean so she was spending more and more time reading the Bible in the living room. Luckily for me that's exactly what she had planned for that evening. I crawled back into the corner between the bed and the wall and carefully unfolded the note from Nelson. I couldn't tell why, but I was kind of nervous dialing his number. I was surprised when a teenage girl picked up.

"Hello?" She said.

"Hi, is Nelson home?" I asked.

"Huh? Like, uh, Mr. Nelson? My Dad?" She sounded confused.

I hadn't even thought about it. Everyone in his house was probably named Nelson.

"Oh, no, I'm sorry. Is Jason home?"

276

"Yeah," she said, putting the receiver down on something hard with a loud *thwack*. I heard her voice call out from far away, "Jason! Hey Jason! Phone! It's a girl!" I could hear a baby crying in the background. A few moments later, he picked up.

"Hello?"

"Hi," I said. "It's Violet."

"Hey, I'm glad you called," he said. "I wanted to ask you about your day."

I was confused. Why did he want to know about *my* day? I thought he was the one who had it rough. I thought this was a call for *me* to console *him*.

"My day?"

"Yeah! Did anybody make up any rhymes about you?" I laughed and the sing-song rhythm of his puke song popped into my head.

"No, nobody made up any rhymes about me. How about you?"

"Nah," he laughed, too. "I've already got one."

I could hear my dad's car pulling into the driveway and the garage door opening.

"Anyway," Nelson went on, "Sara probably already told you she broke up with me."

"Mmhmm." I only halfway listened to Nelson as Dad's dress shoes clipped and clopped up the walkway to the front door.

"I understand why and all," he continued, "and I just thought that since you and I are kind of both dealing with stuff about people in that family, that, I don't know, you might want to talk about it or something."

"Yeah," I said, "we could talk, sure. Only not now. My dad just got home so I gotta go." I barely waited for Nelson to say,

"Ok," before I hung up the Bartphone.

The last thing I wanted was for Dad to pick up the line and find out that I was talking to a boy. He'd made a few comments to Mom recently about what happened over Christmas vacation and I worried that if he heard me on the phone with Nelson he might blow a fuse. The only boy my dad ever liked was Jake and that was probably because he was more like a brother than anything else. Not that there was anything going on with Nelson and me—I just felt like I needed to be as preventative as possible against groundings. Summer vacation was right around the corner. I was going to require some serious freedom if I was going to use it to plan for seventh grade.

Over the next few weeks at school, Sara and I spent our usual amount of time together at recess, but Nelson and I hung out a lot more. Nelson and I started going for evening walks a couple nights a week. Neither one of us really wanted to go over to the Anderson's house anymore. I told my parents that I was going out with Sara, and then I would meet Nelson at the high school and we'd walk until the street lights came on. His curfew was way later than mine so he always walked me home before he turned around. We got to know each other pretty well. I even learned why he had to move away from his old town so quickly.

Jenny was Nelson's older sister. She was a sophomore in high school when she got pregnant. She had a part time job after school scooping ice cream at a Baskin Robbins in the next town over from where they lived by Lake Minnefield. Nelson remembered her crying on the phone to her boyfriend a lot last spring.

"What do you care? You're graduating and going to Australia!" she sobbed into the receiver, while Nelson played video games in his room.

Their parents were never home when Jenny made these phone calls and she wore her work uniform all the time it seemed. Nelson noticed Jenny's belly was getting bigger under her apron but since his parents never really had much chance to see her in the daylight, they didn't notice. Nelson found Jenny crying in her room the day after her boyfriend, Steve Harper, graduated.

"Did Steve Harper break up with you or something?" Nelson asked.

Jenny wailed and cried, flopping down, face up on her bed. Her growing belly was obvious now.

"Well, what are you gonna do?"

"I don't know," Jenny sobbed. "Mom and Dad are going to have to find out and Steve Harper's leaving for Australia and probably never coming back. All he cares about is celebrating his stupid graduation and traveling before he goes to college. He doesn't want to even look at me anymore. Did you know he called me fat the other day? Yeah, he and his buddies were joking around in the senior lounge and one of them told him 'Hey, Steve Harper, your girl is kind of turning into a cow,' and he just laughed and said, 'yeah, I know.' What is wrong with him? I'm carrying his baby! This is a baby in here, Jason, did you know that?"

Nelson stared at his sister's stomach, expressionless.

"No, I guess you didn't know that. You're only in the fifth grade. Have you even had sex-ed yet?"

Nelson shook his head.

Jenny was eight months along when her parents found out about her pregnancy. Their mom was an accountant and their dad was a traveling salesman for cable TV commercials. Nelson avoided a lot of the drama the week Jenny had the baby by hanging around the campground with Sara. Mr. Nelson got a new job in my town around that time and the family had to move quickly to get Jenny and Nelson enrolled in school. Nelson was forced into a fresh start that he didn't even want but he felt better when he learned that the cute girl he'd met over the summer by the lake was from this new town.

I loved the idea of a fresh start. I had lived in the same town all my life and everybody I knew had pretty much watched me grow up. Every embarrassing story about me followed me around. Like the time I went on the school field trip in the fourth grade to the nearby mountain and drank a whole two-liter of pop on the drive up. I had to pee so bad that as soon as I got off the bus, I pulled my pants down and just sat in the snow right next to the bus and went. A lot of people saw my butt that day—people I truly wished hadn't.

"Look out!" Tom cried from the bus window, "*There's a bad moon a'risin'!*" he sang.

I just stared straight ahead like a cat in a litter box and peed. The back of my neck burned with embarrassment but I couldn't do anything about it. Two whole years later, people still brought that up. Living in another town could surely solve a problem like that, so with the memory of that day in mind, I thought Nelson was really lucky to have his life uprooted the way he had.

"What's Jenny going to do now?" I asked as Nelson and I walked along the sidewalk next to the high school one evening. The baseball team was practicing and kids from the band were filing out of the building carrying big instrument cases and folders. Cheerleader tryouts were going on for next year's squad we could see ponytails bouncing up and down as a couple dozen hopefuls danced on the soccer field to Taylor Dane's *With Every Beat of My Heart,* which blared from a boombox nearby.

"She went back to school this year and my mom takes care of my niece. Nobody in the high school knows about it and my mom just tells everybody that the baby is my sister—you know, her own daughter."

"Geez," I said. "Did Jenny get in trouble?"

"What, with my parents?" Nelson laughed, "Oh, yeah! She's pretty much grounded forever. She has to come home from school every day and stay home to take care of Claire. My mom said that Jenny has to enjoy her eight-to-three days as a teenager, because come three-fifteen, she's a full-on adult. Mom won't let her have a job because she thinks Jenny's gonna lie and go sneak off with a boy again."

"What happened to Steve Harper?"

"Nothing, only my dad said he'd kill him if he ever saw him again. I think he went on his trip to Australia and is probably going to college soon. He sent Jenny postcards from Thailand and New Zealand but she burned them as soon as she got them."

Hearing the story about Nelson's sister made me think about my dad. He probably felt about every boy I talked to the way that Nelson's dad felt Steve Harper. I didn't want to get pregnant until after I finished college, or had been in at least a couple of blockbuster movies. I had a long way to go before I did either of those things, which I figured should make my dad feel a lot better.

CHAPTER TWENTY-THREE

The night before the big assembly and sixth grade graduation I talked on the phone with Nelson.

"Are you going to Sara's big party tomorrow night after graduation?" I asked, twirling the cord from the Bartphone around my finger.

"Yeah, probably," he said.

I hadn't been over to Sara's house since the mix tape incident. She and I still sat together on the bus and spent time together at recess. We walked in the evenings when I wasn't walking with Nelson. Things just felt weird because I knew she was leaving. It was a little like I knew she was going to die and I had to find a way to get used to it.

"Are *you* gonna go?" Nelson asked.

"Well, probably. But I'm still pretty embarrassed about Sam—ugh, I hope I don't see him," I sighed. "Who else is going, do you know?"

"Pretty much everybody," Nelson laughed. "I saw Jake when I was signing up to play summer league baseball and he said he was going. He even asked if I thought Sara would get mad if he brought his cousins."

I had no idea Nelson played baseball. I hadn't seen Dan since the rollerblading accident. Even though he went to a different school the chances that he had heard about it were still probably pretty good. He'd probably heard about the mix tape as well. I still had that odd Patrick Dempsey "crush" feeling that I couldn't quite explain about Dan.

"Hey, I'll call you back later," I said, flicking the button on the bottom of the Bartphone to hang up. I had a whole lot to figure out— fast. Sam and Dan being at the same party was going to put me in an odd position. I paced around the house thinking about it.

I went looking for Mom, thinking if I asked her a boy-related question that she might give me some sweet mother-daughter advice. Either that, or she'd just tell me to forget it and avoid boys until I was in my mid-twenties. I found her in the living room, putting on socks.

Mom and Dad were getting ready to go golfing, leaving Victoria, Calvin and me home alone. Victoria was furious that she had to give up her plans with Jean to babysit us. Calvin was glued to a VHS tape of *Teenage Mutant Ninja Turtles*, already in his little blue fuzzy footie pajamas for the night.

"No friends over, no phone calls, don't use the oven or the stove, and if there's an emergency, call Grandpa," Mom instructed.

Victoria listened, making the world's snottiest annoyed-face. Dad kissed me on the forehead as he walked between Victoria and me.

285

"They'll be fine," he said, straightening his visor on his head, "let's just go."

As soon as the car was gone and the garage door was closed, Victoria was in my face.

"I'm going to Jean's," she said, pointing at me. "You stay here with Calvin and don't get into trouble, all right?"

Typical Victoria. I shrugged my shoulders. Then I got an idea.

"Sounds like you're breaking the rules," I said.

"Mom didn't say 'don't go anywhere,' did she?" Victoria smirked. She was right.

"Okay, but what's in it for me?" I asked.

"How about I won't pound you if you don't tell?"

"That sounds like a threat on top of questionable behavior if you ask me," I snipped right back at her. I felt bold and perhaps a little smarter now that I was nearly an official middle-schooler, not to mention a fairly recently-minted woman.

"Fine. What do you want?" she asked.

"I don't know yet," I admitted.

She stomped her feet impatiently.

"I don't have all night! Money? Clothes? Makeup? Phone time? What do you want?"

I had to come up with something good. I wanted to think on it. I wanted to make this bold move really worth my while.

"How about this," I offered, "you go, and when you get back I'll tell you."

She shook her head and waved her hands between us.

"No way! Then you'll come up with something nuts and I'll be stuck in a hostage situation with you!"

"Take it or leave it." I felt so powerful. Victoria stomped her feet.

"Fine," she said, almost spitting with disgust. "I'll be at Jean's. I'll be home in an hour and a half. If Mom and Dad come home before me, just tell them I ran over to her house to get an assignment and I said you could be in charge. Then call Jean's. I left her number on my side of the dresser in our room."

I smiled sweetly at Victoria and she rolled her eyes at me.

"Don't get cute," she warned. "I'll see you later."

Once Victoria was gone I sat down at the dining room table with paper and a pencil. I had to come up with a way to deal with Sara's party and I had to figure out how I was going to take advantage of the situation I was in with Victoria. I thought a list of ideas would be a good start. Calvin ran up to me and tugged on my arm.

"Want to play Imbatendo?" Calvin asked.

"Not now," I said, shaking him off.

"Want to play cards?" Calvin had just discovered Uno and was obsessed with the game.

"I can't right now," I said, biting my lip and trying to concentrate.

"Play with me!" he whined and pounded his feet on the carpet.

"Later buddy," I said. "Later."

He pursed his lips together angrily and stomped off to his room. I got back to the task at hand. I wrote my name in the middle of the paper. I put Sara's name beside it. I wrote Nelson's name, then Jake's, then Sam's and then Dan's. I added Darci, Mya, Alice, Cristina, and a few other names from my class, just in case. I started circling the names, connecting them with lines. That's as far as I got before I noticed how quiet Calvin was being his room. I went down the hall to check on him. The door to his room was closed. I tried to turn the handle but it was locked.

"Calvin?"

"Go 'way!"

"Buddy?"

"No!" he shouted. "Go 'way!"

I shrugged, figuring he was safely locked in his room and the worst that could happen was that he'd have trouble unlocking the door, get scared and pee in his jammies before he made it to the bathroom.

"Okay," I said sweetly and walked away. I went back to the table and stared at the piece of paper. All I felt as I read over the names was embarrassment. This exercise was useless. I gathered up the piece of paper and crumpled it between my hands.

Reaching for the garbage can under the sink, I heard the scratchy plodding of Calvin's footie pajamas going from the hallway into the entryway.

"Calvin?" I called out. There was no answer. I heard the sound of coins jingling together in a bag. "Calvin?" I said again, and again was met with silence. I closed the cupboard under the sink and heard the front door open. "CALVIN!" I shouted and ran to the front door. It slammed just as I got there. I threw the door open and saw Calvin, in his blue fuzzy footie pajamas, climbing onto his bike that had been parked in the courtyard. "Calvin! What are you doing?" I yelled after him, stepping out onto the concrete steps. The rocks poked into the bottoms of my feet, making me do that little dance that people often do when they're walking on hot sand or piles of Legos.

Without a word Calvin rode off. His *Alvin & the Chipmunks* backpack swayed from side to side across his back as he pedaled.

I ran back inside the house and to his room, which had the best window for viewing the street. I saw a little blue fuzzy streak round the corner out of the cul-de-sac and start down the hill.

"CRAP!" I shouted.

I didn't know what to do first. As I ran to my room to grab Jean's number off of the dresser I noticed a note on the floor in the hall. Calvin had drawn a stick-figure image of himself with tears dripping off of his face.

No 1 liks me. I am leevng.

I picked up the note and ran to the phone in the kitchen. It rang twice before Jean picked up.

"Where's Victoria!?" I shouted at her.

"What's wrong?" Jean asked.

"GET VICTORIA!" I screamed into the phone. My heart was racing and the back of my neck got hot and tingly. Victoria answered the phone with an annoyed tone.

"Unngh, what is it?"

"Calvin ran away. I'm going after him."

"You let him what?" she barked.

"Get home," I said firmly and slammed the phone down. I was about to race to the door and put on my shoes when an idea struck me— I could call Nelson, who lived on the other side of town. He could ride toward my house on our usual back-road route and maybe he would intercept my brother.

"Hello?" Jenny said when she picked up the phone. Her baby was crying in the background again.

"It's Vy, can I speak with Jason?" I said with a panicked tone in my voice.

"You okay, honey?" she asked.

"No! My brother ran away and I need Jason's help."

"Oh!" Jenny sounded sympathetic to my situation and had what I thought was an appropriate level of urgency in her voice. "Jason! Vy needs you--hurry! She's on the phone!" There was a little jostling then Nelson said,

"Hello?"

"Calvin ran away. He's on his bike. My parents are golfing. I'm leaving now to try and catch him. Can you ride toward my house and see if you run into him? If you don't we'll meet in the middle and look for him together. Can you?" I begged.

"Sure," he said, "I'm on my way."

Riding my bike down the hill I had to duck back onto another side road when I came close to the golf course. If my estimation was correct then my parents were probably coming up on the fifth hole by now, which meant they could be teeing off right next to the road by the high school. I couldn't let them see me and I hoped they hadn't seen Calvin ride by.

I rode along all of our usual family bike-riding roads, thinking that he would stick to areas that were familiar to him. I couldn't imagine where he would be going. Our town and the next one over came to an end at a highway interchange about three miles away. At the very worst, Calvin could make it to the edge of the next town and ride up onto the highway. Surely, by that point, he'd be picked up by the police, though I hoped Nelson or I would find him first. I reached the Minute-Mart without seeing any sign of him.

Halfway down the river road I noticed a few pennies pooled together on the ground. Then I saw a few more. Pretty soon I was following an entire trail of pennies. I remembered the jingling sound I had heard when Calvin ran out the door and I thought maybe these pennies had come from his backpack. I was still following the trail when Nelson and I met up.

"See him?" I asked.

"I don't think so," Nelson said. "I've still never met your brother, so I don't know what to look for."

I waved for Nelson to follow me and I rode onward.

"He's six years old, blonde, and right now he looks like a little blue Muppet on a bike," I said. "I think this trail of pennies is coming out of his backpack."

"How long have you been following it?" Nelson asked.

"Since the river road."

"And it's still going? Poor kid! That backpack has to weigh a ton!" Nelson laughed.

I gave him a *get serious* look. I knew that no matter what happened, if I didn't find Calvin and get him home before Mom and Dad beat us there, it was highly likely that I would spend the summer in solitary confinement.

When they got really mad at me, my parents would make me sit on the edge of a stool in their bedroom facing the corner. At first they'd send me to my room, but my room had toys in it. Then, when I moved in with Victoria, sending me to my room wasn't fair to Victoria anymore, so it was easier for them to send me to their room. I loved exploring in there and getting into things that I probably shouldn't, like Mom's sewing machine, Dad's change dish, and the suitcases in the closet. At least the corner of their room had interesting shapes and figures in the spackle on the wall. There was a spot in the paint that looked just like a cartoon duck and I usually found it within ten minutes of being sent in there.

Nelson and I rode on, following the trail of change into the next town. When we were coming around the back side of the park where the summer league kids played baseball, Nelson pointed ahead and shouted,

"There!"

Over behind the red dugout was Calvin, sitting on his bike, drinking a blue Squeez-it and holding a bag of M&Ms. He still had his *Alvin & the Chipmunks* backpack on over his blue fuzzy footie pajamas that were crammed into a pair of yellow galoshes. His face was flushed and he looked sweaty and exhausted as Nelson and I rode up to him.

"Calvin!" I cried out, letting my bike drop to the ground. I ran over to him and hugged him hard.

He stretched his arms out to the sides to keep me from crushing his drink and candy.

"Oh, buddy, I was so worried about you! I love you, pal! I didn't want you to run away!" I gushed and let him pull back out of the hug.

He took another drink.

"You wouldn't play with me," he said coolly, pouring M&Ms into his mouth. With his cheeks full of colorful candies he pointed at Nelson, tipped his head back and asked, "Who's he?"

"This is my friend," I said, "he helped me look for you."

293

Nelson laid his bike down and walked over to Calvin with his hand outstretched.

"Hi," he said, "I'm Jason, but your sister calls me 'Nelson.'"

Calvin just nodded at him, chewing on his candies.

"You dropped a lot of coins along the way," Nelson went on, "you must've been carrying a heavy load!"

Calvin slung the backpack down off of his shoulders and let it fall to the grass.

"It's heavy," he said, drinking the last of his juice. With a sigh, Calvin looked up at Nelson with an exhausted expression. "I'm tired. Will you carry this for me?"

"Sure," said Nelson. "Wanna ride home?"

"Can you carry me?" Calvin asked.

Nelson laughed.

"I don't think so, pal, but we can all walk together."

Calvin nodded his approval. While he walked his empty Squeez-it container and candy wrapper over to the trash can, Nelson unzipped the backpack. I peered in over his shoulder to see that Calvin had packed about twenty pairs of clean underwear, probably forty dollars in loose change (mostly pennies, and not counting everything he'd already dropped), and all of our Nintendo game cartridges. Nelson and I looked at each other and started to laugh but straightened up and closed the backpack as Calvin came back over.

"You ready" I asked.

"Sure," Calvin said. "I'm sorry, Vy," he added as we started to walk.

Before we could get out of the park, Dad's car came zooming around the corner. It had barely stopped before Dad leapt out and threw his arms around Calvin.

"Buddy!" Dad cried. "What are you doing way out here?"

Calvin was still red from riding so hard and his little fuzzy blue body seemed to just go limp in Dad's arms. Dad closed his eyes and hugged Calvin tightly. Calvin's face melted into tears. He let out a wail, right into Dad's shoulder.

"Shhhhhhhh," Dad said, rocking Calvin from side to side in his arms. "It's okay. Let's just go home."

I watched Dad set Calvin in the front seat of the car and buckle him in. Calvin was still crying but his eyes were starting to droop.

"Poor little guy!" Nelson whispered to me.

I smacked him on the arm.

"Shhhh!" I hushed him. I was waiting for Dad to explode at me.

Dad closed the door beside Calvin and went around to the back of the car. He pointed at Calvin's backpack, which was slung over Nelson's shoulder. Nelson quickly took it over to my dad, who was loading Calvin's bike into the trunk.

"Here you go, Sir," Nelson said, handing Dad the backpack.

I winced, half expecting my dad to snatch it away from Nelson angrily. Instead, he paused and gave Nelson a kindly acknowledging look. After he closed the trunk he walked over to me.

"Can you and your friend, um," Dad pointed at Nelson.

"Nelson," Jason interjected, "Jason Nelson." He offered his hand to my dad the same way he had to Calvin.

Dad accepted Nelson's handshake and, dare I say, smiled at him.

"Okay," Dad said, "Jason, can you and Violet get home safely?"

I was speechless. Luckily Nelson answered.

"Yes, Sir," he said.

Dad winked at me. My mouth dropped open. I was beyond shocked. It was late enough that we surely wouldn't make it home before dark. Not to mention the fact that my dad was leaving me alone with a boy. After Christmas vacation I didn't think Dad would let me anywhere near a boy, chaperoned or alone, until I was at least in my thirties, but here he was letting me ride home after dark with Nelson after I'd let my little brother run away while I was supposed to be watching him.

Dad walked over and kissed me on the cheek and then climbed into the car and drove away.

Nelson smiled at me and hopped on his bike.

"It's gonna get dark soon," he said. "We should get going."

"I'm in no rush," I smirked.

CHAPTER TWENTY-FOUR

It was late spring and the water from lawn sprinklers that smacked against the evening asphalt smelled like summer as Nelson and I slowly rode toward home. I was in no big hurry and was still reeling from shock. I couldn't believe that my dad gave me permission to be there. I wondered what was going on at home.

"I bet Victoria is dead meat," I chuckled.

"Yeah," Nelson said, "poor thing."

He obviously must have had a different relationship with his sister than I did with mine. When Victoria got into trouble it was almost always following her doing something terrible to me so I didn't see much reason for sympathy. When I got into trouble it was often either set up by Victoria, something Victoria did and blamed me for, or somehow otherwise influenced by Victoria. I honestly believed that I rarely made any bad choices that would have led to me truly deserving punishment or disciplinary correction.

"I'm sure she'll survive," I said. "Mom and Dad never really lay it on her that bad when she gets in trouble."

I recalled the night Victoria took Mom's car for a drive around the block. Mom and Dad had taken Calvin up to Dad's fraternity brother's cabin on the river, leaving Victoria and me home alone. It was just a few days after Victoria's 14th birthday. She scooped up Mom's key ring from the counter and was tying her shoes when I questioned her.

"Are you seriously going to drive Mom's car?" I asked.

Mom had a nearly pristine 1967 Chevy Camaro. It was black and shiny like my nicest pair of dress shoes. She got it for cheap from one of her old college friends whose parents needed the money to move to New York City. Mom had a more conservative, little four-door sedan that she drove around every day but she truly loved that Camaro. She dusted and polished it and only drove it on the weekends. She noticed any sort of scratch or bug on it and I wouldn't doubt it if she kept the mileage written down somewhere, which was why I considered Victoria's decision to drive it like some sort of death wish.

"You can't even drive!"

"I can too drive," Victoria snapped back at me. "Melissa at my Young Living group took a bunch of us out in the parking lot and taught us to drive her Gremlin and that was a *manual* transmission, Vy—a stick! I can totally drive. Besides, I'm getting my permit in under a year so this is like extra practice. I'm just going to take it around the block a couple times." She finished tying her shoes and stood up. "In fact, would you call some of your friends and tell them I'm going to be out driving today? I wanna make sure people see me."

She had totally lost it. She'd gone insane. My sister was going to die, either behind the wheel or at the hands of my parents.

I couldn't bear to watch as Victoria backed the car out of the garage. It made a rumbly, guttural, heavy-duty sound when she fired up the engine. I didn't understand why they called it a "muscle car." With that sound they should have called it a "digestive car" or something like that. She rolled out slowly, grinding the gears at the end of the driveway as she shifted out of reverse. I closed the garage door and went back into the house to hide under my bed until I heard the car come back into the driveway.

"OPEN THE GARAGE!" Victoria shrieked.

I ran outside, not necessarily to open the garage but rather to confirm that Victoria had returned home alive and before my parents. Sure enough, she was alive. But Mom's precious Camaro had a pretty substantial dent under the front bumper. Victoria rolled the car into the garage and quickly shut it off.

"Close the door!" She hissed at me. I did, and then bent down to stare at what she'd done.

"What happened?" I asked.

"I was driving past Brian McMurphy's house and he was out mowing the lawn. I took my eyes off the road for a little too long and hit the curb."

Surveying the damage I could tell that it was a little more than just a curb she hit.

"And then?"

"And then *what*?" She snapped. "I hit the curb, that's all!"

I learned on my next walk around with Sara that she'd hit the curb *and* a low retaining wall. I knew it was her accident because there were still remnants of the shiny black paint left behind even a few days later.

As if the suspense of waiting for Mom and Dad to notice that someone messed up the Camaro wasn't enough, when they finally did find out they instantly pointed a finger at me.

"Who else would do something so reckless, so stupid?" Dad shouted.

My jaw was on the floor.

"You know that I am *eleven*, right? Eleven. Ee-lev-vin!" I was dead serious but they took my tone as being sarcastic.

"You're on thin ice, young lady," said Mom.

I was even more blown away.

"Why are you not even considering Victoria? Why me?" I asked.

Victoria shot me a glare from where she sat on the couch, doing her language arts homework.

"Because Victoria knows better," Mom said, looking back at my sister, who gave Mom a smile that was so saccharine-filled that just looking at it could have given you cavities. "Victoria doesn't make trouble for us as often as you do and she said she was here the whole time," Mom said.

"No!" I cried out. "*I* was here the whole time! *I* know better! *I* can't drive! I've never even sat in the driver's seat of a car!"

"That's a lie," Victoria said, giving my mom a knowing and disappointed look. "When you were two you climbed into the front seat of the station wagon, put it in gear and drove through the garage door of the Markhams' house."

Mom put her finger to her lips to shush Victoria.

"Yes, that may be true," Mom added, "But that's neither here nor there. The hardest part about all this is that someone did something illegal, immoral, and expensive to my car and now they're lying about it. My heart is just broken."

"Vy, look what you've done," Victoria clucked, disapprovingly.

"WHAT THE HELL IS WRONG WITH YOU PEOPLE?" I shouted.

For that outburst, I spent two whole days in the corner of Mom and Dad's room, staring at that duck shape in the spackle.

Nelson and I were about halfway home from the baseball park when we rode up to the municipal tennis courts. He hopped off his bike and walked it up a grassy hill to the water fountain.

"Mind if we stop?" he asked.

"Okay," I replied. I followed Nelson up the hill and laid my bike down behind his. He went over for a drink while I sat down on the bench next to the water fountain. There were initials and the occasional swear word carved into the big blocks of wood that made up the bench. I traced over them with my finger, stopping when I came to a piece of gum that had been stretched out in a heart shape around the names "Matt & Kathy."

"I don't know how I feel about Sara's party tomorrow," I announced.

"Really?" he sounded truly surprised as he sat down beside me. "Don't tell me you're thinking about skipping it. You're her best friend! You can't miss her going away party, that'd be a horrible thing to do."

I sighed.

"I know. I really *do* want to go, but I'm kind of confused."

"Confused?"

"Yeah. I mean, to start with, I'm still embarrassed about the whole mix tape thing."

"Okay," Nelson said. "So what?"

"So," I said, "There's no way Sam's going to like me anymore. And Jake's bringing his cousins, too, and you know all about the crush I had on Dan?"

"The crush you *had*?"

"Well, I don't know! I told you I'm confused!" I said, picking at the splinters in the bench. "I just don't want to put myself in a situation where everybody's going to be staring at me and talking about me and there's a good chance that's going to happen at Sara's party."

"Vy, you're weird. I thought you loved attention, good or bad."

"Of course I like attention, sure," I said, admitting, "I want everybody to like me. But not all publicity is good publicity," I said, standing up.

Nelson stood up right alongside me. He looked from side to side and over my shoulder.

"What are you looking at?" I asked.

"I wanted to see if anybody is watching," he replied softly.

"Watching?" I was confused.

Nelson stepped in closer to me. We were now facing each other. He stood just a few inches taller than me.

"Because this could probably go either way in the publicity department." He said, leaning down to kiss me.

My eyes instinctively closed. He took my face in his hands. My heart started racing and I don't know why, but I raised up onto my tip toes. I took a breath, noticing for the first time what Nelson smelled like. He was wearing cologne but it wasn't one I'd ever smelled before. It was spicy, like cinnamon. When the kiss was over I fell back onto my heels, nearly losing my balance.

I opened my eyes and saw Nelson in a completely different light. We stood, looking into each other's eyes. It only took a moment for me to realize that what I'd just done was totally wrong. It felt good to be wanted and I liked kissing. But something in my gut told me that Nelson wasn't someone I was supposed to have kissed.

"What's wrong?" He asked, stepping back. He raised his eyebrow.

"Nothing," I said, turning toward my bike, hoping that Nelson would do the same. I wanted to take it all back. He just stood by the bench, staring at me. "Are you coming?" I asked.

"Yeah," Nelson said. "Let's get you home."

CHAPTER TWENTY-FIVE

The assembly started right before school got out on the last day before summer vacation. All of our parents were there to cheer us on as we walked across the cafeteria stage to receive certificates and a t-shirt with the name and mascot of the middle school. The sixth graders all sat on risers with their classes while the younger kids sat Indian-style on the brown linoleum. The room still smelled like institutional canned corn, chicken patties and room temperature ranch dressing from lunch earlier in the day. Most of the kids were sweaty and dusty, having had their "play day" filled with large-scale games of tug-of-war, kickball, red-rover, and flag tag.

We didn't have a play day like the younger grades. Instead, we filled a time capsule to be opened at our high school senior tea, saying goodbye to all of our teachers at a special lunch, and getting our class schedules for the next year. When they handed out schedules they let us wander around on the playground and compare them with everybody. I'd seen most everyone else's and was showing mine to Alice and Darci when I noticed Sara sitting against the wall all by herself with the saddest look I'd ever seen on her face. I walked over to her.

"Hey," I said, sitting down on the ground beside her.

"Hey," Sara responded. She had a little bit of a froggy tone to her voice.

"Wanna see my schedule?" I asked.

Sara smiled.

"Yeah, actually," she said, taking the piece of paper out of my hand. "Nobody else is showing me theirs. Probably because I don't have one to show back."

There were all sorts of reactions going on around us—people excited or disgusted with who was or wasn't going to be in class with them. Since Sara wasn't going to be around next year I really didn't have any reason to care who was or wasn't in my classes. By some strange chance, Nelson and I had most of our classes together except for our electives. I picked woodshop and he chose art.

"Advanced math, huh?" Sara teased, "You nerd."

I shoved her arm.

"When do you find out about your new school?" I asked.

"When we get there I suppose. I've seen pictures of the building but that's it." She handed my schedule back to me. "Are you coming over tonight? You still haven't RSVPed."

"I'm your best friend; I didn't think I had to RSVP."

"So?" Sara asked, giving me puppy-dog-eyed look.

"Duh," I reassured her with a hug.

"I just started to think that you might not, I mean, because you don't come over to my house anymore."

"I wouldn't miss it for the world," I said.

"Good," Sara said. "Sam will be glad."

"What?" I blurted, louder than I should have, because I noticed several people quickly turning to stare. I whispered, "Why will Sam be glad?"

"Because he's been asking about you."

Oh that was just fabulous. All this time I thought he thought I was a brain-damaged cry-baby. I'd been working really hard to avoid him. What if I'd just wasted all the valuable time that I could have spent as his girlfriend? How could I have been so wrong?

My head was filled with questions. What should I wear? Was this going to be the last time I could smell Sam's cologne? Would he talk to me? I went from feeling so embarrassed that I wanted to hide from him forever to really wanting, just one last time, for Sam to like me.

I got so wrapped up in my thoughts of Sam that I forgot about dealing with Nelson until the assembly. I managed to keep things polite during the time-capsule and schedule-comparing parts of the day. He sat down behind me and Sara on the risers, patting me on the shoulder and giving me a sweet smile that I couldn't help but find awkward. I could smell his cologne, and it turned my stomach. Sure, I always loved attention, but for some reason I didn't want Nelson's attention right then. He was getting kind of annoying. I gave him a forced smile and whispered,

"Hi," and then turned my back toward him.

The program hadn't started yet but when Nelson tried to talk to me, I waved my hand to shush him then turned back to stare at the stage. I felt weird about it so I'm sure he probably felt like it was strange too.

I wanted to focus my attention on the Sam situation. I didn't know when the next time was going to be that I'd see Sam and I felt a need to make sure his memory of me was better than that of a girl with a traumatic brain injury holding a mix tape. Also, I had become more experienced over the past year, logging kisses with quite a few boys and still, no one brought about the same feelings for me that Sam did.

A few minutes passed after I shushed Nelson. I started to wonder if my ignoring him was making him mad or if he'd just be confused by it. The thing was, I knew I would see Nelson all summer and we could smooth everything out then. I loved having Nelson as a friend but I was feeling turned off by the idea of us being more than friends. I had him kind of in the same category where I kept Jake. Crossing that boundary seemed exciting in the moment, but the more I thought about it the more I wished we hadn't.

When the principal walked out on stage half of the room quieted down right away. He stood behind the podium and raised his hand, which silenced the rest of the room. I scanned the audience for my parents and found them standing against the wall in the back, next to the door the hot lunch line usually filed through. Mom smiled at me. Dad gave me a thumbs up. I waved to them inconspicuously at waist level while the principal talked about what a "remarkable year we'd all just had." He listed events and accomplishments, asking the Odyssey team to stand up and be recognized. I didn't know if I should have stood up, since I wasn't on the team for the whole year, so I stayed sitting. Sara stood up beside me and tugged on my shirt. I shook my head.

"Stand up!" she whispered.

"No!" I hissed back.

After the applause died down Sara leaned over to me.

"Why didn't you stand up?" she asked.

"I wasn't on the team the whole time," I replied.

"So what! You love applause!" She said. She was right, I loved attention, especially in a performance-related setting, but this time it just didn't feel right.

"Shhhhh," I shushed at her while the principal went on about the year.

He talked about the exceptional sixth grade international fair and called out a few groups individually to stand up.

"This year the first-prize blue ribbon international fair project goes to Sara Anderson, Jason Nelson, and Violet Karchefski's report on Germany," he announced, waving the three of us up to the stage.

Sara grabbed my hand and we walked down the risers toward the stage. Nelson shuffled along behind us like an afterthought. We were each handed a certificate that had been glued to a piece of construction paper. The glue-job must have still been pretty fresh as it was cold to the touch. I brought my certificate up to my face in a gesture of shyness but was really just trying to get a sniff of the glue to see if it was rubber cement or plain white school glue. It was rubber cement. I loved it.

Before we walked back to our seats the principal shook our hands and read an excerpt from our report. Standing up on the stage I could see my parents, beaming with pride from the back of the room, and Sara's parents on the other side. Both Judy and Julie were there with them. That meant that Sam was probably somewhere nearby. I quickly took stock of my appearance. I was wearing a pair of knee-length denim shorts with a loose-fitting white t-shirt and a pink baseball jacket. By no means did I look "cool." If anything I looked my age, which wasn't how I wanted Sam to see me.

Sure enough, Sam was there. I made eye contact with him as Sara, Nelson and I walked back to our seats on the risers.

While the principal talked about the accomplishments of the younger kids, like the fourth grader who went to the spelling bee nationals and the third grader who rescued a classmate using the Heimlich maneuver in class, Mrs. Saltor came around with a box of graduation caps. Sara grabbed two and handed one over her shoulder to Nelson. I could see by the look in her eye as she gave him the hat that she missed him. It was her idea for them to break up in the first place but it was obvious   that   she   still   really   liked   him.

Our class was asked to stand up with our hats on and we walked in single-file lines across the stage to receive little rolled up certificates tied with the kind of gold ribbons Mom used on Christmas presents. Sara stood in front of me. Nelson was right behind me.

I decided then and there that I never wanted Sara to find out that Nelson and I kissed. She didn't need to know. Just like I was planning for Sam to leave town with the memory of me as a beautiful, confident, and mysterious young woman, Sara was going to leave blissfully ignorant, only remembering the romance and friendship that she and Nelson shared. I didn't want to ruin her otherwise sweet memories of her last year in her hometown. Also, I didn't want her to get mad at me.

"Hey, Vy," Nelson whispered in my ear from behind me. "What is up with you today?"

"Shhhh!" I quickly spit back at him.

"Seriously! What is going on?" He tapped me on the shoulder. "Are you ok?"

"Stop it!" I whispered, flicking at his hand. "Leave me alone!"

"Well that's a real nice way to treat a friend who you've—" he said out loud.

I cleared my throat loudly and gave him a wide-eyed look. I needed to shut him up fast before he got any more agitated. Lord knows what he would say. Needy people should never be trusted with secrets.

313

"I'm sorry!" I snapped back at him. "Can we talk later?" I turned around to see the hurt and confused look on his face. "I promise, we'll talk after school. Okay?"

"Okay," he said.

Just outside the door in the hall there was a lady with a teenage girl holding a baby. They were both grinning from ear to ear. The lady was blowing kisses and the teenage girl was giving thumbs up. For a second I thought they were looking at me, but I quickly realized who they were blowing kisses and giving thumbs up to. That must have been Nelson's mom, his sister Jenny, and his niece.

When I looked over my shoulder at Nelson he was smiling proudly, waving at his family. The whole moment seemed so sweet and kind. A tidal wave of guilt hit me. I felt selfish brushing him off the way I did. At the same time, I couldn't force myself to feel something that just wasn't there. Plus, I still wanted Sara to like me.

Sam was leaning against the wall with a disinterested look on his face as he stared in my direction. We made eye contact and he raised an eyebrow. My heart pounded. Nelson put his hand on my shoulder. I whirled around, a little surprised and then a little sorry for him.

"I'm sorry if I'm being weird," I said. "I don't know what's wrong with me."

"It's okay," Nelson said. "I'm sorry for being weird, too. I guess it's just our age or whatever?"

I was so relieved that he felt just as awkward as I did.

"Can we maybe forget about," I paused, looking over my shoulder to see who might be listening, "you know, last night?"

"No," Nelson said, "I mean, you can, but think I'd like to remember it. We don't need to do it again, though."

"Really?" I asked.

"Vy," Nelson smiled at me. "I get it." He raised his eyebrows looking over at Sam and then at me. "You want him," Nelson said. He pointed at Sara, "and I want her. I don't know what came over me. I've been trying to talk to you about it all day but you've either been around Sara or brushing me off. Can we just be cool now?"

I let out a sigh of relief as my parents walked up beside me. My dad reached his hand out. Nelson took it and shook it.

"'Hello, Sir," Nelson said. Dad beamed and gave my mom a look that indicated he was impressed.

"This was the young man I told you about," Dad said to Mom, "the one who found Calvin." Before anyone could say anything else Sam slid up beside me and bumped into my hip with his.

"You coming over tonight?" he asked.

Dad's expression instantly shifted and so did Mom's. I gave my parents the best *oh-this-is-awkward* smile I could and looked at Nelson, whose sister had just walked up to him with the baby. Mom gave me a look that said she absolutely did not approve, but of what? I couldn't figure out what sort of judgment was going on. I thought my parents liked Sam after he brought me home from my skating accident. It was hard enough getting everybody to like me. I wasn't going to be able to get them all to like each other, too.

Nelson's mom stepped in and introduced herself to my mom, which took some of the negative attention off of me. Dad was giving Sam a dramatic once-over. I looked at Sam and realized he was wearing a t-shirt that said "Big Johnson" on it. It had a goofy-looking cartoon firefighter holding a giant hose between his legs while a pair of large-breasted women in bikinis and short shorts posed around him provocatively. It was totally tacky. I instantly understood what my parents were upset with and I struggled for words.

"Hey, yeah, she'll be there," Sara chimed in, popping up between me and Sam. I breathed another sigh of relief. Sara started chatting with my Dad, filling him in about the move and where he could go to buy the vitamins he usually purchased from her dad. Sam stepped over behind and between my parents and was making faces at me. I fought hard not to giggle nervously.

Nelson's mom and my mom seemed to hit it off. They exchanged phone numbers and kept talking as my family started walking toward the door. Sara and Sam took off in the opposite direction toward Judy, who was calling to them from the other side of the cafeteria. Dad put his arm around me and we followed behind Mom and Nelson's family. Nelson walked a few steps behind us.

"Do you want to go to this party tonight?" Dad asked.

"Sure," I said. "I mean, please? It's the last time I get to see Sara before she moves."

"I know," Dad said, squeezing my shoulder. "You two have been best buds for a long time. That's why it makes me sad to see boys come between you."

"There's no boys between us," I protested.

"There's her brother," Dad said, "and there's the young man behind you—I'm not dense, Vy. Just remember, boys will come and go but a best friend is forever, no matter how far away. And stay away from Sara's brother. He looks like a slime-ball."

I gave Dad a reassuring smile. Little did he know, that slime-ball had been in the forefront of my mind all year and probably would be all night.

CHAPTER TWENTY-SIX

I closed the door to the bathroom while I was getting ready for Sara's party. Calvin was having a majorly loud fit about having to pick up all of the Legos from the carpet in the living room. Plus, I wanted to use a little bit of Mom's makeup and I knew that if I asked she would say "no." Mom still wasn't big on me wearing makeup yet. I had ridden my bike to the pharmacy downtown last summer and bought some 99 cent black eyeliner, a blue and pink combo pack eye shadow and some bright pink blush using three dollars in quarters I'd found under the seats in Dad's car while I was vacuuming it out. The first time I wore my makeup Mom noticed it right away.

"What do you have on your face?" she asked, hardly looking up from the clothes she was folding as I walked past the laundry room.

"Um, it's makeup?" I said meekly.

"I can see that," she said. "Is it mine?"

"No," I proudly stated. "It's mine. I bought it at the pharmacy with my own money."

"Young lady, are you allowed to wear makeup?"

"Victoria does."

"I didn't ask if your sister was allowed to wear makeup. I asked if you were."

"May I?" I asked, hoping that she'd retroactively give permission.

"Not until you learn how to do it right," Mom said, gathering up the pile of towels she had just folded. "Victoria sat with my Mary Kay lady and learned how to do it properly. The whole point of makeup is that you don't want to look like you're wearing any."

Mom had obviously never seen a music video.

"And you, Violet," she went on, "look like you were poked in the eye by a box of crayons."

She made me wash it all off and give her the eyeliner, eye shadow and blush I'd just bought. I never saw her do it, but I was pretty sure she threw it away.

Mom had the same rules about perfumes. Every now and then, for special occasions like piano recitals or Dad's company Christmas party, she would give me a spritz of her perfume. She wore a Lily of the Valley perfume that was a sweet, delicate, floral scent. The delicateness was a little too delicate for me, because a few minutes after she'd put it on me I couldn't smell it anymore. She never put enough on. My aunt, who worked in a department store gave me a bottle of perfume two

Christmases ago and I loved it. I would give myself three or four sprays every morning. Mom tried to convince me that one was enough but there were girls at school whose perfume I could smell when they got on the bus or walked by me in the hall and I wanted to have that same impact. Again, I never saw her do it, but I had reason to suspect that Mom threw away my perfume too.

I carefully traced my lips with Mom's "dusty rose" lip-liner and made subtle additions of blush and pink eye shadow. I had trouble noticing if I had makeup on, which I was fairly confident meant that I'd done it right. I carefully applied some of my mom's foundation over the scars on my forehead and temples to try and hide them but Mom's skin tone was a little darker than mine so it just sort of looked like I had dirty smears on my face. I was washing everything off my face with a washcloth when Mom walked into the bathroom.

"Hey, Vy," she said, closing the door behind her and then sitting down on the closed toilet. "Can we talk for a second?"

"Sure," I said, taking extra care to make sure that there was no trace of Mom's makeup left on my face, including the eye shadow.

"I wanted to talk to you about boys."

And there it was. Dad must have said something to her after he bestowed his words of wisdom on me in the cafeteria. I had a feeling this was going to get uncomfortable and would probably venture into the zone of "the talk" that mothers have with daughters. I wished we could have had this chat a few days ago.

"It was pretty dumb," Victoria said when she told me about the talk Mom had with her. "Mom just kind of sat me down and asked if I knew about sex. I told her I did and she told me to never do it. That was it."

Mom smiled while I dried my face. She didn't look as uncomfortable as I thought she would have been, preparing to talk to her almost-teenage daughter about sex. I was so uncomfortable just thinking about it, it was like slugs, spiders and ants were all climbing up my spine at the same time.

"I know that sometimes it can be hard to make good decisions when you want to impress a boy," Mom said. "But I want you to remember that the most important person to impress in absolutely any situation is your grandfather."

I whirled around, stunned.

"What?"

"Your grandfather."

"No, I heard that," I said, confused as all get-out. "Um, Mom? I don't understand."

"Look, Vy," Mom said, "I want you to be happy. And I want you to make good decisions. My mother told me this and now I'm telling you. In everything you do, I want you to ask yourself, 'what would Grandpa think of this?' before you do it."

"Why?"

"Because, if your grandpa would be disappointed, embarrassed, or at all not impressed, then it's a safe bet that you shouldn't be doing it. Make sense?"

"Kind of," I said. "What does that have to do with boys?"

"Violet," Mom said with a somewhat disappointed tone, "think about it."

I thought about it. It just wasn't connecting for me. I think Mom could tell because she dropped her hands to her sides.

"When a boy wants to do something, like, let's say, make out,"

"Ew, Mom, don't say 'make out.'"

"When a boy wants to make out," she repeated and I cringed, "think about how your grandfather would react to your decision. Do you think he'd like to think of his granddaughter making out with some boy?"

Oh. I understood.

"Gotcha." I said. "Is that it?"

"Were you planning on sleeping over at Sara's tonight?"

"Is that an option?"

"No."

"Then why did you ask?"

"I wanted to make sure it wasn't going to be an issue," Mom said, standing up. She kissed me on the crown of my head as she walked by. "And don't use any of my makeup."

I was hoping to be one of the first people to arrive at Sara's party but since all of the Anderson kids were having friends over the house was already packed when I got there. There were cars lined up around the block and I could smell the barbecue all the way from my front porch.

Victoria had gone over to Jean's house to get ready. I was sure it was because she wanted to wear trendy makeup and borrow an outfit from Jean. I second-guessed my outfit several times before deciding on a pair of hunter green knee-length jean shorts and an ivory and blue floral bodysuit. Usually Mom didn't approve of bodysuits because they were too tight but this one still had a little room in it. It fit me more like a tucked in blouse that didn't ever come untucked. I wore my white sandals and had painted my toenails a subtle pink. I'd put a lot of thought into my look for the night. But not nearly as much thought as I had given to my potential interactions with Sam, which I still hadn't completely figured out.

The front door was open and people spilled out onto the front lawn. There were grownups from the neighborhood and people who sort of looked like Sara's mom and dad so I assumed they were her relatives. Kids ranging from Calvin's age all the way up to high school seniors were everywhere. Alice, Mya, Cristina, and Darci were all following along as one of the high school cheerleaders tried to teach them the tryout dance to a Taylor Dayne song. Tom and Justin were sitting on the front porch with a class list printout they'd stolen from the office garbage can at school. They were trying to make up nicknames for everyone in the seventh grade.

324

"Um, what about 'socket-wrench?'" Tom suggested, pointing at a name on the list.

"Good one," Justin nodded, "write that down."

I walked past them and inside to look for Sara. She greeted me in the kitchen.

"Vy!" she shrieked, running through the house. She threw her arms around me and squeezed me into a tight hug that felt more like we hadn't seen each other all year, when in fact, we'd seen each other less than an hour earlier at school. "I'm so glad you're here!"

For a second, things felt more like they did at the beginning of last summer when Sara and I made all of our plans for the year. We were going to sit by each other in class. We were going to be on the Odyssey of the Mind team together. We were going to go for walks every single night, rain or shine. We were going to perfect the simultaneous death-drop on the flip bars. We were going to stand next to each other in the class portrait. Together, we were going to pick the same electives for seventh grade and join the band and pick the same instrument—the bassoon. We were going to win the international fair together and we were going to spend the whole summer before seventh grade at the river getting tan and preparing for the things that usually happened in seventh grade, like first boyfriends and first kisses.

Thinking back on all of our plans and comparing them to what really happened in sixth grade, I realized that in spite of all of the things that went awry, we still did most of what we'd planned. It may not have been the best year ever, but it was certainly something. For how much

Sara and I grew apart, it felt like we grew even closer together. That made the thought of her leaving feel just horrific. As she squeezed her arms around me, I closed my eyes and held on to the moment. I had a best friend. We survived sixth grade together. She may have been leaving the next day, but for that moment, she was there and I loved her.

"I wish you didn't have to move," I whined.

"Stop it!" she said, sniffling. "You're going to make me cry." She pulled out of the hug to wipe her eyes with the back of her hand. "We'll have time to talk about it later--you're spending the night, right?"

I looked down at my feet.

"Um, well, not exact—" I was interrupted by a door slamming upstairs. A girl came stomping down the stairs while Sam chased behind her.

"I'm sorry!" he pleaded, trying not to attract too much attention.

"Whatever," she shot back, putting her palm up in his face. "Keep your hands to yourself, Samuel Anderson!"

I had never seen this girl before. She looked to have found some friends of hers out on the front porch and she circled up with them before Sam could catch up to her. When he jumped down over the last few stairs, he landed just a few feet from the group, who all turned their backs to shut him out. He shook his head and moved on, wandering through the groups of people in the entryway toward the kitchen. When he caught a glimpse of me standing next to Sara he walked with more purpose.

"So are you or aren't you spending the night?" Sara asked, smacking me in the arm to reclaim my attention.

"Mom says I can't," I said, just as Sam slid up beside us.

"Can't what?" he asked, putting his arm around my shoulders.

"Spend the night," Sara said, exaggerating a frown.

"Oh, that's too bad," Sam said, giving me a squeeze. "I was hoping we'd get to say goodbye properly!" He winked at me.

I felt electricity surge through my body. Just as I was wondering why I only felt that with Sam and not with anybody else, Nelson walked in through the front door. Sara walked over to him and greeted him with a somewhat somber hug. Sam leaned in and whispered in my ear,

"Really, I'd love to say goodbye to you, you know, in private, so let me know before you leave, 'kay?"

I knew what that meant: another kiss. My heart fluttered as I watched Sam walk out the front door.

Sara and Nelson were talking closely, both with their heads hung down. It looked like a pretty private moment, so I made my way out to the back porch where Sara's dad was manning the barbecue, loaded with burgers, hot dogs, tofu slabs and a giant pot of simmering ears of corn. Out in the yard Jake and his cousins, Dan and Chris, were playing lawn darts. He looked up as I crossed the deck and waved me over.

"Vy! Come even out the teams," he said, pointing at Dan. "Goofus here needs a partner."

I shrugged my shoulders and hopped down into the grass. Dan handed me two big yellow darts.

"Oh good," he said. "Welcome to the winning team."

I took the darts and smiled, batting my eyes at Dan, who just turned and walked back to the game. I heard squeals coming from the treehouse just overhead. A group of kids were playing in there. They must have been around Calvin's age, laughing together without a care in the world. I missed those days. I turned back to our game just in time to see Jake trip over his own feet and nearly impale himself on a dart.

"I'm a fallin' man," he joked, popping up, "but I'm not a jerk!"

Chris, Jake, Dan and I all burst out laughing. It was in that moment I realized that the days I longed for—the ones the kids in the treehouse were sharing—didn't have to be over yet. I stopped thinking about boys and just focused on having fun playing the game.

The sun was low in the sky, the radio was playing pop music, and the air smelled like summer. Between the barbecue, the smell of the lawn that had been cut earlier that day, the music and the hum of conversation with the occasional laugh, things just felt right. I was twelve going on thirteen. Sure, the past year felt like my life had turned completely inside out, but I could still say that so far it was the best one yet. As I launched a big yellow lawn dart up into the air, I confidently decided that next year was going to be even better.

Dan and I lost at lawn darts, though I wasn't sure exactly how because no one was keeping score. When the game was over Jake threw each dart forcefully into the ground and then scooped me up, tossing me over his shoulder like a sack of potatoes.

"C'mon, goofball. Let's go eat," he said.

It was good to sit down and catch up with Jake. While I was busy focusing so much time on what people (primarily boys) were thinking of me, Jake was investing his time into sports. He had become the best player on his baseball team and was going to be playing on the high school team during the summer. He said it was because he was too tall to play with the seventh and eighth graders and that umpires had started to accuse his team of cheating by putting older kids on the roster. He blended in with the high schoolers size-wise anyway.

As it turned out, Jake had experienced his first kiss in the sixth grade too. It was with a girl who was in the sixth grade at the school in the next town over. Her older brother played on Jake's baseball team, and he met her at practice.

"We're on the phone with each other like every day," he told me as he scarfed down his second hamburger. "I haven't asked her out officially yet, but I am going to call in to the radio request show tomorrow night and do a dedication for her."

"What song are you going to request?" I asked.

"Nelson," he said.

I looked over my shoulder but didn't see Nelson anywhere.

"*I can't live without your love and affection,*" Jake sang out.

Ah! He meant Nelson the band, not Nelson the guy.

"That's cool," I said. I should have done that instead of the mix tape for Sam. Although, I wasn't sure if he listened to the pop music station. I had a feeling he didn't.

"What's your plan for next year?" Jake asked.

"Seventh grade? I'm really not sure." I said, noticing that the sun had just about gone down and that Sara's dad was turning on the strings of light bulbs he'd wound around the trees in the backyard.

"Yeah," Jake said, "I mean, wow. It seems like you kind of need a break from boys and attention."

"I don't know about that," I joked. "I still have a long way to go before everybody likes me." The street lights blinked on. I stood up from the table and gave Jake a hug. "Hey, I gotta get going," I said, "but thanks. For everything."

"See you on Monday at junior golf?"

"Sure," Jake held his hand up for a high-five which I returned.

On my way back through the house I walked past the backside of the couch, right behind where Sara and Nelson sat. I gathered Sara's hair in my hands and brushed my fingers through it to smooth it into a ponytail. I could hear Sam's voice. I looked up to see him leading a girl by the hand upstairs toward his room.

"I'm going home," I said, "and if we have any kind of big goodbye, I'm going to start bawling, so can we just not?" I asked. Tears were starting to well up, and I wasn't totally sure if they were because of Sara or Sam. Nelson smiled at me sweetly and Sara sat perfectly still.

"Me too," she said. I could hear in her voice that she was getting the same knot in her throat that I had.

"I love you," I said. "Promise to write, like all the time?"

"Promise," she replied. "Hey, Vy? Before you go?"

"What?"

"Will you braid my hair?"

THE END

ABOUT THE AUTHOR

Holly Jones is a wife of one and mother of three who was raised in and inspired by her childhood in the small town of Washougal, Washington, located northeast of Portland, Oregon in the Columbia River Gorge. Holly holds a B.A. in English and a Professional Writing Certification from Washington State University and spent her early career in television broadcasting, producing Emmy-nominated local promotions and programming in Spokane, Washington. She also did time as an advertising copywriter before returning to her roots, writing jokes for radio, articles for the local newspaper, and made-up, far-fetched stories—her true passion. At the time this story was written, she was on staff and studying physics at Gonzaga University.

She hopes very much that you like her.

CPSIA information can be obtained
at www.ICGtesting.com
Printed in the USA
FSOW01n1130121216
28463FS